PARIS

# PARIS

## MARCOS GIRALT TORRENTE

*Translated from the Spanish by*
*Margaret Jull Costa*

 Hispabooks Publishing

Hispabooks Publishing, S. L.
Madrid, Spain
www.hispabooks.com

Copyright © 1999 by Marcos Giralt Torrente

Originally published in Spain as *París* by Anagrama, 1999
First published in English by Hispabooks, 2014
English translation copyright © by Margaret Jull Costa
Design and Photography © simonpates – www.patesy.com

A CIP record for this book is available from the British Library

ISBN 978-84-942284-4-5 (trade paperback)
ISBN 978-84-942284-5-2 (ebook)
Legal Deposit: M-11918-2014

On November 8, 1999, Marcos Giralt Torrente was awarded the XVII Premio Herralde de Novela for his novel *Paris*. This was the unanimous decision of a jury made up of Roberto Bolaño, Salvador Clotas, Juan Cueto, Ester Tusquets, and the publisher Jorge Herralde.

The runner-up was *Bariloche* by Andrés Neuman.

*To the one who is no longer here.*
*And to Luz Suárez, who gave me her name.*

# I

It's in the silence of the night, in those moments that precede sleep, when the worst of nightmares are most likely to assail us and make us turn for comfort to the warm illusion of the person sleeping at our side, that's when the memory of my mother becomes omnipresent and knocks at the door of my consciousness like an outcast knocking at the door to reclaim the place from which he was once expelled. It doesn't happen often, but when it does, fears and regrets I assumed to have been long since vanquished overwhelm me and fog my thoughts. I suddenly find myself torn between lamentation, which is a reproach to her, because her presence is no longer enough to fill everything around me with significance, and sadness, which is a reproach to myself, for failing to realize that she was once a child, too, and, like me, will never again have someone who can assuage her dread of failure and oblivion.

It's nostalgia. It's fear. It's a dream state. It's the loneliness that looms in the darkness. It's not knowing and yet wanting what I feel and what I imagine to coincide. It's doubt, too. It's all those unanswered questions. It's wanting to run to the place where she's waiting for me so that I can tell her, *It's all right, I know everything.*

To be honest, I'm not entirely clear what my feelings are, and I simply can't understand why it is that whenever I'm a bit down, I'm always drawn back to the thought of something that may never even have happened and only exists in my imagination as a way of neutralizing the different emotions the image arouses in me. I will never know more than I know now, and perhaps it's the impossibility of getting beyond mere speculation that continues to endow with significance an event which, if it did happen, would have to be considered less important in comparison with others I *know* to have happened, and which she very bravely told me about when few people in her situation would have dared to so much as mention them. And I'm drawn back to that event even though, were my mother capable of filling what seemed to be the void of my memory, I would still not ask her about it, knowing that there would be no point in probing the reasons for or the consequences of her actions, because after all these years, anything she said would not be so very different from what anyone in her place would say or from what I can so easily imagine for myself.

For example, I can see them on what might have been their last morning together. I can see them waking up, I can hear what they're saying. My mother is still in bed, and my father is shaving or washing up on the other side of the partition wall. On the bedside table are some earplugs, a clock, two ivory bracelets, and yesterday's newspaper. It's the second or third day that they've woken up in that room, and they probably won't stay longer than a week. My mother isn't smiling, she has no plans and no idea how she will fill the next few hours. It's the only moment in the day when she allows herself to look back and when she feels any remorse. She wants his presence there to act as a kind of guarantee of oblivion, and she listens eagerly for each sound coming from the bathroom. She waits expectantly for the gurgle of water as it's gulped down the plughole in the sink, she hears a cheery whistle and knows that he's finished sprucing himself up now and is beginning to put on the same clothes he left hanging on the door handle last night. She knows they are in pristine condition and will remain so until their owner decides to take them to the laundromat. She knows that she should follow his example but is incapable of imitating him and, instead, leaves hers in a heap on the floor, lacking his foresight and as yet unaccustomed to this new life in which every gesture must be gauged and measured.

I can see that time of awakening, but I can just as easily imagine a world in which such a scene never took place and my mother never spent the night in a hotel room with my father or with any other man. That is just as convincing a possibility. Even if she herself were to corroborate the one and reject the other, the dilemma would remain. After all, everything I know, I owe to her, and I have no way of finding out if she is also the reason I don't know certain other things, things she deliberately kept from me. When our knowledge of a subject depends on the words of others, we can never be sure if they've told us everything or only a part. That's why, even if she had been totally honest and described to me every minute they spent together, every argument, and everything they could have done but didn't, nothing would change. There's no point imagining or asking. Words don't exist in the present. Words come later, and we all use them in the same way, we can all describe and offer an opinion even though what we describe or have an opinion about didn't happen to us.

In order to speak about my parents and about the nightmares that assail me during those moments before sleep when we move closer to the person slumbering by our side, and who is oblivious to our all-pervading anxiety, I must make do with what I myself saw and heard. I must try to speak only of the things of which I have direct experience, even if that depends in large measure on what I don't know but can only intuit. Since it's not my intention to convert doubt into certainty but simply to make sense of what happened as a consequence of my suspicions, there will be nothing contradictory about my course of action as long as everything I say is told from my point of view at the time. Any gaps other than those in my own memory will have to continue to exist, because even if it were in my power to do so, what purpose would there be in trying to investigate them further? Indeed, their fate might be precisely that, to remain unassailable in order to illuminate other gaps that actually do exist in my memory.

My father was arrested at home one night when we had guests over for dinner, and it wasn't until the meal was well underway that my mother discovered, too late, the reason for his boundless excitement. I was nine years old at the time and fast asleep, and so I have no idea what happened during the initial confusion. I have a vague memory—although I can't be sure it isn't just an image I created later on—that my bedroom door opened and two men came in, preceded by my mother. I remember that, at first, she didn't turn on the light but, rather, given her nervous state and her concern lest I be frightened, showed them in with the room still in darkness, and it was only when one of the strangers asked where the light switch was that she made her way over to it in the dark and turned it on. I remember that I didn't feel afraid, because when the room filled up with light and the two men emerged clearly out of the gloom and I saw their eyes fixed on me, the taller of them made a joke and my mother smiled reassuringly. I remember that while this was going on, the other man glanced quickly around him, and after opening the closet door a crack and peering in, he tapped his companion on the shoulder, and they both left, leaving my mother with me. The whole incident could only have lasted a matter of seconds, because I have a feeling that my mother immediately came over to me and gave me a kiss, and that after she had stroked my hair, turned out the light, and closed the door behind her, I fell asleep again without noticing that I could no longer hear the hum of jolly conversation that had accompanied the first half of my night's sleep. I did not see the sad, downcast departure of the guests nor that of my father, handcuffed and under escort. Of the following morning, all I can say is that when I woke up, he was no longer in the apartment. I went into the kitchen and found my mother tidying up after the party, and if she *was* feeling nervous or upset, she obviously did her best to hide it, because nothing in my memory indicates that she was. I've even forgotten what happened afterward, as the hours passed and my father still did not come back, and as the days passed, too, and the fact of his disappearance became unavoidable and my mother was obliged to offer me some explanation. Indeed, not even once she had given me that explanation, or when my father's absence continued and she had to come up with new excuses, not even then did I make a connection between our sudden solitude and the men who had come into my room on the night of the dinner party. My father simply vanished from my life without warning, and not only did I not register this as the tragedy that it was, I did not even miss him in the two years that followed, at least not to the point where one begins to have suspicions and seek answers. My memory blanked out that sudden nighttime visit to my bedroom, and only years later did it return to me in the nebulous form of some past event that did not, in its day, arouse any interest.

Before that happened, and after I had found out about my father's police record, my mother had spoken to me about his arrest and explained that the way it was carried out was as ruthless as it was unexpected. As she told me when she felt I was old enough to know, and as she continued to tell me over the years, my father had been in a state of extreme agitation for some weeks, and yet despite this and the fact that the dinner party had been his idea, and though she hadn't exactly been feeling optimistic herself, she had never guessed that he was in any real trouble. She neither feared nor suspected anything until, halfway through that evening, he took her away from their guests and led her into the bedroom, where, from under the bed, he produced a suitcase she had never seen before, and which, with growing excitement, he set about opening. It wasn't until she saw him take a small key from his pocket and open the last lock that something like a sixth sense stirred inside her consciousness. However, once he had removed the lock and opened the suitcase and turned to her smiling, any hunch she might have come up with herself paled in comparison when she saw that the case was stuffed with cash. She later described to me how it was arranged in neat bundles and looked brand new, as if it had come straight from the presses and no one, apart from him, had touched it. Always sparing in such details and reluctant to say much about them, she never told me what words were exchanged over that suitcase once its contents had been revealed and she was beginning to have some inkling as to where they had come from. She didn't tell me, but I can easily imagine. After her initial perplexity, I guess my mother would have said, "What's going on? Are you crazy?" and that he, still smiling, would have answered, "Don't worry. We're not in any danger." My mother would then have responded rather sarcastically and he in a firm but conciliatory way. Only then, having properly absorbed what my father had said, would my mother have given in to the desire to learn the origin of that money. My father doubtless proved evasive, and after a time, during which the tension between them grew to the point where words became redundant, they rejoined their guests. Between that moment and the moment when the police burst into the apartment demanding to see everyone's papers, I would not, I think, be wandering too far into the realm of speculation were I to say that they carefully avoided each other, my mother unable to think straight and wishing she had someone to confide in, my father observing her from a distance and not looking forward to the argument they would be sure to have once their guests had gone, but meanwhile enjoying his temporary good luck, blissfully unaware that someone was already heading his way to snatch that luck from him and confirm what his worst fears had been when he had first thought up his scam or someone else had planted the idea in his head.

# II

Even though I may have to consider such disagreeable hypotheses as the product of mere haste or a sense of gratitude born of necessity, the question inevitably arises as to why my mother chose so badly. That isn't intended as a reproach—that would be stupid. It's the never-resolved temptation to turn her into a victim, to assume that she married my father out of ignorance and not because she thought she could make him change. That last possibility, though, is not only more probable, it's also more realistic. Don't we all believe ourselves capable of changing the behavior of those around us? And she was no exception. She thought she would have more influence over him than any of his other interests, that she would be able to impose rules on him, if not conventional ones, at least some minimally reasonable ones. Otherwise, I can't understand her tenacity. I could understand her taking that first false step, but not the determination with which, for so many years afterward, she refused to abandon the many meandering paths of deceit he chose to follow.

I keep looking for a word to define him, but I can't find it. The only one that comes into my head is "fly-by-night." I like it because it suggests a degree of irresponsibility that fits well with the kind of person he became in the end and, at the same time, contains an element of madness essential to his character. I like it, but it falls short. It isn't exact enough. It attracts more than it repels. It sounds too amusing, or cheerful, or frivolous, or innocuous, and he was neither cheerful nor frivolous, and certainly not innocuous. My father was somber, destructive, and selfish. Capable of dragging you with him in his fall, capable of ruining your whole evening, or however long it took to wheedle out of you the money he needed so that he could then buy a drink or a meal for someone he *wasn't* asking money from, capable of lying obsessively even when the pain he might be inflicting was far greater than any shame or embarrassment he might feel were he to relent and acknowledge his deceit.

Obviously, he must have had something about him. I'm not saying he didn't. We all carry within us a plan of what we are as well as what we could have been, and whether we end up being one rather than the other depends not on the appearance or disappearance of new characteristics but rather on the way in which certain already-existing characteristics win out over others. If my father was the way he was in my memory, it's only because that particular combination of characteristics won out in the end, not because he had never been any other way or because he had lost the possibility of being any different. To know what he was as a whole, one would have to look in between those two poles, between what he could and could not be, between his potential to be different from the father I knew and the determination with which he devoted himself to destroying that potential. But I could easily get lost in a labyrinth, trying to reconcile the uncertainty and despair he caused with what my mother saw in his face one rainy day in Madrid when someone took him along to a party at her place, which he left, carrying off with him as plunder a far better

18

overcoat than the one he was wearing when he arrived, and I don't think I could find a midway point between what his image evokes in me and what my mother tried to see in him for so very long, which may or may not have deceived her and possibly inspired the penultimate step that was never proven to have taken place, never questioned or spoken about between us, and about which I will never achieve a sense of certainty I do not even seek. In order to find that middle ground, I would need to have shared in my mother's first, dazzling vision of him or to be quite sure that, at some point, she stopped being deceived, and if the former is impossible because my opinion of my father only came about indirectly, the latter is equally impossible, because I have no idea if my mother's view of him really did change or if, on the contrary, it was weariness, or prudence, or the final, definitive payment on account of a debt contracted long ago, or merely a sacrifice on the altar of her maternal responsibilities that finally made her want to be free of him and to put an end once and for all to the anxiety of never knowing where that constantly renewed hope was leading her.

I have no idea, I don't know what that middle ground might be, and I cannot, therefore, give a balanced portrait of his personality, but I have to say that I really don't miss him. Not since the moment when, just at the point when my own observations were beginning to tarnish the rather idealized image I had of him, my mother seemed to make up her mind to admit defeat, to get rid of him, to be no longer available.

There's an anecdote that reveals a lot about the kind of person my father was. It dates from long after we'd lost all contact with him, from a time when we rarely even mentioned him, and it's neither shocking nor spectacular, merely illustrative.

It must have happened toward the end of the 1970s or the beginning of the 1980s, and I only know about it because its protagonist, a woman with whom he was living at the time, came to my mother seeking help, something to hold on to, someone to listen to her story. He was, it would seem, a lost cause by then, beyond redemption, and apart from information gleaned from the occasional phone call from people asking for him—which for years gave us an approximate idea of where he was—and apart from one occasion when we happened to see each other in a bar, I've had no direct news of him.

The story, as my mother told it to me, is so sordid as to be almost funny were it not for the pain caused to the woman involved. At the time it happened, which was when my mother found out about it and told me, there was no need to tone down any of the details. Had it happened shortly before, when I might still have been affected by who my father was and how he behaved, the version I would have received then would definitely have differed from the original. The bare facts of the case revealed him in a most unfavorable light, and my mother would probably have preferred to say nothing rather than risk giving me the unexpurgated version too soon.

Apparently, my father and the woman had been living together for a year in a rented apartment in downtown Madrid, and no rent had been paid for nine months. My mother told me very little about my father's previous record, perhaps because she herself did not know or perhaps because she thought it unnecessary to tell me, but it's not hard to infer that she knew about my father's capacity for fooling people. To begin with, I imagine he had impressed the woman with his easy way with money at a time when his luck was in, that he had subsequently persuaded her to go and live with him and leave her own apartment, and then, in the end, when the money ran out, she had found herself landed with an unexpected bill, although she nevertheless still trusted in his inevitable assurances that he was expecting to get a windfall any day now or to land some well-paid job or something of the sort. Anyway, this was how things stood, with the landlord threatening to evict them and phoning her every day in increasingly imperative tones, when my father presented the woman with a most unusual solution: moving out into the country and taking over an old battery-style poultry farm that belonged to some acquaintance of his and growing marijuana plants there under artificial light. According to what the woman told my mother, my father had been so excited about this scheme, so convinced it would work, that even though she was aware of the risks she was running, she ended up agreeing to it. They didn't even have to invest any money, she said by way of an excuse. The neon strips intended to keep the birds in perpetual daylight could be adapted to this new use, and on the understanding that they would share any profits fifty-fifty, the owner of the farm agreed to take care of everything, including providing them with food. It appears that, even so, my father considered that his associate was taking too large a cut, bearing in mind that he was not the one running any risks, because if the police intervened, he would simply have to play the part of the innocent landlord whose trust had been betrayed and he would get off scot free, but it also appears that my father did not, at this point, complain, and, initially at least, he kept to their agreement. After purchasing a few chickens to give some semblance of verisimilitude to the situation, my father and the woman had moved into the farmhouse, fitted out a broken-down old tool shed to make the tiny dwelling slightly roomier, ordered and prepared the hundreds of rectangular planters, sown them with the seeds ready-germinated in rolls of damp cotton wool, and set up an irrigation system, which would mean that when the time came, they wouldn't have to water each and every plant. From then on, they would have nothing to do but wait until the plants had grown, except, of course, that the irrigation system never worked and they ended up having to water them manually. This, however, was not the woman's biggest problem. The cannabis plants grew as rapidly as expected throughout the long, hot summer, and when they were ready to be harvested, she and my father picked the leaves, laid them out to dry, chopped them up, and put them in plastic bags. That was when events took a turn for the worse. On the day she visited my mother, the woman said she could not understand how she could possibly have agreed to his suggestion, but she had thought it perfectly natural, even generous on my father's part, when, in order to keep her from running any unnecessary risks, he proposed that he take charge of the cannabis and come back for her when he had sold it, "in a matter of days," he said, "just as long as it takes to find a distributor." She herself couldn't understand why she had agreed to this, but that is what happened. My father loaded the transparent plastic bags onto a van, disguising them in thick, brown paper sacks that had previously contained fertilizer, and set off with the merchandise one evening as the sun was setting behind the mountains. The problem was that he never came back. He left her alone, with no car and almost no money, to sort things out with their associate, who turned up a week after my father's departure, demanding his share of the profits. Such was the woman's trust in my father that not even then did it occur to her to think that she might have been duped and that she would probably never see him again. She resisted the pressure from their intrusive colleague, saying that the fact that she was still there was proof that no one had any intention of running off with his money, and she chose to think that my father had merely run into some difficulty selling the stuff and that it was only a question of waiting a few more days. Not until a whole two weeks had gone by and the pressure had become unbearable was she forced to admit that he would not keep his promise. This happened one night when the owner of the farm visited her again and was more aggressive than usual, insulting her and telling her that he'd heard that my father had been seen in Madrid, in a restaurant he could never have afforded unless he had plenty of money. He said that if my father was still not there the following day to pay him what he owed, then she would have to face the consequences and the police. She ignored his threat and waited until he had gone, then she herself left, walking three miles in the dark to the nearest village, with the surprise and shock of this inexplicable situation still imprinted on her face. She never saw my father again, and when she finally found *us* a month or two later, it would seem, from her conversation with my mother, that she was still clinging to the possibility that he might have been arrested or had an accident. That was the only explanation for his silence, the only explanation for something that had no explanation.

# III

I looked after my mother when she was ill, I watched her cry and listened in the darkness to her breathing, I cheered her up when she was down and celebrated with her whenever there was something worth celebrating. No one was as close to her or knew her as well as I during that time. For as long as I can remember, whenever her world was falling apart, I was the one who was there by her side to encourage her and help her find a solution. I was the person she saw before she fell asleep each night, the one she said goodbye to in the morning and who was there to greet her on her return from work. Even during the times when my father lived with us, he never played such a role. For years, even when my mother and I were apart, I was the one constant reference point in her life, the only one she could be sure of finding again.

When, with the definitive disappearance of my father, my mother announced that she was moving to Paris, she did not, of course, tell me she was doing so as a result of her latest failure, but given the level of my confidence in her, that is how I interpreted it. I sensed somehow that a change was needed, and moving to another country seemed the best way of bringing about that change. She was seeking refuge in another city, leaving me with her sister. I was quite sure about this and didn't feel she was abandoning me, and I believed her when she said this was a purely temporary measure while she adapted to her new life, found a place to live and a school for me. When I think about it now, now that time has passed and the reasons for her leaving are less clear, it no longer matters whether she undertook that journey for her sake or for mine, whether she made the decision to put a stop to the uncertainty as represented by her husband either then or later—the fact is she left. Whether or not that step was a sad one, or whether or not she first had to suffer bitterly, would make no difference to the end result.

What was their relationship like exactly? What was it that attracted them to each other? What were they hoping for? Did they waste time arguing or did they just accept their differences as given? Were their reunions passionate affairs or did they get back together with a sense of ill-digested disappointment?

As with everything one has not experienced directly, for me, the beginning of their relationship, albeit devoid of all symbolism, belongs to a territory that is more mythical than real. According to the idealized version my mother gave me in my childhood—which was the one destined to last and which, even now, I have no reason to doubt, because she never amended it—they met in the late 1950s in a Madrid that I imagine to have been like the dusty skin of the elephant in the old Natural History Museum but that, when my mother spoke of it, was lit by the blue of a nostalgia that consisted in equal measures of partying into the small hours and a sense of life lived at a slower pace, which had to do perhaps with the general tone of the period and, in equal measure, a complete and proper youthful disregard for time. My mother said that my father was fun to be with and that although some of the characteristics that would later mark his life were already there, they were so subtle that they were not so very different from the habits of other friends of hers who went on to lead a perfectly normal existence. She was always quick to emphasize that he was the youngest and most attractive of a family of four brothers, all of whom, apart from him, were happy to follow the family tradition of making a career in the judiciary. And it isn't hard to imagine that it was precisely this mixture of scoundrel and gifted young man that proved so seductive to someone of my mother's age at the time. His desire to reject the fate decreed by his family found some justification in certain intellectual ambitions; he had travelled, he played tennis, and was as at ease in the wealthiest of Madrid's social circles as he was in other very different circles where fights frequently broke out and feelings of resentment were always quick to surface.

My mother said of herself that she came from a similar family background of high-ranking civil servants, in her case diplomats, but what expressed itself in my father as rebelliousness and a genuine desire to break the mold being imposed on him, in my mother's case may well have been mixed up with her feelings of abandonment. She had no mother, and her father had remarried, his second wife being an Englishwoman fiercely jealous of everything in her husband's life that predated her, and my mother's one bulwark was a sister three years older than her, to whom she had always been very close but whom she rarely saw. My mother was studying French at college and her life was lived between two poles: on the one hand, the freedom allowed her by the relative neglect of a father who tended to give precedence to the often arbitrary demands of his new wife and, on the other, certain social impositions that, because she associated them with the figure of her father, she flatly rejected, while never daring to openly call them into question.

That is the starting point, according to what my mother told me when I was growing up. Oddly enough, she never went into any detail about how they came to marry, not that I can remember, at least. What I do know is that the early days of their marriage were calmer and less troubled than one might expect. After I was born, she took a job as a high school teacher, and my father, who dropped out of college, got the family involved in a business importing sportswear, something, he said, that would provide him with a basis so that, later on, he could devote himself to what he really wanted to do. It seems that, even then, he loved the high life, and any little luxury acquired licitly was as insignificant to him as the unworthy, exhausting work he had done in order to pay for it, although whether other people had any sense that this might become a problem, I don't know. I can't recall her mentioning any great financial disaster or when precisely it all began to go wrong. The sportswear business failed, as would all the various other businesses he set up subsequently, and my father was reduced to freelancing as a translator and proofreader, but the mere fact that this was a chain of events rather than a single, isolated incident means that it's impossible to speak of one particular determining factor that prompted his drift over to the dark side. Rather, it was a slow process in which the withdrawal of his family's trust in him played a large part. Even so, the first signs of conflict must have already appeared, because the range of his business experiments began to expand into other areas outside Madrid, as if he felt an increasing need to put some distance between them and his family, my mother and myself included.

The knowledge transmitted to me about the years that came afterward is not very much clearer. Apart from what my mother told me when she thought she could allow herself to and what I myself observed in the brief time during which I lived with him, I learned nothing, or very little, of what happened at home. I know that he lived with us until I was six or seven, but I'm not even very sure of that. The mechanisms of memory work in strange ways, and all I can remember from that period are a few completely irrelevant anecdotes in which he plays a more or less central role. I remember an afternoon at the movie theater, a day when he came to pick me up from school, and a few summer mornings when he tried to teach me how to ride a bike—but these memories are all in black and white, there's no intensity, no awareness that those incidents were in any way exceptional. From 1968 on, and for six or seven years afterward, when the real change occurs, the bonds between us are not broken exactly, rather they become more loosely interwoven. In theory, he continues to live with us, but there are also long periods when he disappears and we have no news of him for months at a time. The most significant thing about this situation is that it doesn't appear to affect my mother. There are no arguments, no complaints. She has obviously begun to realize that he frequently lies, and she sees, with some concern, that his life is gradually dissolving into one of constant flight, but she nevertheless still greets every return home with joy and barely turns a hair whenever, quite unforeseeably, he disappears again. In a way, it's as if the role she reserved for him were not so much that of occupying a physical space at home as merely continuing to be a possible reference point, as if his role in our lives consisted of his willingness to take on that role, rather than him actually fulfilling it. She's quite sure he's not going to replace us with someone else, and yet is afraid that putting pressure on him might make him leave for good; I suppose she has her reasons for wanting the relationship to carry on with a certain appearance of normality and that, deep down, none of his absences matter to her as long as they do not become definitive. Meanwhile, without my noticing, my father's life has begun to grow chaotic, he has lost friends and set off along a path on which there is no room for anything that might tie him permanently to one place or one project. He frequently changes job, spends money like water if he has it—and very often he doesn't—but he still continues to do nothing definite with his life. The adventures we know about are limited to the theft of some silverware from his parents' house, the continual fabrication of catastrophes and excuses in order to borrow money and not give it back, and generally presenting the world with a façade that looks far more respectable than it really is. He's already becoming a trickster, and as his life proceeds, he's caught up in that spiral in which every deception serves only to cover up the previous one, but his misdeeds are still amateurish affairs. They can still not be considered crimes, because there is still far too narrow a margin between the thefts he plans and the unjustifiably trusting nature of the parties being swindled. We have to wait until 1972, when I'm nine years old, for everything to fall apart.

# IV

During the whole of my childhood, my position in the family hierarchy was, I felt, not much different from that occupied by my mother. Even during the times when my father was there, she and I formed the nucleus. It was, if I can put it like this, my father and us, and us and my father. There was no other possible combination. It was a feeling born of my condition as an only child, which was reinforced one morning on our way to Burgos, a feeling that survived both the months during which I was separated from my mother and my father's definitive absence. Of course, in the intervals when the three of us lived together, I was always conscious that, however peculiar, they were still a couple and there were, necessarily, intimate places into which I could not enter, but such intimacy, to my mind, was limited to what went on inside their bedroom once the door was closed. I never thought there was anything I didn't know or in which I couldn't be involved, nothing hidden. If my mother didn't talk about my father or ask my opinion about matters relating to him, it was because she, like me, didn't know anything, or because there was nothing to give an opinion about.

It was as a result of the last period of time my father spent living with us that I found out exactly what he had done to deserve arrest, and also that I managed to retrieve the memory of that night of the dinner party when two strangers came into my room while I was sleeping. It must have happened in a moment of despair, when my mother considered that I was old enough to know the details, or at a moment, perhaps, when my questions were becoming less easy to avoid, and more specific, too. Besides, I've spent so many hours in my mother's company, we've talked about so many things, and the memory of the occasions when we spoke about him has become so mixed up with other occasions when things were better left unsaid that I can't pin down one precise moment or separate out the first time from all the other times that followed, not even once he'd already been expelled from our lives.

Apparently, the beginning of the 1970s marked the end of the line in my father's career and life—the removal of the safety net that had previously allowed him to leap onto the trapeze of each wild impulse with complete disregard for the results. A few years before, his father had chosen to give him his inheritance while he was still alive, in order to provide him with the capital he needed for one of his many failed projects, and when his father died, his brothers, invested with an authority that my father entirely lacked, came out in full force to defend their share of the inheritance and robustly blocked any attempt by their mother to give him any money at all. He was still doing the occasional translation, whenever he had no other source of work, but found this increasingly difficult. His contacts in the publishing world resented the many unfulfilled commitments, the rushed translations, his general unreliability, and even were he prepared to go in search of new commissions, it was not easy for him to find them. Deprived of the family money that would allow him to launch new enterprises, and with his credibility seriously damaged among his oldest friends and his wider circle of friends of friends, he was once again spending most of his time in Madrid, and his friendships were beginning to come almost exclusively from just one end of the social scale, the two sides of which he had manipulated with such consummate skill up until then.

My mother used to say that anyone else finding himself in that position would have taken it as a sign to get a firm grip on the wheel and change direction, but not him. More than anything else, my father needed to be admired. Regardless of the social sphere in which he was moving, he liked to shine, to put on a kind of aura. In the world where people, on seeing him, immediately associated him with his reputation as a freeloader, he needed money to back him up, and in the other world, where his impeccable manners were what shocked or attracted attention, it was enough that they should *assume* he had money. But in both those worlds, money was essential to him, either as his real reality or as the shadow reality that gave him his self-assurance. The weapon was the same. With no fixed profession, with neither the determination nor the fortune required to undertake new projects, part of his drift toward the darker side must have been an awareness that he had nothing to offer in his own milieu. He took refuge in those places where the least was demanded of him, where he needed only to dress as he dressed and speak as he spoke. What before had been a mere pastime, whether aimed at feeding his own legend or not, then became a necessity. Starting to frequent the underworld, and distancing himself more and more from the people he had known up until then, must have seemed to him the only way out. Whether he considered this to be a possible path to recovery right from the start or whether the opportunity only presented itself later on is something I really don't know.

Whatever the truth of the matter, this was, broadly speaking, what triggered and hastened his downfall, at least in my mother's experience of events. She only found out the full details of what happened later, at the trial following his arrest and, to a lesser extent, from what my father was willing to tell her.

According to my mother, it was such a straightforward affair that had she not witnessed the outcome herself, she would have thought it was pure invention. If she is to be believed, my father was not the brains behind the scam, his role was simply to provide a respectable façade, the face and manners that would lend the whole thing credibility. With the aim of creating a dummy company that would serve as a cover, he and the real architect of the plan had used false documentation to rent an apartment on the Calle Serrano, which they then fitted out as an office, hiring a couple of secretaries to add greater realism to the whole performance. Later on, they registered the business and, after that, using counterfeit title deeds, applied for a business loan from a bank where a third associate worked, although he knew neither of them by name. The idea was to dismantle the "company" and vanish without a trace once the money from the loan came through. It had all been meticulously thought out. The principal player was in charge of planning and sorting out the necessary documentation; my father had the most dangerous role to play, that of actually going to the bank, negotiating the loan, and, finally, picking up the money; their contact inside the bank was supposed to speed up the paperwork and raise the alarm should any difficulties arise. The execution was impeccable, and the trick would have worked had fate not intervened in a somewhat comic guise. When the bank realized they would not be getting their money back and reported this to the police, the latter had no clue as to the identity of the fraudsters, and not knowing where to begin, they did what they usually do in such cases and put the bank employees under surveillance. Up until then, everything had gone swimmingly. Their inside man, however, failed to follow the most elementary of security rules and made the mistake of buying himself a luxury car and phoning my father on a couple of occasions—on the emergency phone number he'd been given—to say how pleased he was and to keep in touch with the one person to whom he could boast of his newfound wealth. My father began to get nervous after the second phone call and decided to follow the example of his main co-conspirator, who had gone to Italy early on, leaving the country until the dust had settled. The night of the dinner party and the arrest was, as my father told my mother, the last night he intended to spend in Madrid, and he had shown her the money with the intention that she and I should go with him. It doesn't really matter whether those plans were real or not, because the police eventually found out about the bank clerk's lavish spending, and his connection with my father was discovered that very night, when they listened in on a phone call. The most regrettable part did not happen then, however, but a little later on. For when the police burst into the apartment demanding to see everyone's papers, they knew who they were looking for, but not his real name. They were hoping to arrest one Antonio José Domenech, and that was the name on the identity card that my father instinctively produced instead of his own. By presenting his false ID instead of his real one, he thus contributed to his own arrest. It's hard to know what would have happened had he presented his genuine ID, but, according to my mother, the memory of that fatal error was enough to make the next two years of his life even more bitter.

# V

Just how bitter those two years were for my mother, I have no idea.

Things happen, and later on you might recount them to someone else with more or less exactitude, and the image you convey will not be so very different from the original events. What you were feeling, though, what was going on inside you while those things were happening, is more a matter of silences. We can get quite close in our description of events, but we will never be able to describe their very essence, an essence tinged with despair, or joy, or with both at once. You might be able to give some sense of the intensity of those feelings, but not the whole diverse chain of connections of which they were composed. With the passing of time, feelings grow more impersonal, and their very impersonality renders them impenetrable.

That's why it's impossible for me to know what went on inside her during those two years, what waves of indifference broke over her spirit or where she found the necessary consolation, what she did or didn't do, what she thought, what she regretted, what she missed—if, that is, she missed anything at all—and what depths of despondency she plumbed. When all of this was going on, she told me nothing, her life was a pretense, a permanent charade intended to allow me to carry on as normal, to sleep, eat, laugh, wake up, go to school, and even cry, without worrying about things I had no reason to worry about or that she didn't want me to worry about. My mother was a rock, and if there *was* a chisel chipping away at her, if it caused dust or flakes of stone to fall onto the floor of her spirit or allowed time to erode her, revealing gaps and flaws and fractured veins, all of that happened while she was alone, without me as a witness, or, of course, as a confidant. After those two years, and with the return home of my father, things changed superficially but not fundamentally. I came to know about certain events that had affected me; she confided a truth that had previously been kept from me; I would talk to her and she would explain that something had happened this way or that, but we never touched on feelings, she never told me what went on inside her or what pain she felt, if indeed she felt any pain.

Leaving aside my age and the likelihood that any mother would have behaved the same, I cannot help but think that her personality played a large part in her behavior—her fear and her stoicism, her distance and aloofness from everything, the mixture of confidence and helplessness that made her such a complex person, simultaneously whole and divided, part fearless and unshakeable, part defenseless and vulnerable. My mother was a strong woman and had a capacity for resistance I've never encountered in anyone else, but, in a way, it was as if that strength existed outside her, like an ornament or an autonomous organism, a parasite, like those that coexist with certain mammals, and which she used in order to do things she would have been incapable of doing on her own. She could spend hours with other people, listening to their complicated unburdenings, advising them or consoling them if necessary, but never, ever putting herself in a similar situation. She inspired trust, and I doubt you could have found a better listener to whom to reveal your innermost thoughts, your most profound or superficial of anxieties, but I never heard her talking about herself or demanding attention. On the contrary, she always did everything she could to avoid the personal and, instead, would make someone else the center of attention, thus ensuring that no conversation would take her as its focal point or put her in the position of having to talk about things she didn't want to talk about. I had more than once seen her crying, but I almost had to force out of her anything remotely resembling a confession or a confidence. There was no point in my alluding directly to what I knew to be the cause of her pain—the death of her mother and her subsequent life with her father, for example. Whenever I asked a question, she always replied in the same way: *What do you want to know?* And I would ask her to tell me about this or that, and she would begin a gentle, melodious story going nowhere, full of insignificant details that in no way added to my knowledge, just a collection of anecdotes that showed her in everyday situations, which were utterly neutral and interchangeable with those experienced by anyone else: the day she spilled some soup on the tablecloth, the day she discovered her father's gun, the day her sister left home . . . I even questioned her about events I myself could remember, like the death of my grandfather, which, although it happened when I was only four, I can remember vividly, because that was the first time I saw her cry, and there was a clear contrast between her evocation of that incident and the substance of my memory, almost as if she were two different people, the one who was there at the time and whom I'd seen crying, and the one who was coolly answering my questions years later. To listen to my mother, you would think she'd never had any problems at all, that no one had ever raised their voice to her or treated her unkindly. Then, of course, I realized that this wasn't true and that the very doggedness with which she avoided talking about the subject concealed more repressed pain, more signs in need of interpretation, than all the words she spoke. If I cornered her and she was unable to avoid answering my questions any longer, she would cast her eyes heavenward as if to keep them from filling with tears and remain silent for a moment, just long enough to ward off temptation, then she would take my hand and squeeze it briefly, timidly, drumming on it with her fingers rather than remaining in prolonged contact, then deftly change the subject. That was with me, of course; with strangers this was not even a possibility. Talking about herself would have meant allowing her "self" to surface, and that was something she simply could not allow. What she felt and how she really was had to be covered up, concealed beneath hundreds of protective veils— either learned or innate—beneath hundreds of habits—either learned or innate—that established a distance between her and the suffering or hopes that were watching and waiting inside her. I suppose what this revealed, deep down, was an intense shyness, an exaggerated rejection of any kind of exhibitionism or attention-seeking, of surrendering to other people's pity. She would have found it demeaning to talk to someone about what she missed or what was hurting her, and she could never allow that. My mother was very proud and kept her head held high at all times. Family was one thing, and that, of course, included my father as well as her sister and myself; friends and acquaintances, though, were quite another thing. They were not to be provided with a single fact that might later be used against her; she could not show them the slightest weakness or allow them to know too much or give them the opportunity to offer an opinion.

This was also why she was lonely. People seemed to sense a kind of aloofness in my mother, and there always came a point in any relationship when it collapsed in on itself and they would slip away. It wasn't that they sensed in her a lack of generosity, it was more that she was too openly generous. People liked my mother and felt drawn to her and sought her company, the feeling of calm she gave off, the intense, devotedly maternal friendship she offered; she was a person one could go to for help, she represented order and strength. The trouble was that their initial bedazzlement did not last, and sooner or later, those same friends would leave just as they had come. They would come into our lives, my mother would adopt them, and for a time, a close, unconditional friendship would spring up between them; then, after a while, for some inexplicable reason, a gradual distancing process would set in, until there came a point when she only ever thought of one of those same "close friends" when, later on, she happened upon their name in her address book. I imagine that the fault lay with the dynamic imposed by my mother, but whether it was because they grew weary of the lowly role they were allotted and finally fled in shame, or whether they tired of my mother and her inability to give of herself, the fact is that they all ended up leaving, and none survived either change or the passing of time. They would simply stop phoning, and she did nothing to bring them back, rather, she seemed not even to notice or be affected by their absence.

My mother's life, and mine at her side, was a constant parade of people, first childhood friends, then fellow students from university and work colleagues who would, for a while, become regular visitors and then, without exception, vanish from our world.

# VI

The only relationship that survived over time, the only person my mother phoned and who she seemed to need, apart from me, was my Aunt Delfina, her sister. With her, the roles were reversed and my mother became the daughter. From long before the death of my grandfather, of whom we spoke very little, my aunt was the one with authority, the one my mother turned to for help, the only person whose company she sought and the only one whose advice she would listen to. I don't mean that there were no differences between them. In more ways than one, my aunt was the polar opposite of my mother. She lived in La Coruña, where she had married very young; she had no children, and apart from reading books about bullfighting—which provided some compensation for the fact that this pastime was impossible to cultivate in a region so little given to bullfighting—her main occupation consisted of accompanying her husband, a naval officer, to the numerous social events organized throughout the year by the local yacht club and golf club. She found it hard to make friends and was one of those people whose self-image is so bound up with certain habits mechanically repeated over the years and never questioned that she could, on occasion, be somewhat inflexible. She was herself an extremely anxious person but felt an acute sense of responsibility toward my mother, and the role she took on with her was more that of mother than sister, and with me, more grandmother than aunt. And yet, although their relationship was based more on emotional needs than on any shared ideological or personal characteristics, it more than fulfilled its purpose. For her, my mother and I were, if I can put it this way, non-negotiable items. No distance was too great and no difference of opinion so serious as to be considered worth bothering about. Not even my father—who, as I've since found out, was a not inconsiderable bone of contention— caused the slightest rift between them. My mother would tell her all her problems and keep her up to date on each new catastrophe as it occurred; my aunt would listen and give her opinion, but she did so almost always with the intention of consoling rather than destroying, of consolidating my mother's position rather than advocating a break-up.

I hardly knew my grandfather, but I knew my Aunt Delfina very well, and anything I say about her, any anecdote intended to recover the past, will be influenced by the time we spent living together, those months when my mother was absent and about which I will speak in due course, and which I call her Paris period. This doesn't mean that my aunt had not been important to me before or that we had grown apart, rather, the idea I have of my aunt—the collection of intuitions, incidents either described or experienced, and various other data we collect about people, the things we turn to whenever we try to define them—that idea dates in large measure from the time I lived with her. For as long as I can remember, my Aunt Delfina has been part of my landscape, and I owe to her many of those childhood moments that stay forever in the memory because we think we can find in them the keys to the inexplicable, the unknowable and unimaginable. One such moment, the most relevant, perhaps, happened during the two years that my father, unbeknown to me, spent in prison. Now it almost makes me blush to remember it, because I would be lying if I said that I personally discovered anything or began for that reason to ask questions I'd never before asked myself. The only reason the memory endures is not because I drew any conclusions I did not have time to draw then but because, in a very vague and needless to say unconscious way, that was when I first became aware of a side of my mother she had never shown me before.

My Aunt Delfina rarely came to Madrid, but my mother and I often went to visit her, and we spoke to her on the phone twice a week, taking it in turns to call each other, not counting other calls made ad hoc, without my knowledge. I have the feeling there were hundreds of such calls—furtive, barely suspected moments when my mother would shut her bedroom door, or when she thought she was alone in the apartment until surprised by me sometimes arriving home unexpectedly early, moments when she sought the relief of being able to talk freely to my aunt. Of those phone calls, only one has stayed in my memory, the synthesis of all of them or perhaps the only one where I managed to catch something of what was being said. It was a perfectly ordinary evening, after we'd both turned in for the night, and I'd been in bed for some time, unable to get to sleep. I don't know what I was thinking about or even if I had any particular reason to be so restless. I imagine that nothing of any great importance had happened and that I had simply enjoyed one of those intense childhood days in which the body gets used to a faster rhythm that is then hard to relinquish. Anyway, as I always did when I couldn't sleep, I got up and left my bedroom in search of my mother's soothing company, a few moments of talk that would calm me down until sleep arrived unnoticed. I turned the corner of the hallway, and my unconfessed fear that she might already be asleep vanished completely when I saw that, from beneath her closed door, a bright fringe of light was penetrating the darkness. I crossed the brief distance separating us, and, just as I was about to open the door, a voice—my mother's, but which I did not immediately identify as hers—broke the silence of my two bare feet planted side by side on the narrow parquet floor. I heard only an incomprehensible murmur. I had raised my hand to the door handle, and my reflex reaction was to lower it again and stand very still, unsure as to whether I should retreat or stay where I was until I knew what was happening. Confused by this unexpected situation and fearful lest she should open the door and find me there, I was on the point of retracing my steps. The reason I didn't, but stayed rooted to the spot, holding my breath, was that just as I was about to turn around, I heard my mother's voice again, very clearly now and therefore recognizable. "I just can't go on, I can't." I froze, and I must confess that, at first, I didn't so much register the meaning of the words as the pitiful, complaining tone in which they were spoken. I can't even be sure that those were her exact words and not other, similar ones, but I can be sure about what happened next, after a silence of about two or three seconds: "I know, I do try to keep calm, but it's so hard. I know it's better this way, but I live in fear of the day someone will force him to open his eyes, and then none of my excuses will work anymore. Every morning I think, 'Today will be the day,' and I just don't think I can bear it. I feel like putting a stop to it right now, however much it will hurt him. He'll find out one day, either through me or someone else, and I don't know if he'll ever be able to forgive me." Here there was another pause, and it was then that I realized: my mother wasn't *with* someone but speaking on the phone. As if she herself wanted to confirm this fact, the next thing she said revealed who it was she was speaking to. "But, Delfina," I heard her say like someone trying to buy time in order to respond to a new reproach from the person on the other end. Feeling more at ease now, I was wondering again whether I should knock on the door or retreat, when a series of short words (*Yes, Fine, All right*) strung together and rounded off with a firm "I promise" provided me with the solution. Realizing that she was about to say goodbye, I decided to knock on the door. I did so without delay, before my mother had hung up, so as not to give the impression that I'd been listening. She immediately said, "Come in," this time addressing me, and then, more softly, as I opened the door and went in, "Yes, I'll call you, take care."

And that was that. As I went in, I didn't see her put the phone down. The door concealed this action from me, and when I'd closed it, nothing about her appearance or her attitude revealed anything untoward. And she made no mention of it, either. She assumed that I'd heard nothing and seemed not to care if I had, and I, for my part, merely sat down on her bed, saying that I couldn't sleep. She drew back the covers on the other side by way of invitation, and I seconded that gesture by slipping in between the sheets. For a while, as she began the usual ritual and embarked on a dialogue intended to make me forget my inability to sleep, all I could think of were the words I'd heard just a few moments before. I was troubled by the tone in which they'd been spoken, and I'm sure that I asked myself, however briefly, what it was that had provoked that tone of voice. It's equally true, though, that not for a second did it occur to me that I might be the subject of their conversation. As with everything important that happens in childhood, that realization only surfaced later, on the evanescent screen of memory. That night, as my mother talked to me and I lay at her side, listening simultaneously to what she was saying and to the capricious flow of my own thoughts, my replies became less and less focused, more spaced out, and I finally succumbed, defeated, to her melodious, absorbing voice. I fell asleep, and when I woke in the morning and found her dressed and standing by the bed, my only doubt, the only one that really interested me, was whether she had spent the night with me or if, as on other occasions, she had waited until I fell asleep to go and occupy my empty bed.

# VII

The two years that my father spent in prison are like a bellows that seems to empty and fill in accordance with the contours of memory. Some folds are plump with evocative sensations, circumstances, or moments, and in others the void of the unspoken and unrecorded renders the fertile soil of memory barren. Given that I was so keenly aware of incidents like the one described above, it may seem strange that I was completely deceived about my father and had unquestioningly accepted his disappearance without seeking any answers other than the rather lame ones provided by my mother. It may seem strange, and yet it's very easy to explain. Those two years, which would not necessarily be a time of substantial change for an adult, could easily, at the age I was then, have meant the transition from unconsciousness to a more critical mindset, from nonanalytic, unreflecting acceptance to an awakening of the ability to make my own judgments. I don't mean that none of these things occurred on the night when I heard my mother talking to my aunt on the phone. I'm convinced I found out nothing new that night, nothing I didn't know already, and that what I heard through the door did not make me rethink the fixed elements, the certainties and uncertainties that sustained my life at the time. For a few moments, the moments during which I stood listening at my mother's bedroom door, I could have become a witness to the vulnerability my mother usually concealed from me, but I had neither eyes nor time to seize that opportunity. I had heard my mother complain, weep, and beg for help, and it wasn't that I couldn't have given her that help or couldn't imagine the reason for her distress, simply that I wasn't even in a position to guess how deep that distress went. I *was* troubled by her tone of voice, which was entirely new to me, and I could have been on the brink of uncovering a facet of her personality quite different from those already known to me, but the fact that such a discovery aroused no doubts in me and neither fuelled a desire to know more nor filled me with a fever to seek out further dark, suspicious depths is proof that the incident did not shake the ground beneath my feet and make my whole world totter, did not become a defining, before-and-after moment. On the other hand, I did store it away in my memory, and in doing so, I cancelled out any harmful effects it might have had; this was a major change from what would have happened one or two years before, when something similar could easily have occurred but without leaving any trace or so much as a shadow on my memory.

Something quite different happens in the case of the other vast, unpopulated hours, all that lost time I am completely unable to encapsulate in images or recover by means of words. People say that childhood images return with old age and that they exist in a kind of fog until then, a tunnel growing ever deeper, with smooth, uniform walls from which only a few light bulbs hang, not bright enough to illuminate their whole length. Perhaps that's where the feeling of emptiness comes from, an emptiness that has to wait until old age for the shadows to be filled with light, for faces and conversations, fears and the hours spent together, games and arguments and the inevitable moments of tension to present themselves to me just as they were, each one distinct from the others. My mother waking me up each morning; my mother telling me to hurry up so as not to miss the school bus; my mother leaving the house to drive to work; my mother at home, where she had been since midday, when I returned at six; my mother insisting that I do my homework; my mother worried; my mother happy; my mother as sole spectator of my childish witticisms; my mother reading me books I couldn't read on my own; my mother answering my questions; my mother sending me to bed and then coming to kiss me goodnight; my mother closing the door; my mother letting me caress her or her caressing me ... The journey to and from school; the weekends that would grow in my mind's eye before they arrived, until their glow was doused by the dull gray of Sundays; days that were both different and the same; short days and long days; days when, on returning home, she alone was there to greet me. There are many such instants worth recalling and that cancel each other out, superimposing themselves one upon the other with all the force of the unalterable. And yet, somehow, even though they're not particularly significant and contain no revelation that makes them stand out from the rest, even though they don't pester me or clamor for my attention, there are certain memories that always surface: the Christmas morning when we went out to buy something and had to walk all the way home again because my mother had forgotten her purse; coming back in the car from somewhere or other and, while we were stopped at traffic lights, hearing through the lowered window two drivers engaged in a heated altercation; the afternoon my mother reached out her hand to pick up a cup of coffee and I saw in her large-boned wrist the antecedent or model of my own wrist, which, while not yet as thick as hers, was already preparing to outstrip hers and to grow as it grows now in my memory of that moment; or the steep, dirt track in the park beside our house that I will always associate with the clothes my mother was wearing one midday when we walked down it to go and have lunch at a nearby restaurant—short skirt, polo neck sweater in the same blue as the skirt, knit tights, also blue, and matching low-heeled shoes with rounded toes.

I suppose that, basically, what I need is a candle to light my memory. Living with my mother, seeing her every morning and every night, talking to her more than to any other person throughout the day, it was difficult to find a dissonant note, some ever-widening crack that might put at risk the stability of the edifice she had created in order to give me shelter. When I look back at those distant days, I'm surprised by the tranquility, the lack of color, and the monotony with which they passed. My mother, as I said, was very disciplined, which meant that life with her followed strict rules, not only regarding superficial matters—the organization of time and the tasks we undertook together—but also what could not be observed directly, the inner life that, with most people, is subject to the changeable tides of mood, but that in her case, rarely got in the way of what she deemed appropriate for each moment and its fulfillment. That's why she exuded such confidence, why there were no upsets or unforeseen incidents and why, in her company, few things seemed unattainable. Life with her was like a straight line. There were no particularly serious problems, no enigmas that could not be resolved with a look, a few words of consolation, or a discreet silence.

The time of year in which the most evocative sensations and moments are concentrated—where the bellows of memory fills up most often and leaves the fewest empty spaces—coincides with the arrival of summer. My image of my mother from July to September grows clearer, more distinct. In the winter, whole hours go by without our seeing each other; there are certain times of day when our lives barely touch, and this only makes the fog grow denser. In the summer, we spend all day together, and the frontiers between the hours dissolve, which means that, even at a distance, I know where she is and how she's using her time; I can see her reading, sunbathing, sitting and staring into space, or watching television just for the pleasure of it and not because I'm there and she wants to make the most of having that moment by my side. In the summer, her image grows in importance and becomes, were that possible, even more indispensable. We used to plan the summers together months in advance, and apart from the few visits we received from my father or some friend or other, we spent the time mostly alone. Always in different places, always in houses that my mother would rent for two months and that she would enter like a whirlwind in order to make everything new, moving furniture around, and taking with us sheets, towels, and even pillows from our own apartment in Madrid. Always that same unchanging ritual repeated year after year, until I began to spend the summers on my own. First, two weeks in La Coruña. Then a plane or a train or a day's journey by car, and once we reached our destination, a couple of days were spent cleaning (everything had to be thoroughly washed, all trace of the previous inhabitants expunged, so as to make the house our own), and at last, two whole months lay ahead of us, sixty intense days that ended in the first week of

September, when she had to go back to Madrid to sort out the syllabus for the new term and negotiate timetables with her colleagues.

The summers were a performance put on for our benefit alone, and they provide the best summary of those years, the compendium that best illustrates them. The story of our life together could, I believe, be told entirely through those summers without greatly distorting the sequence of events. Firstly, lost in a time when seasons did not yet exist for me and the year was not divided up according to fixed dates, there would be the summers my mother and I spent with my father. They were the only ones the three of us shared, and yet if I try to remember them, it is she, not he, I think of, she is the person who filled my mind with what little of those summers I know, with the few reference points that allow me to imagine them. Almost immediately afterward, albeit separated by a clear boundary, come four or five summers for which my memories are only slightly less hazy, retaining as they do a few images in which my father is always just about to arrive but never does, or only rarely; these are followed by two consecutive summers when my father does not appear and is not expected; one summer that was supposed to be a reunion but ended up being the first that my mother and I spent entirely in the company of my aunt; and lastly, the one that signaled the final rupture, or depending on your point of view, the onset of normality, another summer spent in La Coruña, a summer followed by a long list of summers in which we waited for no one, summers that are distinguishable only by the different decors of the various houses we rented.

That, let us say, is the chronology, the temporal framework as experienced by me. Then there is what was going on inside

54

my mother's mind, and it is precisely because those summers are the most perfect expression of our very close relationship that they aren't enough and are of no use to me. My father hardly appears in those summers, and, in a way, he needs to appear for the figure of my mother to make sense. I need to feel my father's presence, I need to think about him in order to begin to think about her. About my mother without me, not about the two of us putting up with my father, but about my mother alone. About my mother and what she hoped for and didn't hope for, about my mother being happy and sad, satisfied and dissatisfied, or simply accepting the way things are, perhaps finding compensations for her strange life, or not even looking for them.

I need my father, I need him to leave prison, I need to start thinking about him.

# VIII

My memory grows confused, and I can't separate that morning from all the ornaments and extras I've added over the years, every time I spoke or thought about it. I'm not sure whether what appears in my memory now is a faithful reflection of what really happened or if the truth has become contaminated or modified by later events or by how I've assimilated those events as my personality has developed. I don't even know why I keep remembering it. I mean, we often forget crucial events and remember others that are far less significant. We remember details such as the fact that we were wearing a new sweater on a certain day, or that it was a Tuesday, and we forget, on the other hand, that we received a slap in the face or that our father returned from the doctor's and shut himself up in his bedroom never to come out. Often our memory of important things is built precisely on the banal, often it's the memory of something that had no apparent effect on us that brings with it the memory of what endures, of what is important now, but which, when it happened, was *not* important, or did not appear to be.

So, for example, what I remember most about the morning my father came out of prison is our car, a battered, much-dented, pale blue Dyane 6, which lasted us for years and which, along with other peculiarities, such as frequent stalling (always in the most inopportune places, and usually with half a dozen cars behind us sounding their horns), had a tendency to slow down whenever we were trying to pass someone. It would start well, but after that initial burst of speed, the engine would flood, and however hard my mother pressed down on the accelerator and however slowly the other car was moving, it was impossible to overtake it unless we both helped it along by jerking compulsively back and forth in our seats. Something similar would happen at bends in the road, which we could only get around if we leaned hard into them. Apart from these comical situations or the frequent rages this triggered in other drivers, the main consequence was that my mother did not feel very safe driving it and used it mainly for going to school and back. If we were traveling around the city together, she preferred to take a taxi, and so I rarely rode in the car, apart from at vacation time, when we left Madrid to go to her sister's or to whichever house we had rented for the summer. Since whole months could go by without my even knowing where it was parked, the fact that we broke the rule one day was enough to fix it in my memory forever.

That morning, which was a weekday, my mother had come into my bedroom to wake me up slightly earlier than usual, and while she was doing so and giving me her usual fond, morning peck on the cheek, she told me not to put my uniform on, because neither of us would be going to school, and that I should try to dress nicely, as I knew she liked me to. She then urged me to hurry up and, still without telling me the reason for this change in routine, left the room. We had breakfast together, as we did every day, and when I asked what was going on, she said she would tell me later, that it was a surprise. She didn't seem nervous, just slightly more serious than usual. I suppose it was that she was about to take a difficult step and that, although she had made up her mind and there was now no turning back, she was still unsure quite how to deal with it. While she took charge of washing the dishes and putting the leftovers in the fridge, I went back to my room, where I dressed myself appropriately, in almost exactly the same clothes I wore each day for school, except that everything was of the very best quality and carefully ironed: gray, wool flannel pants rather than cheap flannelette ones; a thick, navy blue turtleneck rather than the thinner V-neck sweater I wore for school; lace-up shoes with heel plates rather than my usual moccasins, which were worn at the toes and heels . . . As we were heading for the door, she warned me that it would probably be cold where we were going and advised me to take my blue balaclava with me, just in case. Not until long after we had gotten into the car and begun the journey did I have any idea where we were going, and she made no mention of my father. It should have occurred to me that anything so cloaked in mystery must necessarily involve him. And yet the idea never entered my head. During those initial minutes in the car, while my mother was busy trying to dodge the issue and talking about things I've since forgotten, and while I was listening to her, and she could see that I was listening— although her dilatoriness was as obvious as my impatience for her to get to the point—the only likely destination I could think of was La Coruña. I thought of my Aunt Delfina and wondered if something had happened to her, if she was sick or even dead. There followed an even less reassuring silence, and it was only after my mother had sat sunk in thought for a while, apparently incapable of speech, and as the idea of some dreadful tragedy was taking definite shape inside my head that she took her eyes off the road and finally looked at me and dared to tell me where we were going. It was one of those clear, crisp winter days in Madrid, with a few white clouds suspended in the bluest of blue skies; we had left behind us the monstrous Arco del Triunfo and were driving, with heavy traffic ahead of us, to the Puerta de Hierro exit.

"We're going to Burgos," she said.

It's many years since I heard those words, and although memories tend to overlap and nothing is as it was, I still remember, as clearly as I remember those words, that I did not reply; it was as if nothing had been said. My mother's eyes immediately returned to the road ahead, and, for a while, silence reigned again. It wasn't until we reached the last traffic lights on the edge of the city, before merging onto the main highway, that she spoke again. She was changing into first gear, the moment after the lights turned green, when, raising a newly lit cigarette to her lips and without taking her eyes off the road, I heard her say in a strangely calm, almost routine voice, "What would you think if someone were to tell you that you had been entirely mistaken about my real profession and that I'm really a professional thief, a swindler?"

At this point, my memory becomes confused, as if it were some now nonexistent building whose shape we can clearly recall, but not where the windows were, or what materials it was made of, or what the decoration on the façade was like. All that remains now is the sound of the traffic, a sense of my own nervousness, and a certain inner disquiet, but all trace of thought has vanished. All that remains are the means used by my mother to tease out the thread of a confession, her half-prudent, half-timid way of tugging at the skein, leading me toward an explanation that would help me understand and forgive, when the real revelation came; her actual words, however, have been erased, they no longer exist. They were probably not quite as abrupt, but even at the risk of making them sounding artificial, all I can do is reconstruct them, although I can't do the same with my own words.

After a pause during which neither of us spoke, she continued for some minutes to ask me more of these rhetorical questions, which she strung together without expecting me to answer them and without answering them herself: "What would you think if I were to lose my job and, unable to find another, devoted myself to stealing? Do you think stealing is justifiable in times of need, or do you believe that you should always seek some other means of earning money?" Although she was driving and couldn't really take her eyes off the road to look at me, she was forced to do so when, having clarified her position by telling me that stealing out of desperation was not the same thing as stealing for convenience's sake or so as to avoid having to work, she began to take a more radical stance: "It may be that other people won't always be able to understand the reasons why someone steals. There may be other reasons apart from necessity. You might be suffering from an illness or mistakenly think that there's no other solution. There are some things whose importance you alone can understand. For example, the way we, as individuals, experience certain problems. What hurts or saddens me won't necessarily hurt or sadden you." Here she gave more examples to help me understand what she meant, and only when she was sure she had convinced me did she dare to conclude with another question: "Who are we to judge the reasons that lead someone to act outside the usual rules, who are we to judge whether they're valid or not?" She underlined this question with a silence and then, trying to sound emphatic, took the next definitive step in her argument: "That isn't the whole story. Anyone can make a mistake. For example, feeling that the future holds no hope and committing a desperate act that you immediately regret. The main thing to consider is that such a slip does not completely invalidate a person or make him less honorable. Unless it becomes a habit, the act of stealing tells us nothing about the thief." After this rather unorthodox statement, spoken in a monotone, she fell silent for a few seconds, then glanced across at me and again gave herself as an example: "Say one day you talk back to me, and because I'm feeling particularly on edge, I respond by slapping you—I would certainly be acting wrongly. However, that slap would not be enough to make me a bad person, and it would be the same if, instead of hitting you, I went into a bank to steal. Everyone makes mistakes, and if only certain people are arrested, it isn't because those of us outside prison are different or incapable of doing exactly the same. It's just that we've never been in that same desperate situation or we've lacked either the courage or the means. I myself am not completely immune. The fact that I haven't fallen doesn't mean that I won't one day. It may be that I haven't needed to up until now, or couldn't run the risk of losing you. But that's no guarantee for the future. No one is immune, not even you, although I hope, of course, that you never find yourself in such dire need and never feel you have no other way out."

That, in my own words, is the long and short of what my mother said that morning—before she mentioned my father. Her words were doubtless gentler and more maternal, as befits someone trained to speak to children. And yet after that very impersonal introduction, she did not move on from the general to the particular. Whether for her own convenience or because she was thinking of me and how I might react, she felt she should have her hands free and thus be ready to deal with whatever my response might be; we had left the main road and were parked outside a bar, with the engine off but with no indication as yet that we were going to get out of the car and into the intense cold that was already making itself felt and go in search of a second breakfast. She didn't beat around the bush this time. She told me directly, and then looked at me like someone studying the effect on another person of a particularly harsh statement. I still can't remember her exact words. I heard the word "prison," I heard the word "Burgos" again, and then I said nothing, absorbing this confession, and at the same time trying to imagine the remote, diffuse figure of my father in a prison cell; a confusion of bars, roll calls in corridors, and prisoners with wicked faces went through my mind, more like a movie than anything that actually related to me. For a moment, neither of us said anything; any explanations came later. My mother was looking at me, but I said nothing. She was looking at me and I was looking at her, and neither of us broke the silence, because neither of us really knew how to. I imagine that what I was feeling was not what my mother was expecting I would feel; she imagined that part of my world must be falling in on me, and yet my only world was her. It could not collapse as long as she did not collapse, as long as she was there studying my face intently, waiting for some expression of doubt or pain to appear, and meanwhile frozen by her own expectations of what she imagined was going on inside me; even when she reached into her purse to take out a cigarette and light it, she still waited, keeping her eyes fixed on me. We must have spent several minutes like that, because the next thing I remember is what she said, first in the bar and then again back in the car, trying to exonerate my father, abandoning the abstract language she had used initially in favor of more concrete terms, painting a picture of him that was real and at the same time comprehensible and forgivable. I can no longer separate what she told me from what I know now, from what she gradually confided to me in later, lonelier years, and from what I've since found out for myself, what I dared to think, or what I made up. I imagine that the resulting notion was more innocuous, more hopeful or less crude, than the one I have now. In what way or to what degree, I really don't care. After all, if that morning has endured over the years and I can speak about it now, it's not because of what I found out then. Even if she had chosen not to take me to Burgos and had told me nothing about my father, what I would have known then is pretty much what I know now. "Listen," my mother said that morning, stubbing out her cigarette and turning to look at me again. "Pay attention and listen."

# IX

There's a photo we took that day, over which I linger whenever I come across it or whenever a pang of nostalgia makes me seek it out. It was taken shortly after that last scene, once we'd arrived in Burgos and walked across the deserted city. It was taken with the camera on delayed action, and it shows my mother and me, along with my father, standing by the side of an empty road. My father is looking very blond and tanned, and at his feet sits a large, old-fashioned suitcase. You would think the photo had been taken in summer if it weren't for the snowy field in the background and the fact that the three of us are wearing overcoats (I'm clutching my blue balaclava). We're smiling, although my father's smile, somewhat blurred and out of focus, seems rather forced, as if he were impatient to be doing something else. They've put me in the middle (I come up to about shoulder height on both), and because they didn't get the angle quite right, next to my mother you can see a concrete wall topped by a sentry box. It's the prison wall, but that isn't why I linger over the photo every time I look at it. It isn't the situation, which I can remember perfectly and which, therefore, doesn't trouble me.

When a fundamental part of the backdrop to our childhood hasn't always been fixed and immovable, when we haven't been shown, right from the start, how it really was, when it's been hidden or disguised up until a certain moment and we then have to go back and learn to see it from a new perspective, nothing ever seems quite certain again. Duplicity and deceit make us suspicious, and what has just been revealed, what we've actually lived through and experienced, and what has merely been a matter for speculation become so intertwined that it's hard to tell them apart. Our intuitions have as much weight as hard evidence, and while there may be occasions when those intuitions turn out to be right, there are, on the other hand, many others when we can't distinguish what we really know from what we've simply imagined, where we see silhouetted figures when there's really only a wall, a shadow, and a plant swaying in the wind. If, moreover, that revealed reality is a very unusual one which then begins to be treated as perfectly normal because it *is* normal for the person who has revealed it to us, the person who has removed our blindfold, then the whole confused skein of events becomes still more tangled.

I began to face up to the problematic figure of my father and what his nebulous personality meant for my mother, and I began this some time after that morning in Burgos, precisely when we had most reason to believe that one era was coming to an end and we were about to begin to lead a normal life. Up until then, any information I'd been given about him had reached me in adulterated form. My mother made use of her position as intermediary, and not only did I never doubt the excuses she gave for his absence, I also considered as normal things that weren't normal at all. If she told me, as she did initially, that my father had had an accident and was in the hospital or, as she said later on, that he lived abroad, working for some international organization, that is what I believed and what I would say if some school friend asked me about him. It didn't even occur to me that this was no justification for such a long separation, that he could easily have come to visit us now and again or we could have gone to see him over vacation, or he could have phoned or written a letter.

As a result of that morning of revelations en route to Burgos, I must have had a lot of questions to ask. I had to ask my mother how and why, if this was the first time such a thing had happened or if my father had often been in similar situations. She doubtless answered as best she could, although, again, I can't remember exactly how, and her answers to my questions have become confused now with other questions and other answers given later on. I imagine, of course, that she concealed certain information from me, details she considered inappropriate for me to know. After all, it cannot even be said that the picture she painted of my father that morning was exactly faithful; it had a touch of the novel about it and, far from presenting me with the crude reality and thus tarnishing my father's image, made him seem a romantic, even heroic figure, which in no way corresponded with what I learned for myself in between that November day when my mother revealed his secret to me and the still distant days when other secrets, as yet unimagined, would take center stage.

It isn't what my mother did or didn't say in the car; it's the reason why she decided to speak that intrigues me every time I look at that photo. Because if she really thought there was a possibility that my father would change and that we would never again have to live through such a situation, why mention it when he was just about to come home? The worst of it, his long absence, was over. She could easily have gone to pick him up alone. I could understand her telling me about it earlier if

I'd become suspicious or started asking questions she couldn't answer, but since this was not the case, I don't understand why she did it then, on the very last day, when the simplest thing would have been to go and pick him up in secret and continue the fiction. Unless, of course, she suspected that my father would not change and she wanted to cover her own back. In that case, I would interpret her gesture as an attempt to establish a pact between us, so that I could never reproach her for not having been honest with me. Her previous lie became justifiable as soon as she decided to tell me that such a lie had existed. It would not have been justifiable, on the other hand, if, over the course of time, I'd found out the truth by myself and my suspicions of further concealments had threatened to come between us.

I did not become aware of the implications of my mother's decision, however, until much later, when my father had vanished from our lives and other things were beginning to occupy much of my imagination and my memories. I only mention it now to emphasize the importance to me of that cold, early-November morning, so brilliantly captured in that photo, because—over the years and through whatever hardships and betrayals there may or may not have been—it's always that day I go back to whenever I feel a need to judge my mother. The moment, in short, that, for good or for ill, sealed my alliance with her. "Pay attention and listen."

# X

Memory is a great temptation, and what could be easier than to highlight some memories at the expense of others and retrospectively draw up a synthesis adapted to what has endured rather than what actually happened?

After the drive back from Burgos, my father's return home, his way of accepting our presence and settling in again, bore little resemblance to what you might imagine in the circumstances. After my mother and I had greeted him with a kiss outside the metal door through which he had emerged only seconds before—slowly and tentatively, with the unfocused gaze of someone emerging from the baggage reclaim at an airport without knowing if anyone will be there waiting for him—my father behaved as if he hadn't been away for very long at all. He clasped my mother's hand, she took the photo with which she wanted to commemorate the moment, and then he climbed into the car as if in a hurry to get back to Madrid. After that, there were none of the gestures or words or signs that form part of that whole ritual of delicate links with which those who return from a prolonged absence ensure their readmission into an almost forgotten routine until bodies and moods, individual rhythms, different ways of looking and moving, and different ways of speaking become familiar again and that period of separation is forgotten once and for all. He, however, asked no questions and never mentioned what he had left behind.

My father's return was like a long-awaited event we believed would transform us or change something in our lives but that, when it happened, failed to do either. Except, in this case, I hadn't been waiting for it, and so our reunion can't really be said to have disappointed me. The disappointment, if we can call it that, only arises now, years later, and it's not just to do with my father's return. If I think about myself at the time, I cannot help but feel surprised by how devoid of emotions my memory is. I have very clear images of him and my mother, I can recall fragments of what they did and those occasions when a flicker of doubt or fear appeared in their eyes, but I find it hard to see myself, I can't remember any particular surge of joy or disappointment. If my memory is to be trusted, I accepted my father's return home rather as I had accepted his absence, almost without feeling it.

And yet he wasn't actually cold toward me. It's true that he never let himself be carried away by an excess of affection, even though he was clearly thrilled to be free and his excitement occasionally broke through the cool, calm exterior he tried to maintain. But I don't think it was coldness exactly that made him behave like that, not a deliberate, conscious coldness, at least. Rather, it was something he couldn't control, a barrier that sprang up between him and us, preventing him from behaving naturally. He wasn't at ease. Years later, to justify this, my mother would say that he always needed the veil of a lie and that since this was impossible with us, his few attempts to establish some complicity were rendered null, because he could never bring himself to mention his time in prison. She may have been right. It's certainly true that there was never any unveiling, any display of trust. Given that I had seen him come out of prison, he couldn't possibly think that I didn't know, and yet he never made the slightest reference, not even a joking one, to his two-year absence.

During the first few days, he was hardly ever at home. He would leave the apartment while still damp from his morning shower and come back hours later, often early the next day, when my mother and I were already up and yawning over our breakfasts. He would do his best not to be seen, to sidle off down the hallway without so much as a "Good morning." If he couldn't avoid running into us and had no option but to say something, he would shoot us a fleeting glance, without even stopping, removing his jacket or tie as he passed, and making some supposedly comical remark—"Sorry your Dad's such a good-for-nothing," or "Don't worry, I'm nearly done, one more night and it'll all be over." Most of the time, though, there was no such opportunity. These were strange days. Not because they were full of tension, complaints, or disappointments. They were strange in the same way as all things that defy definition and leave no trace. As strange as the fact that my father made no attempt to talk to me and that I neither complained about this nor felt hurt. Meanwhile, my mother remained utterly calm and detached from the situation, as if she wanted to give him time or feared provoking some conflict. I don't know what happened between them in private, when they were alone in their bedroom, but in my presence, she was always kindness itself. She made no demands, never complained about anything he did, whereas I, given the oddness of the situation, turned spy. My father's hermetic nature, his desire to draw a veil over his whole person, far from creating the inattention he sought, acted like a powerful lure, and whenever I could,

I would spend my time observing him, eager to spot any gesture or comment that might help me unravel the mysteries of his newly discovered personality. It wasn't premeditated, I wasn't aware I was doing anything forbidden, but however spontaneous and unmethodical my techniques, it came to the same thing. No detail was irrelevant, from how he moved to his curious choice of clothes, for he made no distinction between formal and informal wear but conflated the two styles, showing a complete disregard for convention or the idea that one should keep certain outfits set aside for special occasions; he avoided suits, opting instead for sports jackets and scarves, which he combined with jeans or corduroys or wool flannel pants with the cuffs rolled up. I was ever alert, ever vigilant. I would follow him around the house like an automaton, and whenever he got a phone call, I would hang around trying to catch whatever words I could—unlike my mother, who would hand him the receiver and immediately scuttle off somewhere else.

I don't know who made those calls, if they were people he knew from before or if they were new nocturnal acquisitions. I don't even know if they were as frequent as I remember or just a few calls that grew in number in my child's mind and continued to grow with the passing time, but whatever the truth of the matter, what I heard gave me my first inkling of my father's duplicitous nature, of his need to lie. Not that I caught him telling any untruths. I simply realized that, for some reason, he had no need to pretend to the people who phoned him, or else his pretense had some other aim; he changed completely when he spoke on the phone. His usual tense, laconic way of speaking vanished, and he adopted a relaxed, often humorous tone, which was quite the opposite of how he spoke to us.

Apart from that one furtive discovery, gleaned from the odd moments when I would linger in the hallway or hang around in a doorway, I can't remember anything else, just the look of apparent indifference in my mother's eyes—gentle and lost in thought, as I recall—whenever we sensed or felt his unexpected presence.

That unexpectedness found its fullest expression three or four weeks after his arrival home, one Saturday or Sunday morning, on the twenty-eighth of November. I remember the date exactly because it's my Aunt Delfina's birthday, and my mother and I had just gotten off the phone to her and were sitting in my bedroom deciding on a date for our next trip to La Coruña. My father was in his room, supposedly sleeping, and perhaps because of that or because we unconsciously excluded him from all plans, we were talking quietly. I didn't notice him at first. He crept up so stealthily behind my mother that I didn't realize he had entered the room until he was actually there. After raising one finger to his lips as if asking me not to betray him, he stood stock still and silent, and when, because of some imprudent look of mine, my mother seemed about to discover his presence, he bent down and affectionately put his arms about her waist. This wasn't the first such gesture I had seen, but it was the most spontaneous and, therefore, the most sincere, as evidenced by what happened next. As if she had been waiting a long time for this embrace, my mother did not start or turn around. She clasped the hands embracing her and, smiling, drew them more tightly around her, as if they were the buckle on some strange belt; and while he tightened his embrace and topped it off with a smacking kiss on her neck, she gently turned her head and leaned back against the body holding her close, thus prolonging the contact.

"So what are you two plotting, eh? Aren't I included?" asked my father after a moment, as he detached himself from the embrace. "Why don't we go and have lunch somewhere and talk about it?"

That was the first time he had shown any interest in our plans, the first time he had spoken in the plural. I've forgotten what my mother said in response and what else happened before we left the house to go to the restaurant where we had lunch. The only image I have is of the three of us walking down the street and of my surprise when my father at one point suggested coming with us to La Coruña. Even though his suggestion came to nothing and we never made that trip together, it has remained lodged in my memory because, from that day on, he began to coordinate his schedule with ours, and the only life he led was the one he began to share with us. Despite all her efforts to simulate normality, my mother had clearly been waiting for some such sign and could finally relax, and I, too, stopped being quite so obsessed with my father's activities. I can't imagine what brought about that change in him, whether it was a sincere attempt to adapt himself to us, a renunciation of his own interests in favor of some hypothetical family harmony, or, once again, merely the dictates of his own egotistical instincts just happening to coincide with what was expected of him. The fact is that the months that followed must have far outstripped even my mother's most optimistic expectations.

# XI

As regards my mother, I have only questions. I don't know what hopes she had for that change in behavior or if she ever seriously believed in it; was it so very unusual that she could allow herself to believe he would not slide back into his old ways, or, on the contrary, could she not help but fear or foresee what would inevitably happen even if she denied it to herself moments later?

One thing is sure, once a certain degree of normality had been restored, regardless of whether or not she hoped it would last, my mother's behavior changed, too. It was not a spectacular transformation, she didn't suddenly become more cheerful, nor did she behave in any way that was substantially different from before. It was more subtle than that, almost imperceptible to anyone who was not, as I was, aware of every signal she gave off. During the early days following his return, not only did she avoid mentioning him when she was alone with me, she did her best to never even say his name, fearful, perhaps, of provoking any discussion for which she was not sure she could find the right answers. However, from the time my father began to stay at home, she grew far less cautious. Since there were fewer areas to avoid, fewer areas that, should my father come up in conversation, would have forced us to mention matters on which it was still too early to make any firm pronouncement, she allowed herself to be a little more spontaneous. If she came home and found he wasn't there, instead of falling silent, as she would have done before, she would ask quite fearlessly where he was. If the three of us were sitting around the dining table joshing with my father and he suddenly got up and disappeared for a moment, she would go on joking, rather than stopping either out of fear or prudence. She went no further than that, though. She never referred to him without some specific reason or without relating it to some event in the day. After that morning in Burgos, when she had spoken to me for the first time about his idiosyncratic personality, she never returned to the subject. She didn't offer me any new information, nor did she probe his motives for behaving as he did. Sometimes I would notice a melancholy look in her eyes when some incident aroused painful memories or when she could have done with an explanation, an explanation she never demanded. Day-to-day remarks were fine, but nothing that touched on the very heart of the problem—nothing about my father's possible fears or hopes or misgivings, or what he was planning to do, or if he would stay with us permanently. She spoke only of the present, never of the past or the future.

Now I understand what a difficult balance her life must have been. On the one hand, there was me—ostensibly the most important person, the one for whose stability she was sacrificing everything else. It's impossible to believe that anything she said or did then was spontaneous, or that she would have said or done the same thing had I not existed. She never allowed her feelings to run away with her. Her every gesture, her every action was rigorously assessed according to what she judged to be in my best interests. That's why, while it was inconceivable that she would have told me about my father too soon, it was just as inconceivable that she would have tried to maintain that fiction when he was no longer in prison. She concealed the truth when she thought it best to exclude me and stopped doing so when she thought that deception could turn against her, and fell silent again when she realized that any comment she made about my father's habits—habits I could now observe for myself—might prove to be mistaken or spark questions on my part which she didn't know if she was able or willing to answer. On the other hand, there were her doubts, the fact that, in a way, this whole situation was built on shifting sand. After all, whether she liked it or not, she had to accept that a great deal had to be left to chance. There would have been no point in her drawing up any plans on her own if, later on, my father did the exact opposite. That was where the silence came from, that's why she never mentioned him at first, and afterward only referred to him in safe, everyday situations, avoiding any confidences that could create a dangerous precedent between us.

This meant that I was unaware of his shortcomings until they were the past and not the present, when they had ceased to exist; and those that survived were different ones that, again, I didn't notice until they, in turn, had been replaced. In this way, we passed through various phases, and I only discovered what the previous phase had meant once it already was the previous phase. In a way, my mother always seemed quite assured, accepting what was going on around her. She never appeared anxious or sad, or surprised by the pace of events. She seemed to accept them, and it was only when those events had passed that I understood what displeasure they had brought her. This also explains why I was always rather slow when it came to judging her state of mind.

Something similar happened with work. My father never said a word about finding a job, and I was completely unaware that normality could not be considered to have been fully restored for my mother until he took the first step toward seeking employment.

It happened one weekend when we were coming back from Toledo. We'd gone there to see an exhibition, which we weren't able to do, in the end, because the palace where it was being held was closed in the afternoons, and we didn't arrive until lunchtime. I don't recall whose idea the trip was or what we talked about while it lasted. I vaguely remember that my father was very lively and full of jokes and that my mother, although she laughed at every humorous remark, gave off a certain air of unease, as if she distrusted that perfect family scene. After our failed attempt to visit the exhibition, we spent the rest of the day wandering aimlessly up and down the steep streets, and before picking up the car to go back to Madrid, by which time it was growing dark, we went into a bar right next to where we'd parked. It was a very cramped place, with a layer of sticky sawdust on the floor and, at the back, a few tables topped with faux-wood Formica. We chose to sit on the brightly colored padded stools at the bar and did so gladly, eager to rest our legs. We'd been there for some time, with the lone waiter occupied in cleaning the coffee machine, when, behind us, during a moment of silence, we heard a man's voice addressing someone as "Professor." We all turned around, and I was immediately conscious that while my response had been purely instinctive, there was a degree of urgency and alarm about my parents' response. The scene that followed has remained engraved on my memory because it was the first time I'd actually seen anyone from my father's secret world. There before us stood a man of about sixty, looking expectantly at my father, while my father scrutinized his face and gave absolutely no sign of recognition. After a few seconds, during which the stranger grew noticeably nervous, my father suddenly got down from his stool and shook the other man's hand while the latter loudly clapped him on the back. Then, avoiding looking at us, although my mother and I were observing both men minutely, my father began to talk animatedly, undoing his initial silence and hesitation and the long moments it had taken him to react. I've forgotten how my father addressed the other man—in fact, I'm not even sure he used a name—but I do remember noticing a marked difference in attitude. They spoke warmly, like old friends, but the stranger seemed far less at ease, as if the title by which he had addressed my father embodied a spontaneous degree of respect. He wasn't tense and was obviously enjoying the encounter, but equally obvious was the tenuous wall that interposed itself between them, a veil tinged with a sense of admiration or respect that my father did not share. The strangest thing, though, was that this submissive attitude in no way affected their evident intimacy. They joked, and asked about people I didn't know, of whom I'd never heard him speak, and they did so using harsh-sounding nicknames. Apart from that and a few other banal remarks, I could understand almost nothing of what they said, with my father behaving as if my mother and I weren't there at all. I understood the intention behind what they said, and certain general ideas, but nothing specific. It wasn't that I couldn't understand their voices or that they spoke too quickly, it was like listening to a language I knew only imperfectly and whose meaning I had to extrapolate from individual words and tone of voice. In this case, they were speaking the same language as us, but their conversation was so sprinkled with strange terminology and odd turns of phrase that I had the impression that these, rather than anything else, contained the real essence of each sentence. I now know that what I heard that afternoon was prison slang, but I didn't know it then, and I remember feeling utterly perplexed. But this conversation did not last nearly as long as it has taken me to write about it. After a few moments of silent waiting, my mother said to my father that we would wait for him in the car and that he should hurry up. He turned briefly and said, "Yes, fine," and then, making no attempt to introduce us or involve us in the conversation, he immediately turned back to his companion. Even more curious was the fact that this rudeness was not exclusive to him. I mean that the other man could at least have directed a look or a smile at us, some gesture that might indicate if not interest, then a willingness, however insincere, to keep us there. It was clear from the very start that he was aware of our presence and had not only guessed who we were but knew it for certain; however, just as he had not said a word to us or so much as glanced at us out of the corner of his eye, as we do when we meet an acquaintance accompanied by someone he or she has neglected to introduce, he made no attempt to prevent us from going, either. As if he were acting according to a code of conduct of which I knew nothing, he behaved exactly as my father did—after shooting us the very briefest of glances, he turned away and allowed us to leave.

I've often thought about that scene in Toledo, and in a way, I consider it a turning point, the moment when I realized how futile it would be to try and penetrate my father's private world, not in order to try and understand his behavior, but to establish some kind of relationship between us, if not one of equality, then at least of complicity. After all, if my father behaved as he did, it wasn't because he was trying to hide anything from us, it wasn't that he'd foreseen that encounter and had things to discuss that he didn't want my mother or myself to hear; in that case it would have been far easier not to take us with him to Toledo. He was merely trying to keep the two worlds that constituted his life quite separate. My father wanted money and success and to be admired, and while he was capable of committing crimes in order to achieve this, he found it hard to accept that the rest of us knew this, too, because he was the first to disapprove of his divided state. He was aware of that division, of the trap he was falling into, but to recognize it openly or simply take its existence for granted would be to admit his weakness, his tragic dependence on other people. That's why he built a fence around himself, that's why he never spoke about prison or the friends he had made there. He was the complete opposite of my mother, who had no problem calling a spade a spade, and the only reason she wanted my father to change was so that she could continue to live peacefully by his side without any unpleasant surprises. She suffered because this was impossible, but she didn't condemn my father morally or feel ashamed, nor was she concerned about what people might think of him. If she said nothing and kept certain information to herself at times, this wasn't because she found it hard to admit to others what she herself would have preferred did not exist. It was just that she believed there was a right moment for everything, a belief she clung to implacably. When that moment arrived, however, she would be sure to tell me. Just as on that morning in Burgos she had told me about my father being in prison, later on, she told me almost everything else about him, too. It was clear that this gave her no pleasure, but she made no attempt to dodge my questions. For example, I found out from her that the name "Professor," which I'd heard in Toledo, was the nickname given to him by the other prisoners in the jails in which he'd spent time, and she was the one who explained how complicated it was to live in a prison if you had no friends, that prisoners use whatever qualities they have to establish alliances, and that my father, who was neither strong nor powerful, had learned to use his education to gain the support and respect of his fellow prisoners, teaching some of them to read and writing letters for others.

But she only told me this long afterward, not on the evening I'm recalling now. That evening, after we left the bar and got into the car to wait for my father, everything happened predictably enough. We sat in the back seat, with the engine off, and talked about the icy weather, about Toledo, about school, and what we were going to do the next day—unimportant matters that would perhaps have helped to pass the time had it not been for my father's encounter with his friend, but given that the encounter *had* taken place and that, having been rather rudely dismissed, we were now waiting for him to rejoin us, our banal conversation seemed somewhat forced, because, as both she and I knew, neither of us was thinking about what we were saying but about what was happening a few yards away, behind the glass, not the glass of the small, narrow, misted car window, but a few yards beyond, behind the equally misty window of the bar where we had left him.

It was another twenty minutes or more before my father rejoined us, and yet he seemed neither worried nor nervous.

He opened the rear door so that my mother could get out, accompanied her to the driver's side, waited for her to get in, and after closing her door, walked around the car and got into the passenger seat. We set off, and a tense silence wrapped about us. What had happened in the bar hovered over us, but no one seemed prepared to lay their cards on the table. My father, because he knew that the right thing would be to give us an explanation he had no intention of giving; my mother, because, once again, she chose to keep her cards close to her chest until the next hand was dealt; and me, because while I was aware of having caught a tiny glimpse of my father's dark side, I didn't know how important it was, I didn't know if it was good, or bad, or quite how to judge it. My mother was concentrating on the tarmac road ahead, and my father, equally absorbed, was silent, trusting that the matter would be forgotten. When we reached Illescas, about twenty minutes or so after leaving Toledo, twenty minutes of silence in which he didn't even open his mouth to say *Step on it, Pass this one*, or *Be careful*, as he usually did when travelling with my mother, I suddenly saw a rabbit appear on the right-hand side of the road, between us and the car in front, trying to dodge the traffic. We had just passed a yield sign and were travelling slowly enough to be able to brake without the car behind running into us. I don't know if my mother had noticed the rabbit or if she judged that it had time enough to get across. But when I saw that she wasn't slowing down and that, in a matter of seconds, the rabbit would be under our wheels, I let out an anxious cry about what only I seemed to notice was about to happen. At that moment, my father, as if emerging from a daydream, said to my mother, "Don't worry, there's enough spa—"

He hadn't even finished the sentence when a soft bump contradicted him—too late. My father turned in his seat, and before I too had turned and knelt on my seat in order to look back, I saw my mother's eyes in the rearview mirror—she was also looking back.

"No matter," said my father, seeing the animal lying motionless in the road. "It would have been much worse if we'd had an accident."

He paused, and seeing that neither my mother nor I said anything, and drawing out the sentence as if he weren't quite sure what he was going to say, he added, "Yes, that would have been most unfortunate, just when I'm about to start work . . ."

"Work?" asked my mother, taking her eyes off the mirror even before he had finished speaking.

"Yes, I was going to use this trip to break the news to you. I've been offered work as a translator. Nothing grand, nothing permanent, but something I can be doing while I'm looking for a more stable position . . ."

"What do you mean? Have you been given a book to translate?"

"No, it's not a book," he said quickly, placing his left hand on my mother's right knee. "I'll be working for a company. They pay much better, and I won't even have to work at home. I'll go to the office in the mornings and do whatever needs doing that day, you know, economic reports, legal stuff. They pay per page, and the work's much more regular than it is with books."

For a few seconds, no one spoke. My father withdrew his hand from my mother's knee, and she, who had listened to him intently, seemed once more to focus on the road ahead, thinking.

"But why didn't you tell me before?" she said after a few seconds, without turning to look at him. "You don't keep something like that to yourself."

"It was a surprise. It's still several days before I start. I begin work next Monday."

"Even so, it's quite enough of a surprise without you keeping it a secret."

Those last words were said more in order to reestablish an affectionate harmony than as a genuine reproach, so I need hardly say what a deep impression they made on me. My mother and father had never before broached such serious subjects in my presence, and I had never before had the opportunity to observe so clearly the effect that a gesture or a few words from my father could have on my mother. Nothing strange about that. Often, especially at the age I was then, we don't know what we want or miss or what's right at any given moment until someone puts it into words, and it had simply never occurred to me that my father would have to work. I knew he'd had dealings with publishers and had once tried to set up his own publishing business, but I hadn't thought that this would have to continue now that he had become part of our lives again. My mother hadn't mentioned it, and I had no idea that it would be a necessary condition, a proof of his determination to stay on the straight and narrow. That day, driving back from Toledo, I was aware of this for the first time, and of my mother's difficult position, caught as she was between simulating some kind of stability for my benefit and the uncertainty into which she was plunged by having to depend on my father to achieve that stability. Not that she said anything out of the ordinary or, afterward, allowed herself to be carried away on a wave of euphoria. It was enough for me to see her unease during that brief conversation, and the gleam of pleasure in her eyes in the rearview mirror as my father explained the situation to her.

# XII

There's no gleam now in my mother's eyes, they're veiled, inexpressive; they communicate nothing. She opens them and looks at me, but there's nothing in that look. Her eyes tell me nothing. It isn't like it was before, when although she hardly spoke and rarely talked about her feelings, I could at least sense what was going on inside her.

I no longer talk to my mother, it's impossible. I think about her, but I hardly see her. What's to be done when we still have questions to ask, when we have not yet run out of questions, and when the person of whom we'd like to ask those questions, with whom we'd like to continue talking, isn't there to answer us, can't speak, and has no idea that we're counting on her? My mother *is* there, but she doesn't say anything—or nothing that makes any sense—she doesn't answer, she isn't her. Her body is there, you can touch her, she hasn't really changed, apart from getting a little thinner, but she's a body without voice or memory, a body that doesn't recognize anyone and has neither past nor future. Something that neither she nor I foresaw has swooped down on her body and torn it apart forever, even though it still exists and can go on existing. Sometimes, like now, I think that since she clearly isn't her any more, nothing binds me to that empty body, which moves and speaks but doesn't feel, or whose feelings are distorted, and at other times

I resist losing her; on those occasions, I take her hand and try to make her recognize me, to rediscover some trace of the person she was. Sometimes when I visit, I spend hours looking at her, then I leave and don't come back for weeks, because I can't bear seeing her like that. I prefer my memory of her to a present in which she has no voice, I prefer to let her grow inside my memory rather than accept this alien, jarring present. And yet I can't help thinking about her still; not like with my father, who breathes and speaks and doubtless still recognizes people, but I don't think about him, I don't know or care what happened to him, I don't care about his past, about his future—he simply disappeared, as if he never was. I don't want to see him, I wouldn't know what to say. There's a strange similarity, though, the two of them equal at last—my mother, one of the living dead, and my living but voiceless father, who doesn't come to see me, doesn't speak, and for whom I don't wait. One, forever silent; the other, never missed, never loved. The two of them ultimately incapable of telling the story, of sharing the past with me. Who would have thought it after that trip to Toledo, when my father had left prison behind him and grown closer to us, or so it seemed? Not my mother or myself. I only have myself now, I only have myself to turn to if I am to reconstruct those months, only I think about them now, only I keep them in my mind. Aunt Delfina's no use. She doesn't know, she wasn't there, she didn't see. Besides, she isn't my mother and I'm not her son, she didn't choose me. She thinks about other things, she lives a life apart, she protects herself. Memory hurts, and for her, I am that memory, I remind her of my mother, I represent her.

I no longer speak to my mother, she can't tell me her feelings, she can't tell me if she believed what my father said, if what lay behind the gleam I saw in her eyes that evening driving back from Toledo was real and survived the days that followed, or if there was a glimmer of distrust inside her. I think about her, and it seems to me impossible that the memory of those days has ceased to belong to her. I'd like to see her again as she was then, as she was when I used to come home from school and everything seemed to be going well. I'd like to hear it from her, I'd like her to still be able to tell me what was going on in her head when my father started to arrive home punctually, when there were no more nasty shocks, when there was no need to worry and everything appeared to be under control and going according to plan, as it used to be when it was just the two of us. I'd like to know what she thinks of that period of her life, now that time has passed and it no longer matters if the cheerful, relaxed face she used to put on faithfully reflected what was going on inside her.

What I remember is really very little and of no importance, and hardly representative. I was always looking in from the outside, without feeling or being involved. Each considerate or affectionate gesture from my father during those months, each day that he came home from work with some new suggestion for how we should spend the evening, each regularity, each description of what he'd done during the day had little impact on me, failed to satisfy any previous wish of mine. Unlike my mother, I had no great expectations of him, I didn't need him. It's true that those months brought changes—we were less alone, and the days were not as long as when we only had each other to seek out or avoid around the apartment. Life was a bit more agitated, more novel. We often went out to dinner or to the movies or on trips, and my mother slightly relaxed her emphasis on discipline and orderliness. Even so, I didn't see this as an improvement, which would have been the normal response, but the truth is that I always saw this period as an exception, not so much because I sensed it wouldn't last as because I didn't have time to incorporate it into my life. I found my father just as strange as I had when he first arrived. His initial furtive behavior had vanished; he not only appeared to do his best to please my mother, he made a considerable effort with me, as well. He still never mentioned his time in prison, but as that episode moved farther off, he adopted a more easygoing attitude and began to ask me about my classes and tried to establish an alliance with me, sustained either by the joking comments he made whenever we were alone or by little ironic remarks aimed at my mother in her presence, with me in the role of knowing accomplice. His former caution and reserve remained palpable, however, in the fact that he never suggested doing anything that did not include my mother. If for some reason we spent too much time without her, if conversation lagged or his jokes began to fall flat, he would become nervous and, as soon as he could, leave the room in which we had happened to coincide.

Seen from my current perspective, I think the problem was that he found my presence troubling. It wasn't just that he didn't know how to talk to me, although obviously the two years we'd been apart didn't help, and although my mother used to show him current photos of me every time she went to visit him in prison, it must still have been a shock meeting me again. Suddenly, nothing of what he remembered was of any use. I had grown and he had to adapt, to alter his habits. On the other hand, it wouldn't be fair to lay all the blame for his difficulty in establishing an easy relationship with me on that failure to adjust. I don't honestly think he would have changed over time. It went deeper than that. It was partly that he didn't know how to talk to me, but also that he hadn't learned how to include me, that in the fragile equilibrium of duties and desires that dictated his relationship with us, he had not reserved a definite place for me. I was there, and he had no option but to accept my presence, but I was not important, nothing that he did, he did for me. The performance he put on, if performance it was, was purely for my mother's benefit. Any regrets or debts, if there were any, were owed to my mother. I didn't count. He wasn't living with us because of me, I wasn't the one holding him there. My mother had her own, intrinsic value, I did not. I was merely an addition to her; in his eyes, I was more an observer than an interlocutor or a victim. I was a bothersome presence, a witness he did not wish to have, one who could testify to any neglect or lack of love.

As I say, these are my thoughts now. I have no actual proof. During the period of calm that began with the trip to Toledo, I did not once witness anything that my father would not have wanted me to see, not once did he do anything that could have hurt my mother or for which he should have felt guilty. And yet my impression, despite everything, is that he had a great fear of disappointing my mother and that whenever he did anything that went against her wishes, it troubled him deeply and he hated himself for having done it or for not having taken her wishes into consideration.

I was different.

I was a concession.

But what did my mother think? Did she see him as I do now, or was she genuinely pleased and happy with his behavior? Would she have been happy had she suspected what I know now? I imagine not, although that is pure speculation. With my mother, as I've said, we talked about facts, not feelings, not how she had been or felt, not about her frustrations or joys or hopes.

Only once did we come close to talking about him. It was many years after that trip to Toledo, closer to the time I'm writing now than to then. My father had vanished from our lives, we knew nothing about him and assumed he would not come back. The tunnel of forgetting in which she now lives was still a long way off. She could have had no idea of what was about to happen to her, but her body must have known in some way, because something was telling her to say goodbye, urging her to take stock. We no longer lived together, and often, when I went to see her, we would talk about my childhood years. These were not conversations intended to dig up painful memories, nothing that would cause us to reflect. We amused ourselves with old anecdotes, brief, insignificant snapshots that served to illustrate past joys, those dead times that, while they're happening, we never imagine thinking about in the future and that, when that future arrives and becomes the present, are nonetheless the most palpable representation of what was transitory and has now passed. That day was an exception, however tiny. We were recalling a period of my childhood when I'd had to spend three months in bed with rheumatic fever. At one point, my mother asked how I used to feel in the mornings, when she'd gone off to work and left me alone, and then she asked if I felt lonely being an only child. Then she fell silent for a few seconds and—deliberately avoiding looking at me, as if she were going to broach a subject she found it hard to talk about—she asked if I would have preferred it if my father had stayed with us. There was no need for her to specify when, we both knew perfectly well.

"Would you have liked him to stay with us and to have had a normal father?" she said.

"Would *you*?" I asked in turn, so as not to have to answer.

My mother blushed slightly and said nothing, as if she weren't quite clear about her own feelings or feared disappointing me with her response.

"And now?" I asked, seeing how long she was taking to reply and trying to help her out of that awkward silence. "Would you have preferred him to have stayed?"

Despite this attempt to help, my mother remained silent for a few more moments, then, after shooting me a troubled, inquisitive look, like someone preparing to tell another person some fact that will give him power over them and wanting to first reassure themselves that their confession will not be used against them, she said, "No, not now."

I could have asked, *Not even if he'd been a real father?* but I didn't.

# XIII

The first dark cloud arrived, suddenly and unexpectedly, after two months during which my father went out to work every day and it seemed that no obstacle would appear that might cause him to stray from his chosen path. I don't know the exact chain of events—how my mother found out, if she found out by chance or if she first became suspicious then stumbled on some clue and decided to gather the necessary evidence that would confirm her suspicions. The only thing I really know, the one thing that has remained and that I can speak about without the mediation of other people's words or someone else's gaze directing mine, is that when it happened, she did not suffer in silence or wait patiently for the *denouement*. She confronted my father and, in order not to delay matters further, didn't even wait for a moment when I would be out of the apartment.

It happened one afternoon when I came back from school after having been out all day. That morning over breakfast, everything had followed the by then familiar script, whose broad outlines, though subject to a few variations, were firmly established—the same jokes, the same gestures, the same relaxed or sleepy or inexpressive looks on our respective faces, the same questions, the same answers. My father, who was always up first, would be impeccably turned out, with either a tie or scarf around his neck, my mother would be still in her dressing gown or already dressed, while I, as usual, would be halfway through the process, putting on my shoes, tucking my shirt into my gray flannelette pants while I hurriedly drank a cup of hot chocolate and ate my toast and jelly, either strawberry, blackberry, or lemon, depending on what my mother gave me.

I arrived home feeling excited and contented, eager to rid myself of my backpack full of books. I walked up the four flights of stairs, and the first thing I noticed was the darkness; there was no light on in the entryway, or in the hall, either, and a second later, as I closed the front door, I heard a murmur of conversation, too loud and agitated, coming from the hallway area connecting the bedrooms and the kitchen. My initial impulse was to walk straight past and go to my room without being seen, to allow my presence to become known little by little, not suddenly. However, as I passed the kitchen, where I now realized the voices were coming from, I could not resist peering in, almost without thinking. I did so timidly, it's true, without speaking or fully opening the door. I'll never forget what I saw, it's one of those moments that remain fixed in the memory and become an obligatory reference point for a whole period of our lives. My father stood with his back resting against the sink, his legs at a slight angle with his torso, forming a diagonal with the floor, although his back remained erect; he was clearly very close to losing his cool, but not entirely. The impression he gave was of someone behaving as if the fence penning him in did not exist. He was obviously very upset and made no attempt to hide this, only to disguise it, as if what he felt were not guilt but indignation. He kept his eyes fixed on the floor, his arms behind him, determinedly gripping the sink. However, that very determination revealed a desire to reproduce the gesture of someone who, though powerless, is certainly not someone who has been caught out, as if his affected gesture were the product of resignation rather than dejection or surrender. He didn't speak, he didn't defend himself, but before he noticed me, he gave a couple of short, nasal grunts, followed by a scornful backward movement of the head, like the silent rebuttal of someone faced either by a very serious or a totally unjustified accusation. The rather unconvincing result was ambiguous, and this might very well have had the effect my father was intending, had it not been for the presence of my mother at the white, marble-topped table where we ate breakfast and sometimes dinner and where she was now seated immediately opposite my father and sideways to me. Her mere presence was enough to negate my father's whole performance, it was far better than any accusatory words. At the moment when I peered around the door, she was looking at my father, and her gaze seemed to contain all the dismay and concentrated disillusion in the world. She was hunched over the table, and her posture, one arm hanging by her side and one hand glumly clutching her head, expressed both despair and weariness. Hers was an angry weariness, a robust weariness in which there was no hint of surrender but rather patience, not defeat or paralyzing despair but quiet determination. She was silent, as if she had just asked a question and was waiting for an answer she knew would not be forthcoming.

This was the scene that greeted me as I entered the kitchen. Had the scene lasted any longer, they would have noticed me, but they were both so intent on waiting for the other to take the initiative that neither of them saw me. I had time to ponder whether to say hello or to beat a silent retreat, then I saw my mother change position; she raised her eyes and sat up very straight in her chair. "Give me the phone number, then, all offices have phones," I heard her say, "what could be easier?" Those three short phrases were spoken in a much softer voice than the ones that had led me to the kitchen, but they had the effect on my father of a whiplash, making him withdraw still further into himself; he removed his hands from the edge of the sink and folded his arms across his chest. It was then that he saw me. He had looked briefly at my mother and was about to go back to staring at the floor when something made him glance in my direction. Contrary to what one might expect, he reacted very swiftly. A flicker of embarrassment crossed his face, but he immediately corrected this expression and smiled at me rather too broadly, as though he didn't want to give the impression that this change concealed any selfish desire, if not a desire for a patently impossible escape route, at least for the brief truce my presence would allow him. What happened next is the reason why I remember that day so clearly. I've thought about it a lot, and yet I still can't bring the necessary distance to bear on any analysis of it. I don't really know how to explain; it's a fragment that endures on its own—isolated and unresolved. The fact is that when my mother realized from my father's expression that I was there, she turned in her chair, and when I saw the look on her face, my instinctive response was a desire to run away and leave them alone. For the first time ever, I saw that she was not in control of her feelings. She didn't seem aggressive, nor was it her intention to make me feel that my presence there bothered her; it was simply that I thought I saw a warning light in her eyes signaling that she was about to do something rash—and I feared the consequences.

"Your dear father has been deceiving us."

My mother was not the ironic sort, not in normal situations, and of course not in situations that were no laughing matter. I imagine that she regretted these words as soon as she had spoken them. What disturbed me was not what her words revealed about my father but the irony, an irony even more troubling because it belied the calm, almost tender tone in which she said them. Of course, that isn't what I thought at the time, although, in a way, that *is* what I picked up on. Somehow, only that word "dear" made any sense to me and spoke faithfully to me of my mother's state of mind and prevented the contents, the phrase itself, from shaking my world more than it did. True, I was speechless and shocked, but it didn't honestly affect me that much. The proof is that although I was, inevitably, looking at my mother—since it was she that had addressed those words to me—I have no memory of what I saw and observed while she was saying them and no recollection even of what happened afterward. Time has remained frozen and empty. I can recall nothing until the moment I decided to leave the room, and then it was my father, not my mother, who caught my eye. I made as if to withdraw, and before I left, I noticed that he turned very pale then immediately regained his composure. All I remember of what happened as I walked down the hallway, leaving the two of them behind me, is the click-clack of my mother's heels on the floor and the sound of the kitchen door slamming shut.

The shouting did not start again until I'd reached my bedroom. I was aware of the aggression and anger in their voices, but I was far enough away not to be able to hear their actual words, and for what seemed an interminable length of time, I had to make do with listening only to the tone in which they spoke, but without understanding and, therefore, without knowing whether I should be worried or if it would all blow over. At a certain point, their comments became more and more spaced out, they spoke more and more softly, until, after a long silence, I heard footsteps on the parquet floor and the sound of the front door opening and closing. Then more footsteps came looking for me, and I did not have long to wait. My mother walked into my room, sat down on the chair next to my desk, drew me to her, and, resting her hands on my shoulders, forced me to crouch down as she pressed my head to her breast. I felt her tears running down my neck, but neither of us withdrew from that embrace until she had grown calmer and her tears had dried. We said nothing, we didn't even mention my father. In the end, when she was feeling stronger, she lifted my head from where it lay nestled against her breast, slid her hands down to my waist and, raising me to my feet, said, "We probably won't see him again." I never found out how she knew that he'd been lying about his job; we never again talked about it.

# XIV

My father came back the next day. And I was faced by a completely different scene from that of the previous afternoon, because when I got home from school, I found him sitting quietly in the living room with my mother. There was no music playing, they weren't speaking. They were both immersed in their respective books, but there was no hint of yesterday's storm. They both looked up when they heard me come in and smiled as if it were the most natural thing in the world to find them there together.

Practically all that remains of the days that followed is my feeling of bewilderment. My father continued going out and coming back at regular hours, integrated into the daily rhythm of the household as before, working, he said, at the same office where he had told us he was working before the argument. The normal thing, or so it seemed to me, would have been to see some sign, some remnant of embarrassment or even an explicit reference that would serve as a reminder of what had happened, as well as a recognition of the clean slate we had apparently decided to make of things since. However, during the days that followed, he behaved as if I hadn't seen or heard what I hadn't been able to help seeing and hearing. My mother, too, appeared to have accepted the situation, and she maintained her usual cool, reticent self, with not a trace in her eyes of the tears she had shed in my presence. This situation drove me to despair, I couldn't understand the reasoning behind it, and I resented being excluded, especially when no one offered me any explanation; I resented being excluded from the pact they seemed to have sealed between them. In a way, that was the only time in my childhood when I had any real reason to feel betrayed by my mother. Since I couldn't believe the comedy they were acting out, my desire to know her real state of mind was transformed into rancor and wounded pride. Then, gradually, I began to notice cracks in their performance (a look that lingered slightly longer than usual, an untimely sigh), and the tension eased. I began to understand and, I suppose, to forgive. I understood that there was no pact, only resignation, that I was not being marginalized, that my mother was only avoiding me because she had no way of explaining the situation. I didn't understand then, but now I realize that my mother's behavior was based on patience, on reasoned calculation, and not on an unconditional acceptance of the rules imposed by my father. Once the skirmish was over, she changed her approach, as if making a preemptive surrender were better than risking further upheavals. This meant that while everything seemed normal, it wasn't, although that false capitulation threw up more anomalies than if the standoff had continued. We all knew what had happened: my father's lie, his non-existent job. And yet not only did he continue leaving the apartment and coming back again just as before, going to a job that did not exist, my mother also behaved as if everything were perfectly all right. She asked nothing and said nothing. Everything continued as it had before the argument—the time the three of us spent in the living room talking, the same or similar weekend trips and outings. My mother made every effort to ensure that life carried on as normal. She laughed, made plans, and talked about the future. Her determination was praiseworthy; in retrospect, however, the results were not, I think, beneficial. On the other hand, there was my father, and although he was apparently doing the same as she, there was a considerable difference. He was the victor, and he had the confident air of someone who knows he has the right to dictate conditions. Slowly but surely, he began to introduce new elements that he would never have dared to before. He again began to receive frequent phone calls and sometimes disappeared for hours without a word of explanation.

As I said, my father was not in the habit of giving much away about himself. He was a compulsive liar, which means that his lies were not always necessary. He was always exaggerating, and depending on the effect he was trying to make, he would grotesquely inflate or deflate any sums of money central to the story he happened to be telling. He was, moreover, the kind of liar who, in order to conceal one lie, tends to make up a bigger one. If he had to justify being late, rather than saying that he'd met a friend or gone into a bar for a drink, he would come up with some bizarre tale about his taxi being involved in an accident or how he'd been the victim of arbitrary arrest. Almost as commonplace as his lies, then, were the confusions he created—someone spotting him in a particular place at a time when, according to my father, he had been somewhere else entirely; an acquaintance he supposedly met frequently but who, when he happened to bump into my mother, would ask after my father with the keen interest of someone who hadn't heard from him in months; whole skeins of lies intended to hide other lies that had failed or been unmasked; excuses made up on the spur of the moment to cover his back whenever he was caught contradicting himself. My father lied continuously whether he needed to or not, and, naturally, like any habitual liar, he could never admit defeat, even when all the evidence was stacked against him. Once he began, he could not even contemplate retreat or defeat. He had an amazing ability to improvise. The worst thing is that he lacked all caution and always went full steam ahead. If something didn't ring quite true in whatever he was saying, or if someone figured him out, he didn't try to come up with a solution that would allow him to emerge unscathed, instead, without exception, he would merely dig himself still deeper in. This meant that when he did fail, he failed spectacularly, and at that point, his only alternative was to disappear. This isn't something I observed during those few months, I couldn't possibly generalize from that basis; it was something he did systematically, with anyone, in any situation, whenever he found his options reduced to zero and he either had to back up his words with deeds or admit that he had lied. There wasn't even any need to catch him out, because such failures were usually the consequence of something as unnecessary as, for example, promising more than he could give or pretending he had certain contacts or a position in life that did not correspond to reality.

I only began to see this facet of his personality in its full glory once all contact with him had ceased and seemed unlikely to be resumed. My apprenticeship happened quite spontaneously, with no need for my mother to enlighten me. Women to whom he had promised a trip somewhere; "colleagues" he had known for a few short hours but with whom he had built up the nocturnal mirage of some business deal; recent acquaintances to whom he had promised a favor.

The range was as varied as the needs of those who met him and whom he, for whatever reason, wanted to please. The only thing that almost never varied was the end result—after waiting vainly for him to call them or waiting, equally vainly, with their bags packed or having initiated proceedings on some plan for which he had promised his support, those affected, filled with the disquieting suspicion gradually forming in their minds that they had been deceived, would end up phoning our number. In those cases, my job and that of my mother consisted of encouraging them not to wait. As I say, no one taught me this. My mother didn't tell me what I should do or how. After the first few calls from these worried or indignant people, from people who did not understand or who did not want to stop believing in him, an ability to explain without explaining came of its own accord. It was something that my mother and I did automatically and often without telling each other about the calls. Excusing him as far as possible, trying to defend him while ensuring as best we could that the person at the other end of the line would not continue to harbor any illusions. It wasn't a matter of telling them about his life, but of making sure that they did not continue to wait, that they wipe him completely from their minds.

Maître d's, real estate agents, town councilmen, private individuals selling or buying a car, architects, cleaning ladies, writers in search of a publisher or someone to read their manuscript, motel owners, haulage contractors, dry cleaners, gallery owners, stock breeders, commercial travelers, decorators, journalists, foremen, PR representatives, tailors, priests, would-be translators, antiquarians . . . Weary voices, hurried voices, prudent voices, neutral voices, voices accustomed to giving orders and voices accustomed to obeying, awkward voices, strange voices, mercenary voices, unforgiving voices and pleading voices, blunt voices, insinuating voices, voices that faded at the first sign of trouble, preferring not to be heard; cheerful voices, sad voices, timid voices, unpleasant, overconfident voices, lying voices, voices that faltered or threatened revenge, arrogant voices, humble voices, voices that had nothing to lose or had already lost everything. There's no point listing them all, there's no point trying to reproduce the script of every conversation. My mother and I would answer the phone, listen for a few seconds, then immediately begin the slow process of demolition, spiraling around the main point, which we rarely reached but which, by dint of turning and turning, was finally revealed. "Don't worry"; "He's probably forgotten or couldn't make it"; "I'm sure he must have had a good reason for not showing up"; "He was unexpectedly called away"; "No, we don't know, either"; "It often happens"; "It's not the first time he's done this"; "The best advice I can give you is to forget all about him"; "Don't wait for him"; "I promise I'll tell him if I see him." Every call was both different and the same, and the difficulty of dealing with it depended on the extent of the deceit and on the reluctance of the people on the other end to understand.

For years, thanks to the phone, which was in my father's name, we were kept informed of his movements, even when we hadn't seen him for quite a while. I wonder why my mother waited so long before changing the name or number on the account, why it wasn't until we changed apartments that she finally took that step, and the only answer that occurs to me is that she didn't want to cut all ties, that despite their separation, she wanted to know where he was and what he was doing. For quite some time after he left, those strange voices—

never repeated, because they rarely called again—were the only means we had of keeping tabs on him.

In the days following that first dark cloud—the argument in the kitchen—there were no such phone calls, and although they later signaled the start of my apprenticeship—when I began to see clearly without the filter of deceit—I could not have said that I had yet grown used to deceit or considered it normal. That did not happen until my father had lost all contact with us and no longer cared that we knew of his deceptions. Like the complicated or frankly improbable excuses my father gave us to explain his long absences or new ways of behaving, those phone calls from strangers, anxious people wanting to know where he was, were still, as yet, few and far between. I didn't even think they were my business. As far as I was concerned, any lies, if he told them, any deceptions, if there were any, were born of whatever problems he had with my mother and directed exclusively at her. Naturally, I sided with her and, like her, felt concerned. But if I paused to think about the matter at any point, I'm sure I considered it an isolated phenomenon, the product of the particular difficulties they were going through, never as something ordinary or systematic. It was one thing for my father to conceal facts from us, to exaggerate, to invent exorbitant sums of money, or to pretend that he knew everything, but lying all the time, on any pretext, was quite another matter.

Despite this, I underwent a very real and understandable change. The need to observe him that I'd felt months before, my curiosity about and interest in everything he did, my alertness to his every gesture, custom, and habit kept me in a state of constant vigilance, of active rather than passive espionage. It was no longer enough for me to observe him in normal, everyday situations, to notice his way of speaking or dressing, eating or moving. I began to seek out what he himself did not reveal, to look in his jacket pockets, to open drawers, and eavesdrop on his conversations for far longer than was justified if I just happened to be walking down the hall where the phone was.

Inevitably, my vigilance soon bore fruit. Five months after his return to the house in November, two months after that scene in the kitchen, and therefore three months after the trip to Toledo when he had told us about his phony job—so it was probably in about mid-April—my father went away. He didn't say where he was going, or at least not in my presence. He announced it the night before his departure. We were watching a movie on TV, and it was when I got up to go to bed, after my mother had once again reminded me of the lateness of the hour, that he told us. If he did offer an explanation, I don't remember it, probably because I was already beginning to pay far less attention to what he said. It was enough for me to look from his face to that of my mother, as I was kissing her goodnight, to realize that this trip was news to her, too.

I don't know what happened between them after I went to bed. The only thing I do know is that my father's trip lasted three days and that, during that simultaneously very brief and very long period of time, my mother took great pains not to betray the slightest hint of sadness or anxiety. True, it may not have required much effort on her part and her behavior may merely have reflected how she was feeling, however, the reason I tend to feel that this was not the case, and the reason why I spontaneously wrote what I did just now, is not because I saw even the tiniest crack in her composure, but because she was far too composed. How else to explain why she turned the day of my father's departure into a celebration? Given that my mother was a very methodical and orderly person, as well as a great believer in discipline, how else am I to understand why, when I came out of school, she was there waiting to take me to the movies? This was definitely not normal weekday behavior. Especially since, instead of going straight home after the movie had ended so as not to keep me up too late, we lingered over dinner in a nearby café. So some effort must have been involved, an effort that was doubtless intended not so much to make her look more confident as to instill me with the confidence that all was well, and while this did not necessarily mean that she was under any particular strain, she clearly didn't want to cause me any strain or anxiety; so, yes, all that must have taken a certain amount of effort. She tried harder to please me and was more attentive. At one point that evening, when we'd left the movie theater and were sitting at the bar in the café, eating sandwiches, she even suggested, when she saw me yawning, or perhaps simply to break a sudden silence, that I needn't go to school in the morning if I didn't want to. She didn't insist, she only said it once, and I can't remember what the conclusion was, if she herself rejected the suggestion or if I was the one to let it pass or if we both did. Again, while I probably didn't interpret this as an expression of alarm on her part at my father's sudden departure, such anomalous behavior must have struck me as odd, because, otherwise, why would I remember it, however faded and faint the memory? Especially because the following day, and, indeed, until my father came back, my mother moderated her attitude and normality was restored, a somewhat hesitant normality, different from what we had thought of as normal before my father's return home some months before, and different from the normality the three of us had shared since, but I would still not describe it as forced. She decreed a general spring-cleaning, polishing furniture and cleaning windows and beating rugs. She barely spoke, apart from greeting me when I got home from school, making some lighthearted comment, and asking how my day had been, before assigning me some chore to perform and continuing her own frenetic, silent, solitary labors until it was time to make dinner and sit down to eat.

My father returned on the day he had said he would return, and the moment he arrived, my mother could not disguise her joy. She had finished the cleaning only a few hours before and was sitting in the living room reading a book when we heard the front door open. She didn't get to her feet, but merely glanced up before settling herself more comfortably on the sofa, and in the way she uncrossed her legs, I thought I saw the reaction of someone relaxing after a period of great tension, finally free from all her accumulated anxiety.

That same evening, while they were out at dinner together, I ventured into my father's room, not the one he shared with my mother, but a small room next to the kitchen, which was where he would go to be alone and where he used to work during a period I can't even remember. Apart from a quick, nervous look around, a brief reconnaissance visit while he was out, I had never before dared go in there. On that occasion, I did so not with the intention of unearthing some secret he was keeping from my mother and myself. It was more a desire to understand, to comprehend my father through an act so common at the age I was then, and which only shame or an artificial sense of decorum prevents us from continuing to practice later on, namely, rummaging around in someone else's belongings as if those objects or the way they're arranged might provide us with some clue about their owners that the owners themselves could not reveal, as if the very breath of a room, its smell, the areas covered in dust and those worn clean with use, the things carefully stored away or stuffed willy-nilly in the back of a drawer or in a box that is never opened might tell us something that cannot be put into words.

The first thing I noticed was that he had already unpacked his luggage. The suitcase had been put away somewhere out of sight, and the only thing that hadn't been was the jacket he'd been wearing, a light gray, three-buttoned jacket that remained in the apartment for years after he left and, at that moment, was draped over the back of a chair beside the bed where my father occasionally slept. After removing it from its improvised hanger and slipping it on with shamefaced speed, I put my hands in the pockets, but found nothing of interest, only a packet of tissues and some nail clippers. I restored the jacket to its proper place, keeping the metal nail clippers in my hand, and after a quick glimpse inside the closet, I went over to the part of the room that served as his office. On the desk stood a typewriter in its case, and all the other neatly arranged objects were just what one might expect: a pewter vase containing a black Pelikan pen and four perfectly sharpened pencils; a ream of paper; a bookrest; and a brass box in which I found half a stick of sealing wax, a tiny eraser, a couple of buttons, some scissors, and an ivory letter opener with the carved head of an owl on the handle. I investigated the old-fashioned rolltop desk where he kept his books and papers, gingerly opening the rather fragile lid, but I found nothing of great interest— typescripts of translations left unfinished years ago, a calendar, an address book, old postcards, and then something I had never seen before: two large envelopes containing the letters my mother had written to him when he was in prison in Burgos. As I hesitantly opened the first of those envelopes, the nail clippers slipped from my hand, and when I tried to catch them, I inadvertently emptied the contents of the envelope out onto the parquet floor, with the letters scattering in all directions, including under the furniture. Once I had picked up all the others, I went crawling under the table to get those that had slid underneath, and something unusual caught my eye. Stuck to the underside of the tabletop, with blue insulating tape, was a very small packet made from a white plastic bag, which was impossible to see unless you actually poked your head in beneath the folds of the tablecloth. I was really shaken by this discovery and immediately abandoned the caution and hesitancy with which I had been conducting my search up until then. Certain of what I was doing, knowing that I now had a clear, achievable goal, I did not, I remember, immediately devote myself to that goal, but carefully put all the letters back in the envelope, and only after restoring the envelope to its place in the desk and closing the lid did I return and remove the package from the tabletop. I did this carefully so as not to tear the plastic, first separating the package from the wood, then unsticking the bits of tape holding it together and laying them on the floor sticky-side up, so that once I'd investigated the contents of the package, I wouldn't encounter any unexpected problems when I tried to reverse the process. In the end, none of these precautions proved necessary, and five minutes later, I was holding in my hands my father's identity card and a transparent, plastic box containing a wad of business cards bearing a stranger's name. At first, I was quite simply bewildered, unable to understand what those two very different things were doing together or why something so apparently ordinary should have been so carefully hidden away. Then, after looking more closely at both things, I began to get an inkling of why they were together. The identity card bore my father's photo but not his name; the address and profession were different, too. However, the address, name, and profession were exactly the same as those printed in raised Gothic lettering on each of the two hundred and fifty business cards.

# XV

I didn't tell my mother about my discovery. I wanted to for days, but didn't. That would have meant making it more real than it already was, and, initially, I just couldn't do it, fearful of how she might react. Later, when I was ready to tell her, my father preempted my decision, and it was no longer necessary and would have solved nothing. Maybe my silence was no more than an innocent and slightly clumsy way of refusing to see the beginning of an end whose approach I had started to feel the moment I found the package. That night, however, while I was crawling around under the table, as well as during the days and weeks that followed, everything was much vaguer. I didn't think about it. I could feel the danger, sense its worrying proximity, but that was all. I couldn't come up with any satisfactory explanation as to what the contents of that package might mean or how they could be translated into something concrete. I could see how carefully it had been hidden away, and I had understood at once, with no need for further thought, the fear felt by the person who had hidden it—fear of me, but, above all, fear of my mother. Anyway, she was the person I thought of, not myself.

I kept trying to ward off the threat, turning my back on it, refusing to think about it, as if it would be less likely to materialize if I didn't name it. I didn't tell my mother about my discovery, and yet the memory of my failure to do so lives on in me. It's more real than many other things that were perhaps more important but my memory has nevertheless failed to retain. It's true that for many years, that scene remained forgotten and not until much later did it come back to me, but it's also true that afterward, that moment or that decision—which I made almost without thinking or even considering the possible consequences—has become one of the cornerstones by which I judge my relationship with my mother, far more than many other things I did consciously, after having carefully pondered the consequences. What troubles me, basically, is the age-old dilemma of whether *not* telling someone something is the same as lying: Does real lying have to be deliberate? Are we lying from the moment we choose to conceal something from someone because it seems inopportune or inappropriate? Or, on the contrary, if deceit—to call it by another name—arises in such cases by accident, with the passing of time, when after waiting for the right moment to tell someone—a moment that never arrives—it becomes ever more difficult to speak out, does that mean that not telling and lying are one and the same? And this brings me inevitably to another question. However close we feel to those around us, can we ever be sure that what we know about them is true, if what they tell us is the whole truth or just part of the truth, and does knowing or not knowing change anything in our lives?

Would anything have changed if I had told my mother about my discovery? Would the ensuing years have been any different? Would my image of her be any different from the one I have now? Would I be different?

If these questions still preoccupy me now, when so much time has passed, it isn't because of the remorse I can't help but feel whenever I think about that period of my life. I'm not even sure I regret my silence, or that I wouldn't do the same again, or that I wouldn't have continued to remain silent even if my father had not preempted my decision. Nor is it my fear of having at some point been a victim myself of the very thing I inflicted on my mother. If these questions still trouble me, it's because the answer is related to something that affects me most directly—my own relationship with my mother.

When you're an only child, when you don't have the mirror of siblings, your insecurity about who you are seems greater than if you had grown up with someone else who shared the same influences, the same parents, and who is nonetheless clearly different from them, and, of course, from you. But when there are no brothers and sisters on whom to offload responsibility, parents are all you have, they become your sole reference, your sole viewpoint. Everything begins and ends in you, and phenomena like betrayal, love, admiration, and duty are felt with greater intensity. The bonds are stronger, or leave a deeper mark, and it's often hard to distinguish what's yours and what's inherited. You have no one with whom to compare yourself, your solitude is suffocating. Who do you share with or offload onto? Who do you ask, who do you answer to, who do you blame? How do you get any kind of perspective? How can you use your memories to construct a balanced history when you have only one way of looking and that way of looking is filtered and influenced by your own solitary self? When you have no brothers and sisters, everything seems specially tailored for you. The danger is that you tend to magnify things, tend to draw infinite conclusions from every word spoken, every look or rebuff, every event seen or sensed, or that you're told about, or that never even happened.

That's why you get into more of a muddle and make more mistakes, too. It may be that you overestimate your parents, that it's harder to break away, and it may be that you don't always value them as you should. Everything has the potential to hurt you more, but nothing so much as your own solitary self, your utter onliness.

I didn't realize what this meant until long after the time I'm talking about now, when I began to wonder if I hadn't taken too much for granted, and when the weight of what I knew and didn't know about my mother on the one hand and what the two of us together represented on the other first began to intrigue me. But occasionally, albeit only vaguely, I had already felt the unnamed, unimagined void of the absent sibling. The first occasion I can remember was the one I've just described. Kneeling under the table—not immediately after I had discovered the package, but once I had opened it and sealed it up again and restored it to its original place, where I could still see the marks left by the insulating tape, and especially in the days that followed, when the temptation to share the discovery with my mother was greatest, as was the caution that prevented me from doing so—*that* was when I began to feel, as I never had before, the loneliness, and the fear that loneliness creates. My disloyalty, and the wall it erected between us, really hurt me. My mother was my only ally, my only security, and the idea that I might be harming her in some way made me suddenly aware of the precariousness of my position. I realized that without her, I was lost, and that if she failed me or I failed her, if she were to disappear or we were to become separated, there was nothing else. The empty, unknown void of a future in which, unless I myself ever had a child, there would be no such unconditional love.

I didn't ask myself anything at the time. It was a feeling that assailed me suddenly, without provoking or bringing with it questions of any importance, but it was enough, nonetheless, to fill me with renewed unease and disquiet. For two weeks, the time it took for what both of us feared would happen to happen, I felt that a gulf opened up between my mother and myself, that we were not the close-knit unit we had been (she and I alone or she and I vis-à-vis my father), but that, for the first time, there were three of us, including my father, each one the vertex of an imaginary triangle, each one (or at least two of us) with a secret to keep.

# XVI

Apart from the parallels with other occasions when I felt that same sense of separation—through no fault of my own this time—the reason I mention the new experience of those two weeks is because I think they influenced the ease with which I accepted what happened afterward: my father's departure, our move to La Coruña, and, in particular, the beginning of what I've described elsewhere as my mother's Paris period, her decision to set off for the first time along a path that would temporarily separate her from me.

There's no real point in looking for causes, there's nothing so very odd about it. It's likely that the most important things that happen to us are things we would never have predicted. We live our lives thinking we know who we are and how we'll react in any given situation, but we just have to dig around a little in our memories to find significant examples of when we reacted quite differently from how we *should* have reacted. There is no model for how we behave. We can't trust how we think we'll respond to a particular stimulus. There are no constants. The variables that govern our responses, like the variables of memory, are entirely unforeseeable. What do we remember, and why? What is it that affects or moves us, and why? We can't even be sure about our most automatic responses, those that shape our character and allow us to define ourselves and others, to say things like "That's how I am" or "This person is like that." For every reflex reaction, every habit or obsession that forms part of our way of being, how often have we also been moved to tears by things that have nothing to do with us, things we are even ashamed to be seeing? Likewise, how often have we accepted, without a flicker of emotion, other situations that do have to do with us and should touch us, that cry out either for our repudiation or our support? As soon as we explore our memory more deeply, it comes up with a multitude of occasions when we experienced incidents or situations that should have upset us but, despite everything, passed and left no trace, or left a very different trace from the one we might have expected. There are times when we think we couldn't possibly laugh at or be offended by something, and yet we can't help ourselves and duly end up laughing at or being offended by that very thing. Deep down, we know very little about ourselves, very little of what might affect us. Even our reactions or responses to the same stimulus are not always the same.

I'm thinking and saying all this as a way of trying to understand my behavior then. But I'm thinking, too, about how things developed after my father's disappearance, the changes it wrought in my life, the transformation, in part definitive, brought about by the subsequent separation from my mother, and the undramatic way in which I accepted those changes never fails to surprise me. It seems unnatural. My father disappeared toward the end of May, by mid-June my mother and I were in La Coruña, and just over two months later, she went off to Paris, leaving me with my aunt and uncle, but in my memory, this sequence of events is not accompanied by any pain or sadness. For what seemed like a very long time, my mother and I stopped living in the same place, our centers of gravity moved apart, but I can detect no hint of resignation, distrust, or resentment in myself. There is, rather, acceptance, a predisposition to understand the reasons I sensed lay behind her decision. Of course, it's impossible to say what would have happened if I hadn't found those business cards, if I hadn't felt guilty about concealing it from my mother, and if my father's departure hadn't confirmed all the foreboding that my discovery had awoken in me. I don't know if my attitude or my feelings would have been any different. Yet I can't help thinking that, albeit unconsciously, the bad taste it left in my mouth somehow influenced my acceptance of that new phase. I'm not saying this was a conscious calculation on my part, an attempt to compensate for my guilt. I'm just saying that one thing followed the other, and it seems highly likely that the former had some effect, however tenuous, on the latter, even if I myself didn't notice it and had possibly forgotten all about my earlier deceit.

On the other hand, there were no such attenuating circumstances with my mother, and I can't imagine what she would have done if, instead of me being an only child, she'd had three children, because in that case it would have been impossible to leave us all with my Aunt Delfina. I can't imagine what would have become of her if she hadn't been able to temporarily shed her responsibilities, how her life would have changed if she hadn't been able to escape to Paris, if she'd had to stay in Madrid even though doing so meant deepening the wound. What is certain is that, even though I was her only child, even though it was her choice, even though she was the one who decided to take that step, it could not have been easy for her. She must have thought long and hard about it.

# XVII

What I observed in my mother after my father ran away was not insubstantial, but it was all very contradictory and would be of little help in getting even a vague idea of her true state of mind if I hadn't had the example of previous occasions when I was able to glimpse how deeply she was affected by what had now become a reality—her possibly definitive failure. We need not go very far back. For example, in comparison with her joy on that weekend trip to Toledo, when my father told her that he had found a job, or with that more recent example when he went off unexpectedly and she feared she would never see him again, her reaction this time was moderate, one might even say cool, but perhaps that's not so very strange. In a way, it could be considered an indication of the magnitude of her despair: the greater her despair, the greater the effort required to mitigate it.

Firstly, there are the days immediately following my father's disappearance, when it was still too early to give up all hope. After the first night spent waiting for a phone call that never came or for him to come home, the light in my mother seemed to go out. She stayed at home and made no attempt to excuse my father's absence, saying only that he had gone. Her bewilderment was obvious, as was the fact that she had no way of justifying it and was in no mood to come up with a justification. My father hadn't said goodbye, he had simply left with a small suitcase filled with his best clothes, and it wasn't hard to infer from this that he had no plans to return. It nevertheless took two days for my mother to grasp this. For two days, she was caught between two impulses, the more urgent one that drove her to stay in her bedroom, and the perennial one that told her not to lower her guard with me for an instant. One minute she would be absorbed in thought or invisible, the next she would be trying to compensate for this by checking up on me all the time, coming into my room or the living room to ask how I was feeling or if I needed anything. Not until the third day—like a watch that has gotten wet and suddenly starts going again just when we thought it had stopped for good—only then did her customary determination reappear. In an ambiguous gesture in which I sensed both a desire to conceal nothing from me and an equal desire not to have to explain too much, she phoned the police, even though I was there with her. She didn't tell them my father had disappeared, she merely asked about his situation, if he'd been arrested or was wanted and on the run. When she hung up and turned to look at me, her attitude was quite different. I noticed a sudden look of relief on her face and in the way she spoke to me. What she said has remained engraved on my memory: "There's no need to worry." I don't remember what happened after that. I don't know if she stayed by my side or if we just went on with our separate tasks. I have a feeling, although I can't be sure, that she began removing all trace of him from the apartment that very afternoon, putting his clothes and belongings into boxes.

It's as difficult to interpret the days that followed my father's departure as it is the intervening time between then and our move to La Coruña. Two weeks in which the only revealing thing my mother did was to schedule our trip for the middle of June, when normally, we wouldn't go until July. Two weeks during which, if it hadn't been such a short time and I hadn't been in the middle of taking my final exams, it would have been almost as if we had gone back to our old, pre-Burgos routine. My mother waking me up each morning, my mother telling me to hurry up so as not to miss the school bus, my mother out at work, my mother there to greet me at six o'clock when I came home, where she had been waiting for me since midday. There was nothing in our daily life to remind us of our recent loss, there were no startling outbursts, no melancholy looks or unusual behavior. My mother talked and moved about the house just as she had before, as if with the simple act of packing up and putting away my father's things, she had freed herself—if not for ever, at least quite determinedly—from any excessive feelings of grief on his account. She didn't tell me what was beginning to take shape in her head, but now that I think about it, there was one day when she almost did. At the time, I didn't give it much importance, because I had no idea what was about to happen and her question caught me unawares. It was one Sunday morning, after the gymnastics showcase my school always put on at the end of the year. I'd taken part along with my classmates, and my mother had watched from the stands in the gymnasium. When the performance was over and we were in the cafeteria—where, every year, parents had the chance to chat with the teachers for the last time that term—in what was perhaps a chance remark or something she said after she'd done the rounds of the teachers, and while I was enjoying a cold drink and she was on her second cup of coffee, she asked if I was happy at the school or if I felt like a change. Perhaps that isn't exactly what she said or she put it in a slightly different way. What I do know is that I didn't interpret her question as having any hidden meaning, and I replied noncommittally, saying something along the lines that all schools were pretty much the same. My mother didn't press the matter, and we didn't touch on the subject again until after we arrived in La Coruña, when she presented me with a *fait accompli*. I have no idea what would have happened if I'd said I didn't want to lose the friends I had or didn't want to have to get used to new faces and new rules. I suppose, though, that it wouldn't have been very different. My mother could be very persuasive and was always very good at arguing her case, and I suspect, moreover, that she knew better than I did that there was nothing very important binding me to that particular school, nothing I couldn't do without, like those annual gymnastics recitals.

Nothing about the journey to La Coruña ruffles that untroubled atmosphere, it neither modifies anything nor introduces any novelty, there are no anomalies to threaten the flat calm of my memory. We made the journey by car, as we had on other occasions, leaving Madrid in the early morning and, after a leisurely lunch in a restaurant on the way, arriving at our destination eleven hours later, but I have no memory of the preparations made on the preceding days and can't even remember what happened on the night before we set off. I think my mother gave me a quarter of a sleeping pill so that I would go to sleep earlier than usual, but I may be wrong and that could be a memory from other journeys. I obviously wasn't overly preoccupied or alert, since otherwise, I would surely remember something, which just goes to show that my mother gave me no reason to be worried, that nothing out of the ordinary happened. It would have taken very little to arouse my disquiet, but my impressions in the car, despite my father's still recent departure and the suddenness of the journey, were clearly not very different from my impressions on other such journeys. I had no sense that anything was about to end, nor was I in the least worried about my mother. It must have been a very quiet journey, with a lot of looking out the window and long silences interspersed with games or my questions about the landscapes we were driving through. She must have been utterly imperturbable, or was pretending to be, she must have behaved as she felt she should, or as she could not help behaving.

With our arrival in La Coruña, my memory grows very slightly brighter. There are a few signs and a few warning lights, but all very faint. There are two images, two interrelated glimmers of light. One has to do with the very moment we arrived at my aunt's apartment and the other, with a moment on the following day or possibly one or two days later. In the first, I see my Aunt Delfina welcoming us at the door. She has stood to one side to make way for us, she has picked up the suitcase my mother was carrying, and after asking if we've left any other bags in the car, she follows us along the path my mother and I have forged ahead on as if we, not she, were the hosts. I could see she was rather agitated. After leaving our luggage in the room assigned to my mother, and once we were able to say our hellos properly, she barely took any notice of me at all, she didn't, as one tends to do with children and as she herself always did, devote more attention to me at the start, getting the usual questions and jokes out of the way so as to make up for subsequently relegating me to the background because what she really wanted to do was to talk to her sister without any interruptions or abrupt changes of subject. On that occasion, my aunt did exactly the opposite. I could tell at once that she was impatient to get me out of the way. She walked past me, enquired briefly about my exams, affectionately pinched my cheek, and then, from that moment on, devoted all her attention to my mother, asking over and over, "How are you?"; "Are you all right?"; "How did everything go?"— as if the continual repetition of the same question, framed in different ways, concealed a real concern about something she did not dare to name directly. After that image, there is nothing, the final flicker of the candle snuffed out in the cold wax of my memory. I don't know how we spent the rest of the afternoon or if my aunt made any attempt to be alone with my mother. I find myself faced by a void that is impossible to fill. I can't remember, however dimly or confusedly, a single incident or conversation. That faint flame is only lit again when the three of us are in the kitchen having breakfast. On that occasion, the image is rather blurred, and unlike the previous one, it isn't my aunt but my mother who takes center stage. It must have been very shortly after our arrival, because my mother joined us in the kitchen, bringing me a pair of pants from our shared suitcase. She left them folded up on the back of a chair, then sat down without offering to help my aunt, who was feeding slices of bread into the toaster. She waited a few seconds, as if she were angry or bothered by something, then said to my aunt, "I'm sure this is the best way." Her words, spoken in the middle of a long silence, sounded brusque, even though they weren't, and my aunt, who had her back to us, turned to look at her. Then she looked at me, as if to check that I was still there, and said, "It's OK, you're absolutely right, I just find it a bit strange." She said this in a conciliatory but slightly weary tone, like that of someone who concedes a point in the middle of a heated debate, not out of real conviction but in order to avoid an insuperable difference of opinion. For a while, no one said anything, my aunt continuing to watch over the toast. Then suddenly, without saying a word, my mother downed her cup of coffee in one gulp, got up, and went off to take a shower.

That is the last glimmer, the last scene after the sudden disappearance of my father that remains shrouded in darkness and uncertainty. There are no further memories until light finally dawns. A few days later, my mother finally told me her plans, and I discovered that this summer would be different from any other and that after our stay in La Coruña, we would not be moving, as we usually did, to some rented house on the Mediterranean coast. I learned that we would stay in Galicia for the whole of July and August, until the first of September, when my mother would go back to Madrid alone, and that afterward, I would not rejoin her—she would send me my winter clothes and my most important possessions and I would remain with my aunt in La Coruña. I learned that my mother would close up our apartment in Madrid and that, with the possible exception of vacations or the occasional weekend, for ten long months we would live in different cities, me in La Coruña, studying at a school my aunt had found for me, and my mother in Paris, working as a teacher of Spanish, although she had yet to find a post; and this sudden revelation was not in the least traumatic. In a way, I knew the step my mother was taking was not an easy one, and even more importantly, I was convinced that she was taking the step not because it was inevitable but because she had chosen to. No one told me my father was the reason for this, but that's how I interpreted it. In some way, I preferred to feel that, after the great disappointment of my father's departure, she was imposing a radical change on us, and moving to another country seemed to me a convincing way of doing this. My mother would take refuge in another city, would be unavailable, and was simply leaving me with her sister, the only person she could leave me with, her only family. At the time, I had no doubts; I didn't feel abandoned or for one moment cease to believe her promise that this was a provisional arrangement, just while she got used to living in Paris and found a suitable apartment for the two of us.

# XVIII

I don't think I found anything strange or disquieting about what I've been calling my mother's Paris period, not until right at the end, at least, when it was almost the past and no longer the present. While it was happening, I didn't feel that anything significant would come of it. I even remember that on the day of her departure, I put on the phony indifference that children or simpletons or people unsure of their own emotions tend to adopt in highly charged situations. If my memory of that crucial moment serves me right, what frightened me, more than separation from my mother, was having to deal with the unknown quantity of life with my aunt in a city that, up until then, I'd only known in summer, and having to go to a school where, for a long time, I would be *the new boy*, the focus of attention and possibly the butt of jokes or jealousy, *that kid from Madrid*. I don't mean that her departure left me unmoved, as had been the case with my father's disappearance, which only affected me insofar as it might have distressed my mother. I would, of course, have preferred to continue our life in Madrid—it would be ridiculous to say otherwise—but just as I felt no malice toward her as the instigator of that move, neither did the move itself arouse in me an exaggerated sense of loss. I felt neither hurt nor sidelined by it. I suppose it was as much a natural desire not to betray my mother's confidence in me as a more personal and perhaps artificial desire to feel that I was part of the challenge she was taking on—our union preserved despite the distance separating us.

One not insignificant factor in my almost blithe acceptance of my mother's absence was that during the time I stayed in La Coruña, there were no disagreements between me and my aunt and her husband. It seems strange to me now, but during the months I spent with them, there were never any unpleasant surprises, no outlandish impositions or deprivations; as far as I can remember, we never experienced any of the little domestic misunderstandings that, however minor, can be extremely troubling and cause great tension, especially between people unaccustomed to living together. No doubt this was largely because my Aunt Delfina had decided that there would be no unnecessary conflicts. Yet I find it hard to believe that her decision was the sole determining factor. On the one hand, it would have been difficult to maintain a fiction over that many months, and on the other, had it been purely my aunt's decision, it would probably have been accompanied by an excess of zeal, which was certainly not the case—childless couples who find themselves forced to play the role of adoptive parents often try to be so perfect and scrupulous in their inherited role that they turn out to be more rigid and intolerant than the real parents. More important and influential than any single decision was my aunt's personality and the already familiar way in which she ran her household.

My aunt was an extremely restless, energetic person, one of those people who cannot imagine lingering quietly over anything or giving in for any length of time to a single feeling or emotion apart from the one that impels them into the labyrinth of some activity so diverse and so obsessive that it has no end and no beginning. She was extremely thin and prematurely lined, and she spent all her time bustling about, busily doing things that turned out to be nothing at all. She gave the impression that if she'd ever had an ambition, she had either long ago fulfilled it or given it up. She was abuzz with frenetic energy, but just as my mother checked her own natural tendency to introversion with a strong sense of duty that often transmuted into overanxiety, so my aunt never allowed her accelerated pace of life, her lack of any real focus, to come between her and what she considered important. Apart from the times they were together, when my mother would take the subordinate role and delegate some of her power to my aunt, they were very similar in temperament. As I said before, my aunt was considerably more conventional, or less flexible, in her views, but, as far as I could see and as far as I can recall, this stance was more imagined than real and could be put down to the very different world she inhabited, and it in no way influenced her relationship with me. In that respect, she was almost a carbon copy of my mother: the same or a similar sense of loyalty, the same or a similar sense of family and sacrifice, the same or a similar mix of tolerance and rigor. Living with her was very comfortable, since it did not require me to adapt to any new order. It was, if I can put it like this, as if she expected of me what I, quite naturally, was prepared to give her. Her husband's influence, if he had any, was barely noticeable. Tall and gangly, with narrow, sloping shoulders and an almost nonexistent neck, on which sat a ridiculously large head, he was both the complement and the opposite of my aunt. A man of few words, with a permanent frown, as if he were constantly preoccupied or overwhelmed by problems, he gave the impression of being someone who leaves nothing to chance, is never plagued by doubt, and is in firm control of everything around him. His every measured, precise gesture oozed confidence, and he had a high opinion of himself, which he applied to every aspect of his life. When you saw him, especially when he was in uniform, you would assume that these attributes were all part and parcel of his military profession. However, the proof that this was very much an inner quality was that he never imposed himself on others and rarely demanded of them what he demanded of himself. He was a friendly fellow, though, and had a kindly, accommodating nature that made him a very pleasant person to deal with. Whenever we discussed matters that did not affect him personally, he would respond in the same neutral tones, never angry or bossy. Despite the marked differences between him and my aunt and the fact that they seemed to talk very rarely to each other, he clearly had total confidence in his wife, or so it seemed, and he was one of those men who, though very much an old-fashioned male—or perhaps precisely because he was incapable of shedding a particular masculine mode of behavior learned and transmitted over generations—happily did as he was told as soon as he crossed the threshold of his house. I never heard him question any decision made by my aunt. He accepted everything, including her sometimes troubling restlessness. With me, he was affable and even affectionate, in his somewhat gruff, embarrassed way, but he went no further than that and would never advise or criticize me. I fell under the jurisdiction of his wife. I was part of a domestic world in which it would never have occurred to him to interfere, not because he despised it, but because he did not feel he had the right to, it wasn't his job, his field of expertise. My aunt reciprocated by showing the utmost respect for everything that formed part of his professional life, going to the frequent ceremonial or social events that his high rank required him to attend or where his presence was expected, and maintaining a scrupulous silence about everything else. That rigid separation of duties, that mutual consideration, did not affect their relationship. Seeing the two of them together, so cool with each other, so repetitive in their daily routine, with its daily dearth of incident, the impression they made on me (or the impression they make on me now) was one of sadness, of a lack of spontaneity and passion, one of those couples who, perhaps rather arrogantly, one tends to think are held together only by habit or by the material or emotional impossibility of even considering divorce. It seems to me, though, that in their brusque, infrequent displays of affection, in the impassivity with which he accepted my aunt's excesses and in her bland, innocuous response to the consequences of leading a life that I can't help thinking was a long way from any hopes she might have nurtured in her distant youth as to what her life might turn out to be, they nonetheless came very close to the image I had of a perfection I had never known at home with my own parents.

That is what occurs to me now, in the light of subsequent events, but such an idea never entered my head during the months I lived with them. As far as I was concerned, my time spent in La Coruña was merely a rather longer than usual vacation, and it never for a moment interrupted a line I thought of as infinite, the line drawn by my mother and myself with our silent understandings and our almost never mentioned and possibly never perceived differences. Nothing unusual happened until the last week; I never thought of my aunt and uncle as something enviable, and I never compared them with my parents. Even then, separated from my mother for reasons I didn't understand but did accept, there was still nothing lacking in my life. Those months could have been the right moment to start asking a few questions, to come up with a few objections, or find grounds for disagreement with all those things I normally never questioned. The distance and separation from my mother could have constituted the right moment, the initiation or apprenticeship that would suddenly allow me to find my own place, rather than the one I had inherited from or owed to my mother. I had plenty of excuses. It's clear, for example, that my uncle must have found it distressing to have someone like my father in his family, even though he was not a blood relative and had nothing to do with him directly. But if that were true (and I can't help but suspect that it was in those days, when one's personal life was an open book and could have proved problematic for someone of his rank), I didn't think about it until long afterward. Just as, in one way or another, my mother, though absent, was a constant presence, my father was never spoken about, did not exist, no one mentioned his name. I myself only thought about him from time to time. I would occasionally wonder where he was living or what he was doing, but the lack of any answer did not trouble me unduly; it was a bit like when we wonder what happened to someone we used to know but with whom we feel no real connection once we've lost all contact, partly because we can't even be sure he remembers us. I noticed the silence that surrounded his name in my aunt and uncle's home, but I assumed, and still do in the case of my aunt, that it was out of delicacy on her part, so as not to remind me of something she thought would bring back painful memories. Not until two or three years later did I realize how alone my mother was in what she was trying to do, how little support she had.

Something similar happened, although for very different reasons, with my maternal grandfather, who died when I was four years old, and about whom I knew almost nothing because I'd hardly ever seen him and because, once he was dead, my mother never mentioned him unless I specifically asked about him. I attributed her silence to the family rift caused by my grandfather's remarriage, which I did know about, and so I was surprised when my aunt, who must also have been affected by this, was far more forthcoming and not only talked often to me about him but enjoyed saying how much I resembled him. It's true that many of the anecdotes she told me hinted at the same resentment evident in my mother's silence and that often during those conversations, her eyes would darken just as my mother's face would darken on the few occasions she spoke of him, but the contrast between their very different attitudes was still not enough to arouse my interest. I was aware of that contrast and felt intrigued by the figure of my grandfather for the first time, although, as with the silence that my aunt and uncle wove around my father, I never thought about it or did anything more than notice it.

During the months I lived in La Coruña, I did not have the mirror of my mother there on a daily basis, but she continued to be the person I thought about most often, the person whose opinion mattered most to me and who was there in my mind whenever I did something that merited approval or censure. The distance between us made no difference, nor did the fact that any communication between us relied not on unspoken words but on the clumsy or hasty ones babbled into the telephone or set down on paper.

# XIX

During the months she spent in Paris, my mother phoned me every week, but never on any particular day or at any set time. She would sometimes phone in the afternoon and sometimes in the evening. She might not phone for five or six days, or leave no space at all between calls, sometimes even phoning twice in one day. Perhaps that's why I still have the feeling that she was always acting on the impulse of the moment and not according to some predetermined plan. As if she were not entirely sure she was going to call until she picked up the phone to dial the number, as if she were calling for no reason, spontaneously, because the opportunity had suddenly arisen and she didn't want to waste it, or she were taking a break from some other task, on her way from one place to another. They were hurried calls, rushed conversations that usually followed the same concentric pattern: first, my mother would ask me how I was and listen with great attention to what I said, and then, after talking briefly about herself, she would bring the conversation back to me, as if she couldn't quite believe the news I had given her just moments before or as if enough time had passed for me to have undergone some radical change. And this cycle was repeated in ever shorter and more insistent segments as we reached the imminent end of the call, until the dropping of her last coin into the pay phone or a decision she herself made brought the conversation to a close. Perhaps that's also why I still have the feeling there were always things left unsaid and that at the end of each phone call, I knew almost nothing or very little of what was new about her. The calls were too unexpected, too brief or emotional. It isn't that they were disappointing, but I can't deny that after the sudden joy of receiving the calls, they left a bigger void than had existed beforehand. They did nothing to dissipate the fog imposed by distance. For a few minutes, my mother's voice was alive and audible, but there was never time for that artificially created closeness to take on the appearance of reality, to lose the sense that it was all a mirage. This contributed to the difficulty I had imagining her in a particular place, creating an enduring backdrop where I could imagine her sitting or lying down while she was talking to me. During the months that her stay in Paris lasted, my mother changed lodgings often. After a brief spell in the house of an acquaintance, she spent most of the time staying in small hotels she never found entirely satisfactory and never stayed in for very long. She used to call from public telephones, and the background noise that usually surrounded her voice was not the submarine echo of furnished rooms but the cold, metallic, pressurized sound of call shops or phone booths encountered by chance. As far as I remember, or according to what she herself told me, she never had her own phone, and since we could not call her, all responsibility for getting in touch fell on her. We had an emergency number, one belonging to someone she often saw who, in case of anything urgent, could go around to wherever she was living and give her a message. We also had the phone numbers of her neighbors, when she had them, and sometimes, that of the hotel or boarding house where she was staying temporarily, but apart from on special occasions, letters were the most usual and reliable method of reaching her, the only one, moreover, that allowed us to take the initiative. Since she had no permanent address, a few days after moving to Paris, she got a P.O. box number, and that was where we sent nearly all our correspondence.

Time has left no trace of the letters I wrote to her on my own or the ones I wrote together with my aunt; I have no idea how frequent they were or what I wrote about. I know they existed, but memory plays no part in that certainty; it's like a sediment, a remnant that persists long after the more complex substance of which it was made up or formed a part has disappeared. What I know, now that time has passed and I can recall no detail of their various characteristics, is that those letters are not so very different from all those other childhood truths we never question and always assume to be true, when in reality, not only did we not experience them ourselves, we don't even know when or how we found out about them. I know that I wrote quite a lot of letters, but that's as far as I can go. I can't remember any dates or what the letters contained. The color of the paper and envelopes I used has vanished, too, along with any memory of which mailbox I used, what stamps I put on them, or what my handwriting looked like at the time.

I have a slightly clearer memory of the letters my mother sent to me. I haven't kept any of them, and there isn't one that I remember in particular, but my memory is of some use here. There are images and details I can base my certainty on. It isn't a truth without evidence. I can still see myself picking them up from the table where my aunt would leave the mail, or receiving them directly from her hand, and then putting them in my pocket so that I could read them later, when I was alone. I can see the box where I kept them, and I can especially see my mother's narrow, sloping hand, the little crosses she added at the end, like English people do, to represent the kisses she had already sent me in words. I remember waiting for what seemed like ages when she owed us a letter, and my almost incredulous surprise when I received one unexpectedly, because apart from postcards—brief, casual messages written and sent from a curbside—my mother rarely wrote on her own initiative. She only wrote in reply to the letters we sent her, and even then not at any great length. She used to linger over the essential details of the letter to which she was replying, and when the moment came to speak about herself and thus furnish material for our response, she always ran out of words, as if she had lost the desire to write or as if some urgent task beckoned. "I woke up today feeling happy"; "I have a really busy day tomorrow"; "I don't know what I'll do this weekend." Her sentences became short, telegraphic. She almost never talked about her work, she didn't mention the people she mixed with or what kind of life she was leading. Just as when we spoke on the phone, she asked a lot of questions, probing for news of myself and my aunt; she was fond and affectionate, but always very vague about her own affairs. Just as when we spoke on the phone, I imagined her alone, coming from one place or going to another, but, again, this was never something that worried me.

The only way in which her letters differed from her phone calls was that they were the medium through which she endlessly deferred the successive meetings we planned, which involved either my going to Paris for the weekend or her coming to Madrid at Christmas or Easter. It was never a sudden decision announced in just one letter, rather, in every case, the postponement began to be hinted at some time before, with the objections accumulating progressively over various letters: "I don't really have anywhere you can stay comfortably"; "I'd rather you came once we have our own place"; "I have hardly any free time"; "Perhaps it would be better, now that I've found something, if I stay on here to see it through"; "I don't know, maybe we should wait a little"; "We'd better put things on hold rather than risk me losing this opportunity". So when the time came for one or other of us to buy tickets, a final decision was already made and my disappointment wasn't then quite so acute. That doesn't mean I didn't suffer. I accepted it as inevitable, but that doesn't mean that I wasn't also disappointed. However, since every postponement brought with it a promise that the visit would definitely take place later on, because she never canceled a trip without proposing an alternative date, which I immediately began to think of as absolutely fixed, I put up with each delay, believing that the new date would be unpostponable. It didn't really matter that when the new date arrived, the whole process was repeated. I always believed my mother, I always trusted her motives. However strange that may seem, that's how it was.

My aunt and uncle, on the other hand, did notice these repeated postponements. My aunt tried to conceal her feelings but was obviously upset. She would become still more frantically active and redouble her various plans and questions. My uncle never got upset, but whenever he asked me what day of the week my mother would be coming or when it was that I was going to join her and I told him that all visits had been postponed, he fell silent, as if he were mulling something over or didn't know quite what to say. I imagine my aunt's reaction had more to do with her private sadness over the effect all these delays might have on me. As for my uncle, I don't know if he felt the same or if he simply disapproved of whatever it was that was keeping my mother in Paris. In any case, the deep frown line on his forehead, which made him look still sterner, seemed to indicate anger or displeasure rather than real concern.

Nevertheless, as with much of what I have described, I didn't notice this at the time. As long as it was the present and not the past, my mother's trip to Paris meant very little to me. I remained quite unaffected by not having her near or by what I may have heard or seen or intuited during the period of her absence.

# XX

My mother and I didn't see each other even once while she was away, I didn't go and see her in Paris, and she didn't come to see me in La Coruña. Even more inexplicable is her return to Spain at the beginning of May, just after Easter, eight months after her departure and two months earlier than planned.

My mother couldn't stand it any longer, she didn't even finish out her contract. She decided instead to come back to La Coruña and wait until I'd completed the school year so that we could then return to Madrid in September together. Just when we'd all assumed that the plans drawn up the previous summer would continue along the agreed-upon path, just when I was embarking on the final stretch of my stay in La Coruña and beginning to think about the challenge of learning a new language and going to a new school in a new city, my mother phoned and told Aunt Delfina that she would be arriving in La Coruña in a week's time. She had grown tired, or so she said. She couldn't see how we could live on the little she earned there, the work she had found so far was scarce and badly paid, it would be absurd to carry on with her plan if we were going to be so much less comfortable than we could be in Madrid.

I won't dwell on the feelings this news aroused in me. The most striking thing about the afternoon when my mother phoned to say that her escapade was almost the past and no longer the present is that this was the only time since her departure that anything related to her had made me feel uneasy. I don't mean the fact of her imminent arrival, which surprised me and might even have given me food for thought, although it didn't. I'm referring to something that occurred because of that phone call and a little after the announcement of her unforeseen arrival, when my mother had already hung up and my aunt had told me of her sudden decision to leave Paris and abandon both her work there as a Spanish teacher and the plan that I should join her the following year. Everything that happened afterward, everything that I would, if it were possible, ask my mother about now, boils down to that moment. Although it did not occur spontaneously and it had to be wrung from me, that was the first manifestation in me of any genuine unease, the first time I was presented with a truth that did not coincide with my own. It doesn't much matter that I completely forgot about it afterward or that, as on other, similar occasions, the truth did not take verbal form and it wasn't until much later that I found the words to express it. That afternoon was the first time I felt uncomfortable in La Coruña, when my mother was not there and could not, with a single look, tell me if I was right or wrong. That truth came from the person most like my mother, the person closest to her.

At the time, I felt so injured, so deeply offended, that I could not see beyond my overwhelming feeling of indignation. Any concrete thoughts, any doubts I might have had were immediately canceled out by a far stronger feeling of shock and wounded perplexity. I will never know if what I heard that afternoon from my aunt was the only thing that caused me to react like that, although it probably wasn't; it seems likely that behind my reaction lay a feeling I have not yet mentioned because I experienced it almost simultaneously with my mother's last phone call from Paris, such an arbitrary, baseless feeling that I find it hard to put into words or to put those words into written form now.

My mother's announcement was not quite as unexpected as I described a moment ago but was preceded by something that, although it did not forewarn me, at least had the effect of making her sudden return seem somewhat less extraordinary. It did not emerge suddenly but rather at a time when her calls had become more urgent, more emotional, and, if possible, even more unpredictable. Taking a rather questionable approach—questionable because it sets too much store by a supposition that is in itself extremely flimsy—I would say that, for some time, she had not appeared to be responding simply to the perfectly normal, pressing need to know if I was all right, but to a more egotistical need, like when we find ourselves alone and frightened in the dark night, hemmed in and harried by all our doubts, when we can see no way out of a life we imagine we have irrevocably chosen for ourselves and we need to be in touch with someone dear to us, not so much because that person will be able to give us the impossible answer we seek, but simply in order to hear their voice, feel their affirmative presence, and have them confirm to us that we are on the right path, that they support our choice, regardless of what right or wrong decisions we have made or not yet managed to correct. As I say, I did not realize this at the time, and I'm not even sure that's how it was. It's merely a retrospective presentiment, the unverifiable impression that my mother began to linger far longer on the phone, that her calls became more frequent and unexpected, and above all, the feeling I had—and which

I actually did feel at the time, although I immediately rejected and forgot about it—that she wasn't always phoning in order to talk to me, but sometimes actually wanted to avoid me, and phoned when she thought or knew I would not be there, so that she could speak freely with my aunt. There were two such phone calls, two occasions when I came home and found my aunt talking to my mother. Neither occasion was the first time she had called when I was not there, and on neither occasion did I hear anything I should not have heard, and my aunt never denied that she was speaking to my mother. On both occasions, Aunt Delfina told my mother that I had just come in and, having said her goodbyes, immediately passed the phone to me. Nevertheless, although those two calls could be explained quite easily by an error of calculation on either side, I remember noticing a flicker of unease in my aunt when she noticed my presence, something unnatural about the way she announced my arrival, a certain embarrassment on the part of my mother when my aunt handed me the phone, and a certain slowness in the way she began her interrogation, as if the news that my aunt was putting me on the phone had caught her unawares while she was still immersed in other thoughts.

I will never know if my mother really was trying to avoid me during that time, if she needed to speak to my aunt about things she could not or did not want to talk to me about. I have no way of confirming that suspicion, but it's highly likely that my feeling—to which I keep returning and can't help but believe was genuine, even though there are no objective elements on which to base that belief—had some bearing on the way I reacted the afternoon my mother announced her early return and my aunt invited me (alarm bells were already ringing in my head) to go for a walk with her.

We walked to a café on the seafront, through the increasingly heavy rain, with me feeling tenser and tenser and incapable of concealing my strong sense that something was about to happen, my aunt having first stopped at a couple of clothes shops, presumably with the secret intention of putting off the evil hour when she would have to speak to me, and finally doing so only after choosing a table near the bar and ordering two hot chocolates (both of us equally slow to decide what we wanted), and then after a silence that lasted for the time it took the waiter—in a bow tie and a black jacket worn shiny with use—to return with a tray bearing two cups and a jug containing the steaming hot chocolate.

We all know what it's like when someone close to us feels they have the right to intervene in our life and advise us about some matter on which we don't want any advice, but when we look back after some time has passed, we can never recall how exactly they began, what words they used. We can remember whole swathes of the ensuing conversation as well as the atmosphere and the surrounding noises, but it's almost impossible to recall exactly how our would-be advisor launched into their speech. This difficulty is really only the reflection of the still greater difficulty felt by the person struggling to find a way to tell us something they feel we need to know but find it very hard to because they can see that it will upset us. It was no different for my aunt that afternoon, sitting with me at a black-glass-topped table, and no different for me now sitting at this rectangular, wooden table where I'm writing these words. Once the waiter had left us, she paused before speaking, the time it took for her hot chocolate to cool, after much stirring and cautious sipping of spoonfuls so as not to burn her lips, and of the words she spoke when she could put the moment off no longer, I can summon up only what she said after a certain point, but not her very first words. I can see my aunt put her spoon down on the saucer, see her pick up the cup with both hands and raise it to her lips, I can see her take a first sip and begin to speak while she puts the cup down on its saucer again, but her words do not appear, there is no room for them in that particular part of my memory. I see my aunt repeat the process, I see her fall silent for a few seconds, again raise the cup to her lips and put it down on the table, I see her wipe her mouth on the napkin and say something else, but still I cannot hear her words. I'm feeling more uncomfortable now, I've finished my hot chocolate and have started playing with the paper napkin lying unused on the table, repeatedly rolling and unrolling it to form an ever tighter spiral, and keeping my eyes lowered so as to avoid my aunt's gaze, which is becoming too fixed and inquisitorial. At one point, she falls silent and looks at me, and I see that she still has some hot chocolate in her cup. She doesn't speak again until she has picked up her cup and drunk down its contents in long, confident gulps. It is then, when she returns the empty cup to its saucer, that her words become clear in my memory. She says, "We've been living together for eight months now, time enough for me to know you much better than I did before. You know me better, too, and know how much I love you and your mother. I love you both in different ways, of course, but I can assure you that I love you both equally." As if to reinforce her statement with something more than words, or perhaps simply to interrupt an activity that was distracting her, my aunt moves her right hand from the arm of her chair and places it on my hands, each of which is busily twirling the ends of my napkin. She says, "You will never again be the little boy who came here every year to stay for a couple of weeks in the summer, but whom I didn't actually watch growing up day by day. I know now that you'll be able to understand everything I say to you. We only have a few more days without your mother. I know how excited you are to be seeing her again, and I am, too. It's been far too long." Here my aunt pauses involuntarily, lending greater emphasis to that last statement. She keeps her hand on the two of mine, although she has relaxed the pressure, and this allows me to continue playing with the napkin. She says, "And yet despite that, we've had almost no time to talk. We know each other, but we've never talked about something that is as important to you as it is to me, we haven't spoken about your life or your mother's life." She pauses for a moment as if to catch her breath and continues plunging deeper into that as yet unnamed territory. She says, "It's a hard thing to say, but the fact is that your life has not been normal. In the last few years, you've had to put up with some pretty unusual situations. I needn't say what they are, we both know what I'm referring to. They've made you different, more mature, more knowledgeable about life. But it might not have been like that. What you have experienced could easily have damaged you. A lot of people wouldn't cope well with such situations, indeed, many people never get over their childhood experiences. I'm sure you know how important your mother has been in helping you to cope so well." Up until then, my hands have been moving around beneath hers relatively calmly, gently twisting and turning the napkin; now, however, they grow more agitated, and my aunt again presses down on them. I still have my head lowered so as to avoid her eyes. She says, "And obviously you've done your part, too, because you're a bright boy. But that doesn't mean that another

153

mother would have done such a good job. Your mother is quite extraordinary. She's sacrificed everything for you. Ever since you were born, you have been her main concern, and that's why we can talk about all this now. Your mother has always tried to make sure that everything seemed quite normal to you, that you would gradually come to understand things as they are. She's found a way of helping you over all those obstacles without your being affected by them. She's taken care that nothing should get in the way of your growing up." Thinking that I'm feeling calmer than I actually am, my aunt removes her hand from mine and breathes out through her nose to emphasize a timid smile I can sense is there but that, with my head down, I cannot see. She says, "That, I can assure you, has not been easy. Often the gravest errors occur as a consequence of a desire to protect. Like your mother, I want what's best for you, but I would often have done things very differently from her. And I recognize now that I would have been wrong, but that doesn't matter, because your mother *didn't* get it wrong. She knows you and has always given you exactly what you needed. She hasn't made a single mistake, but that has been the cause of a huge amount of anxiety, has cost her many sacrifices, and there were times when she only had you to turn to." I'm aware of my aunt moving her chair so as to get closer to me without changing her posture, and, having unraveled my now unrecognizable napkin, I begin to roll it up again, even more tightly this time, with each new turn, a kind of knot intended to contain the explosion I can feel approaching, with each new turn, an invisible, unspoken refusal to hear the words I know even though no one has actually spoken them in my presence before. My aunt says, "The truth is that she's always been alone. Your father has been

154

no help at all—on the contrary. That may seem like a harsh thing to say, but that's how it is, and the sooner you realize it, the better. Your mother was alone while your father was living with you, and she's been alone for these last three years. Now don't take that the wrong way. She's had you with her, of course, and you have been her main compensation, but it's still true that she's had no one unconditionally on her side. She's done all the work, taken all the responsibility. She's had no one to share you with." My aunt falls silent and reaches out her hand in my direction, her fingers form a pincer around my chin, forcing me to raise my head so that she can see what effect her words are having. I see her searching eyes, I see from the way she keeps blinking that she's still feeling nervous, I see gentleness in her eyes, but also determination. My eyes are, presumably, completely expressionless, frozen or paralyzed, because she releases my chin without any show of surprise or concern and then, as before, places one hand on my busy, tangled hands, but this time without preventing my fingers from continuing to play with the napkin. She says, "Because of this, your mother has given up other things she might have done if you weren't there. Naturally, she gave them up gladly. Perhaps it couldn't have been any other way, but the fact is that she has done without a lot of things." My aunt removes her hand from mine and puts it down close by, on the edge of the table. At that moment, as I'm forming yet another spiral with the napkin, it tears in half, and I immediately begin ripping it into tiny pieces, fingertips and fingernails furiously rubbing against each other. My aunt says, "The problem is that some of these things she did have to do without and others she didn't. At least, that's how it seems to me. She hasn't looked after herself properly. She's suffered too much, she's gone ahead with something that was doomed to failure right from the very start, and she's made mistakes, too. Of course, you're not to blame for any of those mistakes, she made them alone, without asking anyone's advice. The thing is, and this is what I want you to understand, the thing is that it's impossible to know to what extent she made those mistakes for your sake, in order to give you something you were lacking." My aunt breaks off to take a cigarette out of her purse, and while she does so, lights the cigarette, then takes a first puff, I think to myself for the first time—having been listening intently to her words despite the growing sense of dread they inspire—that I have no idea what she means, have no idea what mistakes she's referring to. I also think to myself, as I have been doing for some time, that I don't want to go on listening, that I've had enough, that my aunt knows nothing about my mother or me. "What does she know," I wonder, "about what my mother wants? What does she know about what it's like to have a child, when she has no children of her own?" But neither of those unspoken questions—which I ask myself without much conviction, keeping them in my head for as short a time as possible—has any impact on her. She doesn't even see me, is unaware of these questions in my head. She blows out the smoke, takes another puff on her cigarette, and continues talking, saying words that grow less and less clear in my memory, more and more confused and devoid of meaning. She says, "Fortunately, I think that's all over now. At least I hope so, I hope your mother doesn't let me down again. But everything has its consequences. Your mother isn't happy, she can't be after all that wasted effort, after all those disappointments. In less than a week, she'll be here. She'll appear to be really pleased and will give no sign to the contrary. And her happiness will be genuine. Neither you nor I can even imagine just how much she's looking forward to being with you, how much she will have missed you. If these months have seemed long to you, I can assure you they've been interminable for her. Nevertheless, she'll pretend otherwise and try to appear strong and confident. There will be joy, but there will be sadness, too. Her going off to Paris was her final failure. You should be aware of that, and be especially careful with her. You have a responsibility toward her, you must help her and allow her to start to live a life of her own. Your mother's life doesn't begin and end with you. She needs other things, too. She's young, so young that one day you'll regret not being able to remember her as she is now." At that point, my memory clouds over completely. My aunt has stubbed out her cigarette in the ashtray and is talking rapidly, apparently unconcerned about the consequences her words might have. I don't remember precisely when or why it all becomes unbearable, if it is some particular thing she says or just the whole situation. All I remember is her voice, like a distant murmur, becoming mixed up with the other sounds in the café, and how all that suffocating noise suddenly stops, as if my aunt had stopped talking, and as if all the customers at the other tables had stopped talking, too, stopped clinking their spoons on their cups, their cups on their saucers, their saucers on the tables. I remember that not even a second passes before she again reaches out her hand to my chin and again raises my head, which is now almost resting on my hands, which, for some time now, have lain motionless on the unrecognizable jigsaw puzzle of the napkin torn into tiny pieces. I see at once her look of surprise and how she immediately reaches out her other hand to my face and places her thumb and forefinger on my closed eyelids. Only then, when, with the gentlest of movements, she slides her fingers down my cheeks, do I realize, through that contact with her skin, that my own skin is wet, that her fingers are wiping away the two tears that have run down my cheeks, tracing two shining trails that she has seen and whose mere presence is now making the whole scene even more unbearable, making her words still more humiliating and definitive, both the words I hadn't wanted to hear and the words I hadn't even imagined, as well as those she hasn't even said; my tears are like notaries for posterity, the wax seal that preserves and bears witness to what has happened. It doesn't matter what my aunt does next, it doesn't matter that when she sees my tears, she gets up and embraces me. It doesn't matter that she is crying, too or that she goes on to say, her words as stumbling and incoherent as this fading, guttering memory, "Forgive me. Please, forgive me. You know I would never want to hurt you. You know that, don't you? I'm so sorry. Please, forgive me. Forget everything I said. I'm so very sorry. It was all nonsense. Don't listen to me . . ."

# XXI

When we think about the past, it's hard to resist both dividing it up into blocks in accordance with the pattern of events that have made most impression on us and attributing powers to it that it does not have, allowing ourselves to believe that the arrival of a particular date had the ability to work some radical transformation on us. Until the death of my father, we say, I was like this or like that, when we should really say that on such and such a date, something that already existed inside us began to make itself manifest or visible. Such nonsense is merely the reflection of a still greater error of thinking, the belief that we change suddenly rather than gradually, as if we could not possibly be influenced by opposing but simultaneous impulses.

As it appears in my memory now, the impression I have when I look back at the era that began with the return of my mother, the recommencement of our life together, is one of change *and* permanence; as if when travelling along an old provincial road relegated to premature neglect by the creation of a highway or by steady depopulation, we suddenly emerged, after a bridge or a turn or a particularly tight bend, onto a stretch rather different from all the previous ones, different enough to be noticeable, but in such a vague, indefinite way that we could easily be mistaken—it's no wider, the surface is no better, and yet, nevertheless, there's something different about the quality of the tarmac and the paint used on the road markings. Throughout those years, right up until now, really, the direction of travel has remained the same, as have the passing landscape and my fellow passengers, but there's a tenuous, unpindownable shift in the quality of my memory, as if it had grown denser, with diverse, hitherto foreign elements battling to get into it.

However, I have no idea precisely when those elements began to appear. My recollection of those years is so confused that I can't even differentiate between them. As far as I can recall, nothing changed between my mother and me after we resumed our life together, at least not outwardly; there were no appreciable changes in our relationship or in the way she treated me, nor in the world around us or in the way my mother navigated her way through the world. After her arrival in La Coruña and our subsequent move back to Madrid, our life returned, imperceptibly, even smoothly, to the familiar routine that my father had interrupted with his release from prison just over a year before and that we fleetingly reinstated during the two weeks between his departure and our journey to La Coruña, where, as it turned out, I was to stay. My mother is alone, and as far as I recall, I am the center of everything she does. I'm her most constant companion, the person she turns to when she needs calming down or cheering up, the one who greets her in the morning and says goodnight to her before going to bed, the person she has to take care of in the case of illness and the only person who can look after her when she herself is ill. The two of us are the center of everything, our decisions affect only us, and only we decide what does or does not affect us. My mother organizes her day so that she will be at home when she thinks I might need her, and I rarely disappoint her. As far as I can recall, those years not only do not change the rhythm of my relationship with her but, because of their nearness in time, they provide the reference point and model that allow me to reconstruct that relationship now. The journey to and from school; the weekends that would grow in my mind's eye before they arrived, until their glow was doused by the dull gray of Sundays; days that were both different and the same . . . My mother waking me up each morning, my mother telling me to hurry up so as not to miss the school bus. The years that follow her time in Paris do not modify but confirm, do not truncate but endorse and establish what constitutes the essence of her relationship with me, her solitary dedication, my onliness as an only child. And yet something entirely new emerges out of the interstices of those years, out of the almost identical days and weeks, out of the secrets and sadnesses and joys either shared, or experienced in the solitude of my room—something that allows me to establish a certain separation, to divide time up despite myself, to divide it into a before and an after.

This isn't something that happens suddenly. My mother's arrival in La Coruña draws a line in time, but as with the separation she had wanted and sought and to which her arrival put an end, as with her letters and phone calls and the continual postponements of those successive encounters planned during her absence, there was nothing that led me to believe that anything new or unusual was about to irrupt into our lives. My mother arrived looking very tired, carrying two gray leather suitcases much battered by her months of nomadism; her brown eyes seemed about to fill with tears, and her voice was timid and tentative, holding back the many feelings overwhelming her. She seemed uncertain, her every gesture and movement hesitant, as if she didn't quite know how to behave with me, whether she should give me a long or a short embrace, whether she should look at me or take my hand while I walked beside her to the terminal exit. From the very first moment, her every gesture, her every movement was a faithful reflection of the tension she felt between joy and sadness, between restraint and the need to conceal that restraint. On the other hand, despite this apparent exactitude of recall, I remember that I noticed nothing anomalous about her behavior. Nothing was quite as I expected, and yet it was still perfectly acceptable; it was all written according to a script I would not have agreed to beforehand but would not have dared to reject once it was written; there wasn't the joy I might have expected, but nor was her reaction strange enough to be denied or called into question. In a way, everything was acceptable, correct, and normal. Like the look in her eyes, more expectant and laconic than joyful and relaxed. Like her nervous blinking, or her hand, which, on our way back from the airport, she placed on my wrist, now as wide as hers (the two of us sitting in the back of the car that my uncle drove without speaking to or looking at us). Like Delfina's prudent but continual questions. Like the confusion over who should carry what when we took the suitcases out of the trunk or the awkwardness that came over us when we got back to the house (all of us, apart from my uncle, sitting in the living room, squeezing every banal detail out of my mother's description of her flight, all of us worn out with tension and clumsily struggling to find something to say). Like the presents my mother suddenly remembered she had brought for us. Like her apologies for having had to choose them so hurriedly, or the hours we spent afterward, still sitting in the same place, talking without really talking about anything. Like her early escape to bed or her brief, fearful goodnight to me. It was as spontaneous and ambiguous as it might have been had it all happened exactly as I had expected it would, and not so very different from that, either.

The presence of my aunt and uncle may have contributed to this, but I have no memory of any sudden shocks in the days that followed, either, nor during the whole of that summer. At home in Madrid, with the two of us alone, I would probably have assigned a different interpretation to my mother's reluctance to talk about her time in Paris, I would probably have taken a very different view of her evasive looks and comments whenever I mentioned it; the way she quickly changed the subject, the complete absence of any details, her permanently inward-turned gaze whenever I happened upon her alone, the slow fragility with which she seemed to move, and the hesitant, halting way in which she spoke would probably have made me suspicious. Although I can't be sure. The one thing I can say without fear of straying from the truth is that in the company of my aunt and uncle, whose presence diluted everything, I found nothing strange about the silences or the frequent exchanges of glances, nor did I wonder, however often I may think back to it now, at my mother's willingness to bow to the dictates of others—whether to my aunt's occasional peremptory orders or to my own childish, capricious whims—or at her obvious unease whenever my uncle turned up to join in some family outing, or at his general coolness and lack of interest in such activities.

Everything becomes mixed up in one's memory, and I'm not even sure if that really is what happened or if it's just me finding signs and symbols where there were none, especially when I can put no end-date on it, give no definite before and after. I would like to, but it doesn't really help if I say that our move back to Madrid did not immediately cause a change in the texture of the lines and surface of the path we resumed together, or that my mother's silence and the sparing, hesitant way in which she spoke about those months when we were separated for the first time continued unabated in Madrid, or that the blur of day-to-day routine quickly reinstated itself and I soon forgot what that separation had meant for us. I would like to give a date, but there is no beginning and no definite end. I know when the "before" ends, but not when the "after" begins. It's something that affects all those years that were just about to begin. Something that happens without my realizing it. Something that is there in those identical days following one on the other, in the repeated embraces and expressions of joy at familiar situations or situations very similar to other situations, in my mother's words of advice, in the light from her bedroom at night illuminating my dark bedroom, in our two doors left open, in the breathing of one being listened to by the other.

The years ushered in by my mother's return are years in which my father is completely absent and we no longer expect to see him. They are years in which my image of him is the quick, broad-brush sketch of someone who has neither a future nor a present, when he is forbidden from entering our apartment, and we do not even miss him; years in which my mother does not object to talking to me about him when I ask her to, but when the only regular, constant news we get of him comes from the phone calls made by anxious, worried, bewildered people, phone calls that come in waves depending on whether he's in Madrid or not, and with passing time, they will be our only surviving connection with him, even when we move to a new apartment and my father becomes someone forever erased and excluded from our lives. The years ushered in by my reunion with my mother are years in which my Aunt Delfina resumes her important but secondary role; years in which we still see her every summer, in which she continues to be my mother's closest and most loyal ally, but during which she is not, as far as I know, counselor, accomplice, or confessor; years in which I overhear no behind-doors conversations or eavesdrop on dialogues in which I sense some intimate secret that I do not share, simply because there is nothing that requires any counseling, nothing to confess or to share. The years ushered in by my mother's return are years in which nothing changes, and nothing new or unrelated to ourselves occurs. And at the same time, they are years in which time drags and becomes seemingly endless and oppressive, they are years of struggle, years in which I do battle with myself, in which I change completely and begin to judge and rebel and protest against my solitary existence, condemned never to share my feelings with or offload them onto anyone else, to suffer in solitude—myself as sole recipient, sole beneficiary—all the sacrifices and doubts, all the self-abnegation and devotion. The years ushered in by my mother's return are years in which things linger and calcify, in which my mother withdraws further into herself and shows no sign of any anomalous behavior or perturbation of spirit; years in which only remnants of the past surface to worry me, fears that make the sacrifice still more sacrificial, the self-abnegation more self-abnegating. There is no before or after, the lines blur. During those years, life is just life, it's just my mother and me.

# XXII

It's not easy to separate out in your memory different incidents that happened simultaneously. If your father died in the same year as some other misfortune occurred that seemed to alter the course of your life, setting it off along the tracks of despair, it's hard not to connect the two things, not to fall into the temptation of thinking that your father's death was a determining factor in that other event, in your failing your final exams, losing your job, or messing up your last opportunity to save a relationship. According to that same deductive process, it would be equally legitimate to infer the opposite: that your father died *because* you were about to drop out of college or undertake some venture doomed to failure. If we reject that possibility, we do so only out of prudence and not because it's just as false or unlikely as the first hypothesis.

In the same way, I find it hard to separate out those first stirrings of rebellion and my feelings of detachment from my mother from the shadow of doubt that hung over me all those years. The two emotions have become confused in my memory, and I don't know which caused which, or if they were entirely independent from each other.

But in order to speak about the uncertainties haunting my mind, first timidly and later ever more forcefully and urgently, I must first describe a curious incident that happened before that, when, to me, the city of Paris meant nothing more than the months I had spent away from my mother. It happened suddenly, without warning, at a time I can't pin down exactly, but about one or two years after my mother came back to get me in La Coruña. It was winter, one afternoon when I'd already been home from school for some time. My mother was out, and I was sitting in my bedroom, waiting for her, when the apartment's buzzer sounded. This did not surprise me, even though I knew we weren't expecting anyone and that the street door downstairs was open, what with the doorman carrying out his usual duties as inquisitor and filter. While I slouched off reluctantly toward the kitchen, I thought it would probably be my mother calling up, as she often did, to tell me that she'd be slightly delayed because she had to go to the store or had stopped to talk to a neighbor. A few seconds later, however, the voice I heard on the other end was not hers but the weary, servile voice of the doorman. "Two men asking after your mother are coming up. I told them she wasn't in, but they insisted." I didn't even have time to thank him before the doorbell rang. I hung up and went to open the door, which I did—as usual, disobeying all my mother's instructions—without first looking through the peephole or putting on the security chain. I don't know who I thought I would find there. The fact is that all my confidence vanished when I was confronted by a man wearing boots and a black leather jacket; he had curly hair, a defiant look on his face, and he stood on the landing, smiling at me, but making no attempt to say anything during the time it took me to look him up and down. He was probably in his late thirties, and his impeccable appearance struck me as somehow artificial and showy. I didn't feel afraid, because he was standing very stiffly and some way away from the door, as if in order to ring the bell he'd had to reach out his arm as far as he could. I was, nevertheless, so disconcerted that I was completely unable to speak, until, after a few seconds, the stranger took one short step forward, while still remaining some distance away, and asked to speak to my mother, using her full name.

"She's not here," I said. "But if you'd like to leave a message, or if I can help you at all . . ."

"Are you her son?" His smile had grown still broader, and he took advantage of the softening effect this might have on me by taking another step forward, thus placing himself in the normal position for ringing a doorbell. "May I come in?" he added, without waiting for me to respond. "I'm a friend of your parents. I haven't heard from them for some time, and since I'm in Madrid for a few days, I thought I'd look them up."

At that moment, while still filling the doorway, he stood slightly to one side, and the space created was immediately occupied by a man who emerged from behind the right-hand side of the doorframe. He was a man of about sixty, bald and very short. His clothes, although conventional, were shabbier. He was wearing a gray, striped overcoat and brown sneakers. Like his companion, his face wore a smile, but there was, I thought, something timid and embarrassed about that smile, as if he were there against his will. He somehow inspired confidence, though, and seemed to me capable of keeping the other man in order.

"He's with me," said the man in the black leather jacket. "He's a friend of your father's, too."

Perhaps what tempted me was that unexpected reference to my father, combined with the more reassuring appearance

169

of the older man. Whatever the truth of the matter, after a brief moment during which I hesitated as to whether or not to let them in, I stood involuntarily to one side, a gesture that the younger man immediately interpreted as the invitation I had not intended. It was of little use for me to repeat in a firm voice that my mother was not at home. The younger man had already come in through the door and was walking down the hallway toward the living room. Meanwhile, the older man remained where he was, waiting for me to give him the permission his friend had not felt he needed. I must have taken a while to react, because, with one long stride, he, too, entered the apartment, and pausing by my side only long enough to whisper "Don't worry, it's all right," he followed the younger man down the hallway. I closed the door and walked after them; the first man was already much farther ahead, about to turn the corner into the living room, while the second man was slower, trying unsuccessfully to let me pass. It seemed to me that they knew where they were going, and while I was wondering whether to call the doorman and ask him to come to my aid, I thought for a moment that they must know the apartment. As soon as the younger man went into the living room, however, it was clear that he did not. He was standing in the middle of the room, looking around him, pretending to study everything with great interest.

"Hmm, very nice," he said, shooting a knowing, ironic glance at his companion, who was standing alongside me in the doorway. "Nobody ever told me your parents lived so well."

"My father doesn't live here," I explained. And repeating what I'd said earlier and at the same time lying slightly, "My mother isn't in, and I don't know when she'll be back. If you'd like to leave a phone number . . ."

"It doesn't matter, we're in no hurry. We can chat while we wait."

I averted my gaze. In his voice there was a note of aggression, which he emphasized by fixing me with his eyes, and so I chose to say nothing. I was feeling anxious now and hoping desperately that my mother would arrive soon.

"May I sit down?" he asked, indicating one of the large armchairs facing the sofa, where every night, before we went to bed, my mother and I would sit and talk a little and watch television. I still did not answer, and he sat down anyway, while the other man made no attempt to imitate him. After making himself comfortable, he stretched out his legs, took a cigarette out of his inside jacket pocket, and lit it with a silver butane lighter. He took a long drag on the cigarette, held it between his fingers a few inches from his mouth and, with a gesture of barrack-room coarseness, blew on the lit end to make it glow. Only then did he speak to me again. I was looking down at him, absorbed in thought and still frightened.

"Sit down, don't be afraid. Your parents are going to be really happy to see us. Go on, sit down."

He took another drag on his cigarette, and for a moment, silence reigned again. This made his command seem still more of an imperative, and I had no option but to obey. The older man, who hadn't said a word since he came in, remained standing, resting his hands on the back of the empty armchair next to the one occupied by his companion.

"That's better, I don't want to have to look up every time I speak to you," he added after blowing out the smoke from his cigarette and watching as I walked over to the sofa. "Do you want to talk to me? No, of course not," he said at once, without even leaving a rhetorical pause. "Why should you, when you don't even know who I am?"

On that occasion, he did pause. Sitting on the edge of the sofa, I looked into his eyes, and avoiding answering a question to which there was no answer, and purely so as not to appear weak or cowardly, I asked if he'd like a drink of something, a glass of water or a Coke. Then I looked again at his companion to extend the offer to him and, in passing, gauge his mood. He had taken off his overcoat to reveal a tight-fitting, polka-dot shirt, and he winked at me and shook his head.

"I don't suppose your parents will have talked to you about me," the other man went on, as if, unlike his friend, he had not heard my offer. "That would be too much to ask. Mind, they never mentioned you, either. Before I got here and saw you open the door, I didn't even know you existed. That's normal, I suppose. Things were different then, you didn't matter."

At this point, he placed his cigarette in the ashtray on the table immediately in front of him and began to take off his jacket, pulling at the sleeves from behind. When he had done this, he turned and draped the jacket over the back of the armchair. His shirt matched his denim jeans, and on the collar were a couple of embroidered roses. While he was leaning forward again to retrieve his cigarette, I noticed his boots. They had metal-tipped toes, and the heels sloped slightly inwards. I listened hard, in the hope of hearing some sound that would announce my mother's arrival, but all I could hear was the loud, stertorous breathing of the other man, the breathing of a former smoker whom the slightest physical effort—climbing the stairs or simply standing up—seemed to bring almost to death's door. As if he had read my thoughts and needed to pretend no longer, the older man took advantage of that silence to leave his post and come wearily over to sit by my side. This time, he did not consider it necessary to ask my consent.

"No," his friend went on, "I haven't seen them in ages. I don't live in Madrid, although as you've probably guessed from my accent, this is where I was born, but I don't live here any more. I have business interests elsewhere, and it's becoming increasingly difficult to find the time to visit. I'd like to now and again, but I can't. It would be good, though, even if only to catch up with old friends. Otherwise, well, you know how it is, they forget all about you. Like your father—he's forgotten me. We were such friends before, but now he doesn't even want to know me. He hasn't behaved very well, your father. But I can see that you're different. You're polite, you offer your visitors something to drink. Thank you for that. Do you have anything else apart from Coke? Beer or wine, perhaps?"

No, I said, I didn't.

"Never mind. If I'm going to fill myself up with something bubbly, I'd rather make it worth my while."

He stubbed out his still-unfinished cigarette and leaned back. He rested his head on one of the wings of the chair and crossed his legs. He had stopped smiling now and was speaking in a deliberately ambiguous manner, as if trying to say something while simultaneously not saying it. He took no notice of his friend, he didn't even look at him, and I wondered if this wasn't just part of a game, if they had perhaps divided up the roles the way the police do when they interrogate someone. I immediately dismissed this idea, however, because I thought I noticed a touch of genuine impatience in the older man, as if he really didn't like the tone adopted by his companion.

"Yessir," the latter said, looking around the room as he had at the start. "Very nice, indeed. Yes, your father's got it made, really. I'm surprised he plays the tricks he does. We had some business together, you know. For quite a while. Easy enough, no risks involved. It was just a matter of collecting the money. Slowly but surely. That's the best way. It doesn't pay to be overambitious. Best to take things slowly, rather than rush things and mess them up. Anyway, we could have done well, we could have done very well indeed. We were a good team. We complemented each other. All he had to do was get himself from point A to point B. I was the worker, the one who had to do the hard grift, but that was never the problem. We shared the profits equally and, well, you have to accept your lot in life, don't you? We're all different, after all. I would have preferred to be more like your father, but you don't get the choice, do you? And where would we be if we were all alike?"

I looked at his curly, black hair, his strong jaw and cleft chin, his prominent cheekbones, his small, dark, deep-set eyes, positioned rather too close to his tiny nose, and I thought about the vague, absent figure of my father and about my mother, who was late.

"Not that I really need him, of course. He doesn't need me, either. But it's a shame. It's hard to find another partner. It must have been difficult for him, too. Just as I can't do what your father does, he can't do what I do. He doesn't have what it takes. He has no patience, that's his problem. He let me down. I would never have imagined he would behave the way he did and make such a mistake. He deceived me, you see. He had just blown in from Madrid. He'd gotten a bit of money together, enough to live on for a couple of years, and needed a change of scenery. I could see right away that he had talent, and I suggested a partnership. He had no contacts, he didn't know anyone there, and I provided him with everything. It's my fault, really, I won't deny it. I should have realized there was a problem when I saw how he went through all that money in a matter of months. For anyone else, me, for example—and I like the good life, too, mind—that money would have been enough to live on comfortably for a whole year. But your father spent it all. He doesn't know how to hold back, he doesn't know that the best thing to do with money is to use it to make more money. Otherwise, what's the point? To live like a king for a while and then wait until another opportunity lands in your lap? Your father's in for a hard time of it. In our line of business, people find out about everything in the end, and the one thing you can't afford to lose is your reputation ..."

He turned to look at his friend, who was still saying nothing, and after a pause, he went on.

"I trusted him, I wasn't worried about the way he spent money, although I should have been. When you have no boundaries with money, you have no boundaries with anything else. That's the problem. But why am I telling you this? I imagine your mother knows it all too well."

He picked up a photo of my mother from a shelf and studied it for a few seconds.

"Is this her?" he asked. Without waiting for me to reply, he returned the photograph to its place. "Hmm, very pretty. I hope what you say is true and that she's gotten rid of him. You said before that he didn't live with you now. Where is he? Do you know?"

I said that I didn't, that neither of us had seen him for some time, that we didn't know anything about him. I was still feeling nervous and spoke hesitantly, mumbling slightly.

"Just as well." He gave a faint smile. "Anyway, if you do see him or speak to him, tell him I'm looking for him, will you, that we have some unfinished business, and that I haven't forgotten. Knowing your father, he'll probably turn up as soon as he needs something. He won't do that with me, though. He knows he can't come to me for help. It wasn't really any big deal, but that's exactly why I can't just let it go. Leaving a business partner in the lurch like that . . ."

"Forget it," said the older man. "The boy's told you he doesn't know anything."

They looked at each other, and after a few moments, the one doing all the talking continued, ignoring his companion's advice, as if he hadn't heard.

"And over such a petty amount, too. It makes no sense. However much I think about it, I just can't find an explanation. Promise me you'll tell him that when you see him, will you?"

While he waited for my response, I noticed that his final words seemed to strike a more conciliatory note. I forced myself to nod, and he smiled ambiguously at his friend, who, as if to reaffirm what he had said before, had already stood up, gone over to the armchair he'd been leaning on to start with, and begun to put on his overcoat.

"Yes, you're right," said the younger man at last, intently following his colleague's every movement. "He seems like a nice enough kid. We won't bother him any longer."

And then, addressing me.

"I'm sure you have things to do . . ."

Only then did he get up from his armchair and retrieve his jacket. He didn't put it on but slung it over his shoulder, holding it hooked over the fingers of his right hand. I got up, too, and he held out his free arm and placed his other hand on my shoulder. We stood like that, facing each other, while, behind me, I began to hear the older man's labored breathing.

"It doesn't look like your mother's coming," he added, by way of explanation, his eyes fixed on mine. "We won't wait for her. It would worry her. Frighten her. I told you before that I knew her, but I don't. Your father never introduced us. I would have liked him to, but he didn't. Besides, he didn't stick around long."

He looked over at the photo on the shelf and removed his hand from my shoulder.

"Yes, very pretty," he said again. "What a shame. Your father doesn't even appreciate what he's got here, either."

Without looking at me again, and pushing me gently aside, he walked over to the hallway, where his companion was already heading for the front door. I followed behind, my eyes fixed on his back, on those boots with their inward-turned heels, on his wide-leg jeans and the sticker with a tiger that I discovered on the sleeve of his jacket. He walked to the front door in silence, and when he reached it, he waited for a moment for the older man to open it and let him pass. Once over the threshold and after summoning the elevator, he added, "Tell your mother I came. Tell her and your father, if you see him or hear from him. Tell him that I haven't forgotten, even after all this time—he can call me collect, if he likes. And tell him it would be better for him to get in touch with me rather than me just happening to find him one day . . ."

Meanwhile, the older man—who had been left holding the door as if he were the one living in the apartment and were going to stay there—handed me a business card worn with use. It was for a bar on the Calle Bravo Murillo.

"It's mine," he said, with a hint of pride, pointing with a small, nicotine-stained finger. "Call me or come and see me if you hear anything from your father. Or even if you don't. We can just have a chat, if you like."

I held the card, pretending to read it intently, and heard him cross the threshold. When he was outside, he gave me a conspiratorial wink.

"Take no notice of him," he said, gesturing with his head toward his companion, who was eyeing us indifferently from the same place where I had seen him for the first time. "His bark is worse than his bite."

For a moment, the other man seemed about to intervene, but thought better of it and remained silent. At that point, the elevator arrived, and they both turned their backs on me and went in. Before closing the front door, I caught one last glimpse through the glass doors of the younger man sideways on, for he had entered last this time, and I saw him press the button to go down. Then he moved and completely obscured my view of the older man, who was saying something to him that I could not hear. Then I closed the door and went back into the living room. I sat down on the sofa again and fixed my eyes on the armchair where the man with the leather boots had sat and talked to me. After a while, although exactly how long I can't be sure, I heard the front door open and, shortly afterward, my mother's voice announcing her arrival in clearly anxious tones. I got up, straightened the cushion on the armchair, did the same with the sofa and the chair where the older man had sat, and went to find her. We met in the kitchen. She was carrying a plastic bag and smiled with relief to see me.

"The doorman told me that a couple of shady-looking characters were here." I didn't reply at once, as if it were a matter of no importance.

"Yes, it was a mistake. They were looking for someone with the same name as you, but it turned out they were after someone else."

# XXIII

There are no strategies we can reliably adopt in our dealings with other people, there are no fixed patterns, not even if our overriding feeling is one of love. Why is it that I react to the same stimulus sometimes with anger and sometimes with sympathy or even satisfaction? Why is it that, depending on the day, something as ordinary as watching someone I love pick up their morning cup of coffee can fill me with either pleasure or revulsion? Why is it that sometimes a look is enough for me to feel forearmed against any future misfortune and yet, at others, that same look can plunge me into the blackest of melancholies? We tend to think of ourselves as immovable beings, firmly rooted in certain fixed codes and tastes, when, in reality, we are constantly at war with ourselves. We say things like "I love you" or "I can't stand you any more" and think that those words define the state of our soul, when the truth is that we change with the ever-mutable winds of the emotions. That's why young lovers, who are closest to the age when the flow of desire is as yet untamed by convention or self-interest, speak constantly about their love. "I love you," they say. "Do you love me?" they ask. They need their affections to be constantly confirmed, because they know that nothing lasts and that while something may be true at this very moment, the next moment, it might not, that even the sincerest of feelings can change in a matter of minutes.

Not even those who can no longer answer us are free from these vacillations of the mind, not even my mother, who neither listens nor speaks nor even thinks. Why did she not make a better choice? Why did she not get out sooner? Why did she enlarge my solitude with hers? Was it just because she married in haste? Did she sacrifice herself for me, or was I the sacrifice? The questions pile up, the justifications and complaints follow thick and fast. It doesn't matter that there is no reply or that the only person who could reply keeps silent. We felt happy or angry with our living father just as we feel happy or angry with our dead father, the only difference being that in the latter case, the sorrow is greater. Remorse haunts us because we know that it depends entirely on us which pan of the scales weighs heaviest.

I can't remember the first occasion on which either a tantrum or a sharp reply directed at my mother was followed, on reflection, by a hasty attempt to find some justification for it in our strange life, in her kindness, her overattentiveness. I don't remember a single scene in which I responded sharply to some affectionate comment she made, to an inopportune caress, or a perfectly ordinary question like "How are you?" or "What have you been up to?" At first, these were mere flashes of anger that faded almost before they began, like the flame from some pantomime dragon. I remember my confusion, my regret, my attempts to make up for each explosion with subsequent affectionate outbursts. I remember my continuing doubts once I had been forgiven and, afterward, my search for new reasons to exonerate myself, for imagined changes I thought I'd noticed since her return, as if anything that came between us had only appeared since then, as if they were bad habits acquired during her time in Paris. I felt, for example, that she was far more protective of me than before, and I found this irksome. It bothered me to notice how little she went out, and I was sure that before we had spent a whole winter apart, she had been far less preoccupied with me, had had her own life, which she didn't need to supplement with mine. It bothered me that she was always giving me advice on what I should wear or how I should behave, which, it seemed to me, she hadn't done before, at least not so frequently. Of course, I myself realize that these were mere ploys, comparisons dictated by necessity, but they worked. They were not legitimate, but they helped to justify my irritation. Whether rightly or wrongly, I felt that my mother had not been the same since she returned from Paris, and although it's true that I could not have said what that difference was, I was sure she had undergone some kind of transformation. We are, of course, all in a state of perpetual change, adopting new characteristics and new customs as we grow up and grow older. You may not notice it when you live with someone on a daily basis, but you only have to spend some time away from them for that whole evolution to spring out at you. We pick up a certain turn of phrase, an unusual word we find amusing; someone infects us with a particular gesture and someone else with the way he blinks his eyes. Often we don't need the influence of others, we sometimes change of our own accord—the constant jiggling of one leg, which we control one day with our arm in order to disguise the embarrassing tic in front of strangers, only to realize a few months later that it isn't just our leg we're moving, but the arm we placed over it in order to keep it still; the cloud casting a shadow over our face dissolves and disappears if there's no one to look at it. The changes I noticed in my mother were of a different order, they affected the very essence of her being, rather than its parts. That's why they were so impossible to enumerate or define. They were, or so I imagined, tiny details, questions of emphasis or nuance, which meant little or nothing on their own, and only gained force when they came together. I don't know if she always used to leave her slippers neatly lined up next to each other beside the bed, but it's then that I begin to give them a little kick when I go into her bedroom to kiss her goodnight. I don't know if she always used to be such a light sleeper, but it's then that I notice it and can't help but feel annoyed every time I get up to go to the bathroom and hear her voice in the hallway asking if I'm all right. I don't know if she used to submit me to the same interrogation each time I went out on my own, but it's then that it starts to bother me and that I begin deliberately keeping things from her.

Initially, comparing past and present was the most effective antidote against the unease created in me by my sudden attacks of anger or disdain. It didn't matter what provoked those negative reactions. I could always resort to looking back at our previous life, I could always point to some detail in our present life together that made the perimeter fence around me more frustrating, and my irritation more understandable. There's a moment, however, when that recourse to the past stops, when time passes and my mother's return is not so recent, and yet those misunderstandings, those unexpressed feelings of annoyance, that pressure are all still there . . . The old excuses no longer work, and I don't even bother with them. It's from that point on that conflicts accumulate, and I begin sometimes to resent the sheer weight of her devotion.

It's not so much that she's become more demanding or that she behaves very differently or has become more obsessive. It's the tension between the lack of any real grievance or objective reason to justify my rebellious feelings on the one hand and my need, nonetheless, to rebel against my family situation on the other that makes the years since the resumption of our life together different from all the previous years. That, for me, is the main difference between them, the different color of the lane markings, so to speak: the weight of that debt, which I did not accept but which I could not reject, either, the one my aunt tried to talk to me about that afternoon in La Coruña when she took me out to a café and then had to take back her words when she saw my reluctant tears. I don't want to continue being the center of attention, I want my mother to go out and have fun, to begin to lead a life different from mine, not to worry if I'm late and not to postpone things in order to do them later on with me. I don't want to hear her breathing from the darkness of my room.

During the first two years, that secret conflict is the most notable thing that occurs between us, but not the only one. It has its roots in the same cause, but another seed has to be sown before doubt really settles in.

You could say that the process of emancipation I've described happened inside me. You could say that my mother had nothing to do with it, that she remained exactly the same even though what angered me was precisely my sporadic dissatisfaction with a life I believed she had chosen and seemed determined to continue. Naturally, I couldn't always control my sudden feelings of peevish indifference, and when they surfaced, my mother's reaction was never one of annoyance, but resigned acceptance, and this, far from soothing my feelings, only fanned the flames. But, as I say, it was, nonetheless, something that went on inside me, independent of what she did.

In the instance I'm going to describe, my ability to pinpoint the origin of my feelings is, on the contrary, rather more tenuous.

The years following our reunion were also the years in which my mother overcame her reserve and began telling me about my father, about his adventures and misadventures. I mean that these were the years in which she did so systematically rather than when forced to do so by the urgent need to explain some undesirable fragment from the past that had suddenly sprung to life again. It's true that she did not speak of these things spontaneously and that I was nearly always the instigator, but when I did ask her questions, she would reply quite openly and without any apparent embarrassment. Then she would talk freely, letting herself be guided by my demands, illuminating key aspects of my father's personality, the important events in his life, telling me about his family, with whom he had severed all contact shortly after I was born, and about the early years of their relationship. Sometimes she would be overcome by the emotion of the moment and say more than I had asked her to, but that rarely happened, and generally she said only what was necessary. As I have said elsewhere, she never touched on feelings, never explained how she had felt or how she thought my father had felt. She gave the facts with a kind of aseptic coolness, without becoming emotionally involved or drifting into sentimentality. She never mentioned the dreams or nightmares that had accompanied her misfortune, never mentioned any arguments or hopes, or what had happened between them, never spoke of the qualities in my father that had presumably provided her with some compensation, with moments of happiness or feelings of confidence in the future, which, despite everything, she must also have experienced. I don't think there was anything premeditated about this approach. She behaved as she did out of modesty, to protect herself, and not out of rancor or resentment, but it is equally true that she never judged my father, never said a bad word about him. There was, therefore, nothing deliberate about her reserve, but at the same time, it was inevitable that in presenting the facts so plainly, so bleakly, her account of events infected me with that same bleakness. She was harsh without meaning to be, and the resulting portrait of my father was even less favorable, even less flattering than she doubtless intended. Since she gave me no glimpse of their daily life together, no clues to help me understand what had fueled her ever-renewed confidence in my father's ability to change, it was completely impossible to forgive or understand. This wasn't the worst of it, though. The worst thing, given the circumstances, was that I found it as hard to understand her as I did my father. Why did she insist on remaining bound to him? Why was she so patient with a person who had, again and again, betrayed her trust, who, right from the start, had been heading for that point of no return where someone becomes a caricature of the person they might have been? I didn't understand why the thread connecting her to my father had remained intact for so long or why the split had taken place when it did, why she had decided to be no longer available. What had been so different about my father's last departure? She had put up with him until that moment, so what made her decide that enough was enough? What happened then that had not happened before? It wasn't that I disapproved of their separation or that I regretted her previous willingness to try again, over and over. My father was not the solution I was seeking to our wearisome solitude, to our extreme dependence on each other. It was just that the mist covering everything to do with my father was beginning, in part, to spread over her. Gradually, unnoticed, something unexpected had happened, something I did not even dare to confess but that was there, gaining ground: slowly, timidly, I had begun to distrust her. I suppose that to begin with, it was simply a sublimated desire to feel that I had been deceived, to offload some of my guilt by pretending that my mother was not as infallible as I thought. But if that were so, I was completely unaware of it. I told myself quite sincerely that there must be something, that there must be more to it than met the eye.

What I did realize was that my suspicions lay neither in the present nor in the future, that I had no doubts about the life we were living then. And although my father had not reappeared or phoned since his final, furtive departure and my mother's determination had not yet been put to the test, it was clear that she was not expecting him, that she didn't care where he was, where he slept, or what he ate. On those occasions when I asked her questions and we spoke about him, she didn't speak with guarded prudence about the future, she made no provisos or predictions, and even in delicate, unexpected circumstances, like when she would tell me about the phone calls from those anxious, worried, or bewildered people asking for my father, there was not a trace of melancholy in her voice or face; she merely told me about them, just as I told her when I was the one who answered the phone, and that was that—no pregnant silences, no evasions, no revealing anxieties. My father had been expelled from our lives, he was not needed or expected. I had no doubts about that. It wasn't the present or the future that worried me. It was the past. I felt somehow that there must be something in the past that I did not know about, and incidents like the visit by those two men who had come looking for my father only confirmed me in that belief. It cannot have been weariness alone that had finally driven my mother and my father apart, it could not simply have been a case of the straw breaking the camel's back, my mother could not possibly be so perfect in her goodness nor my father so alone in his guilt.

# XXIV

You could say that suspicion settled inside me without my having anything on which to base it. It was a confusion, a futile delirium that would doubtless have faded away beneath the weight of my bad conscience; however, even if that were the case, and even though I'm the one saying it, that doesn't take away from the significance of the moment when I found something real to be suspicious about. Especially since I did not seek it out but came upon it accidentally.

It occurred some time after the visit of those two men who came looking for my father, but not so long afterward that I had completely forgotten it, a few months or a year, perhaps, and two or three years after the end of my mother's time in Paris. That afternoon, it was pure chance that guided my steps toward the place where it happened, an area and a street where I never normally went. There were no warnings, none of those signs or symbols that we always look for after any significant event, in the ingenuous belief that the things that affect us most deeply never happen singly or unannounced. It wasn't even during one of those periods when we were getting a lot of calls from people asking for my father, which were usually an indication that he was somewhere near at hand. As far as I recall, no one had mentioned my father to us recently, and we had no idea where he was; or at least my mother hadn't said anything to me in that regard. It's that absence of related events, along with the coincidence of my being there, that confuses my memory and, on this occasion, covers it with a thin membrane of incredulity, which I find it hard not to feel even when I think about it now.

I no longer went to school on the school bus but traveled there and back alone, with a change on the subway and a bus ride. I didn't always go straight home but hung around with a school friend, making secret forays into the city, which I was just beginning to get to know. Sometimes I didn't bother going to class in the afternoon, and after a hurried lunch—eaten at a local café rather than in the school dining hall—I'd go to a movie theater with continuous showings and get home at more or less my normal time, as if I'd come straight from school. I don't know if it was on one of those days when, after eating lunch, I decided to skip the last part of the day or if it was one afternoon, after five o'clock, when I took longer than usual on my journey home. The only lasting image I have is of the already fading light and of me sitting at a bus stop reading a book. It was one of those glazed bus shelters with advertising posters on the end panels. Sitting on the narrow metal bench that ran along the inside wall of the shelter, I could see only what was directly in front of me on the other side of the quiet, narrow, one-way street: a green door, a mailbox, a shop selling household appliances, and a café whose windows were slightly steamed up, at least those I could see from my rather limited viewpoint. A light drizzle had been falling for some time, and the passers-by were walking along with heads down and shoulders hunched against the fine rain. My reading, which had been very focused to begin with, had gradually become more distracted and fragmented, and I spent more and more time watching the hurried footsteps of the people a yard or so away on the other side of the gray asphalt and the swift, fleeting mist of passing cars. Apart from occasional sideways glances to see if the bus was coming, I observed their comings and goings, whether to the right, where the last thing I could see was a store selling dried fruit and nuts, or to the left, where my visual boundary was provided by the corner of a building at the intersection with the next street.

Everything happened very fast. Just as I was despairing at the lateness of the bus and had closed my book and placed it on top of the folder on my lap, I noticed a blind man emerging from the café opposite and heading off to the left, with his guide dog at his side. I watched their slow, deliberate passing, the man apparently more confident than his dog, which seemed uneasy and hesitant, and saw them turn the corner and disappear. I had not even had time to look elsewhere in search of some new prey when I saw *him* appear around that same corner, but heading in my direction, walking so quickly and keeping so close to the wall that he had probably had to flatten himself against it in order not to bump into the blind man and his dog moments before. I recognized him at once. He was wearing a brick-red jacket, a scarf, and boots. He had a folded newspaper under one arm, was carrying a furled umbrella, and walking along with head held high, not hunched against the rain like the other passers-by. I didn't think anything, I wasn't even startled. In the few seconds it took my father to reach the café and go in with the determined air of someone who has reached his final destination, I merely followed him with my eyes as indifferently as if he'd been just another anonymous pedestrian.

As soon as he disappeared inside, as soon as the glass doors closed behind him, all the things that I could or should have done rushed into my head; my initial coolness was shattered by curiosity, by a cascade of voices and memories, in which my mother was a constant presence, observing my indecisiveness from the stage of memory. For an indeterminate length of time, I remained sitting on that bench, and a few minutes later, while I was still debating what to do, the bus I had been waiting for finally arrived, but I let it pass without getting on. I could have caught it, I could also have gotten up before it arrived and walked to the next stop, as I had considered doing during the time that had passed since my father's unexpected arrival. Either of those things would have preserved me from witnessing what happened next, and yet I did not move.

Shortly after the automatic doors had wheezed shut and the bus itself had lurched off, I began to look around me for a place where I could safely watch what was happening inside the café, because its broad window was too far to my left for me to be able to see in. For a moment, I wondered if I ought to cross the road, but that seemed too dangerous, too indiscreet, too exposed in the event that my father were to leave the café suddenly. After getting up from my seat, I went over to a wooden bench on the same side of the street as me, next to a newsstand and behind two parked cars with enough space between them to allow me a clear view. I sat down with my book and folder clutched against me to protect them from the rain and so that I could easily beat a hasty retreat if my presence were discovered. I was now in an excellent position directly across from the café window, but when I peered through the glass in search of my father, there was no sign of his tall, slim figure. The problem wasn't that I was too far away. As I said, it was a narrow street, and for a young person like myself with perfect vision, it was easy enough to see across.

The café, however, went back quite a long way inside, which meant that most of the bar, only the near end of which was next to the door, and the tables at the rear were completely invisible to me; the former because it was obscured from my perspective by the glass doors, and the latter because the fading, orangey, late-afternoon light clashed with the café's scattering of bright neon bulbs, and the collision of the two bathed everything inside in a kind of nebulous penumbra, apart from the tables nearest the window and the central part of the bar, which was full of mirrors and lit by various spotlights. I got up and moved three or four yards further to the left, in search of a more diagonal sightline, to a point where, instead of a bench, there was a tree and two more parked cars, and from which I could see my father leaning on the corner of the bar. He was sideways to me with one foot up on the foot rail, facing the door that I could no longer see. He still had his newspaper under one arm, and in the hand closest to me, he held a glass of some dark liquid, probably wine, while the curved, black handle of his umbrella was hooked over the edge of the bar and resting against his raised knee.

Once again, I don't remember what went through my mind that afternoon as I observed my father after having spent two or three years with no news of him; meanwhile, I grew increasingly wet in the rain, which, while it failed to soak through, was gradually dampening my hair and the folder and the book I was clutching to my chest—for either out of forgetfulness or adolescent disdain, I hadn't bothered to protect my head with the hood of my red parka. I knew that I wasn't going to approach him, so I don't know what my plan was or what I was hoping to achieve by watching him standing at the bar, finishing his drink, summoning the waiter, talking to him and nervously changing position, then receiving a glass of wine identical to the first, along with a small plate, which he rejected with a brief, dismissive lift of the chin, before once again turning his gaze toward the door. I imagine that very little went through my mind in the few minutes my father was alone in the café and I watched from afar, incapable of making a decision and oblivious to the rain slowly impregnating me with the smell of moss and wet grass. Soon after the waiter had served him his second glass of wine, when he had picked it up with his right hand and taken one or two sips, my father removed his foot from the rail, took a step forward, smiled in the direction of the door, put down his glass, drew himself up to his full height, as if to welcome the person coming into the café, whom I tried in vain to identify when all I could see were the two closing leaves of the door, which was slightly set back in the colonnade. At the time, I couldn't know that the person he was preparing to greet was my mother, but that was what I thought in the seconds it took me to glance over at the window and again peer inside, trying unsuccessfully to find out who it was, because my father's back was blocking my view. There was nothing to make me suspect it could be her, but that was what I continued to think and fear during the brief but, to me, seemingly endless time they remained standing, one in front of the other, only a few feet from the bar, saying words I could not hear or see them speak. I had no reason to suspect that the person was my mother, but I did—however strange that may seem now, and even though she was indeed the person who finally emerged from behind my father when he, taking a step back, stretched out one arm in my direction, ushering her toward one of the tables nearest the window through which I was spying on them.

Because I had sensed it was her, I should not, therefore, have felt uneasy when I saw her, her face silent and indecipherable as she proceeded in the direction indicated by my father. The truth is, though, that the moments that followed were moments of confusion, during which my heart beat faster and I felt something akin to panic. My parents reached their chosen table, pulled out the chairs, placed their respective jacket and raincoat on one, then sat down, but I didn't see any of those actions, because I had hidden behind the tree next to me, afraid they might look out, and with just one solitary thought occupying my mind: who could I talk to about this, to whom could I confide my surprise and my doubts? It was an absurd thought, I know. There before me were my mother and my father, together for the first time in years, when she had given me no indication that they were going to see each other, but I didn't spend time wondering how that meeting had come about, if it was simply what it appeared to be or if it had been arranged very recently, a few hours ago, if my father had phoned while I was out and she had had to go and meet him without telling me first. No, rather than asking myself that question—to which I would have no response until my mother left the café and we saw each other later on at home and she either did or didn't tell me what she had done that afternoon—what was worrying me was an entirely unnecessary question, one that answered itself. I had no one to confide in apart from my mother, no one to whom I could describe what I'd seen and would continue to watch, because she alone fulfilled that role, and clearly on this occasion, she could not. After about a minute, I did ask myself about the nature of that meeting, but that was when I had finally dared to emerge from my hiding place behind the tree and look directly across at them. They were both seated, my father with the glass of wine he had brought with him from the bar and my mother with a tall glass of tomato juice before her and her raincoat neatly folded up on the chair that served as their cloakroom. They were sitting across from each other and sideways to me, so it was easy for me to scrutinize them with no danger of being seen, unless, during an awkward silence, one of them needed to rest his or her gaze on some neutral spot, although that seemed unlikely just then, because when I emerged from the tree's protective bulk and all the questions I had not initially asked myself began to rain down upon me, they were deep in conversation, oblivious to what was going on in the bar and, of course, to what was happening out in the street, where I was now sitting crouched on the curb between the two parked cars.

For a while, I didn't notice their very different attitudes, evident in their looks, their posture, their pauses, and their silences, the moments when one of them began speaking and the other intervened and interrupted, the imagined abruptness with which some answers were given, and the very definite way in which heads were shaken, far more emphatic than mere words, which I could not hear anyway. For a while, I looked at them both almost without seeing them, impervious to all gestures, paralyzed by the fact that they were together right there in front of me, and incapable of overcoming my surprise, of hearing or feeling anything other than silence as the sole answer to the questions I was asking myself and no one else heard—How was this possible? How had this happened? Had my father been the one who wanted to talk to my mother, or had she sought him out?

Little by little, and still without any of those questions having been answered, everything arising from the fact that they had met without my knowing, everything that was vaguely indicative of their inner lives and yet had remained unseen—because it had more to do with the way they were sitting and the looks they exchanged—began slowly, irreversibly to become clear to me. I began to observe them and realized then that, contrary to what I would have expected, it was my father who did most of the talking, who seemed most solicitous, who tried hard to hold my mother's evasive gaze, and who was, apparently, making the greater effort to keep the conversation going. He was the one who maintained and sustained it, while my mother, looking nervous and upset, resembled the engaged but dispassionate reader of the few final dramatic touches added by someone else to a play of which she was the principal author. She was the one who remained largely silent, who seemed to be thinking about something else, who seemed least affected. So, almost without realizing, I began to observe them and notice things that gave new meaning to what I was seeing and allowed me to guess at and understand what I had not known and was only now beginning to grasp. It soon became plain to me that this was not a casual meeting at which the topic of conversation had been left open. It appeared, rather, to be a meeting arranged in order to discuss a particular subject and clear up some unfinished business. Given the seriousness with which they acted out their respective roles, it would be easy to infer that this was a negotiation in which both parties were equally involved, however, my mother—and I noticed this with growing surprise—seemed in no mood to play the game. Despite the nonchalant air my father tried to impose on the conversation, despite the jokes he made, which, to judge by the frequent smiles that died on his lips, failed to find the hoped-for echo in my mother, he was the one with the more difficult role, the one who wanted something and was trying to shape and present his argument to gain the other person's agreement. My mother, on the other hand, seemed to be in the stronger position, that of the person who could say yea or nay, and who could also, if she chose, give in to his requests. She was sitting very upright in her chair, slightly back from the table, looking down at my father, whose free hand lay diagonally across the table top, prepared, at any moment, to invade her territory. He wasn't nervous or afraid, he didn't seem embarrassed or prepared to surrender. There was a stubbornness in his attitude, and a touch of shamelessness. Not that he was preparing to eat humble pie, but there was something shocking about such a prolonged struggle with such poor results. This was never clearer than when, after a silence in which they both sat looking hard at each other, he reached out his hand to intercept my mother's as she reached for her glass. She did not remove her hand, but the cutting coldness with which she left it there, motionless and inert beneath his gently stroking fingers, contained the very essence of a decision on which there was no going back, and which inevitably left me feeling deeply perplexed.

I was witness that afternoon to my parents' definitive separation, to my mother's refusal to remain caught up in the chain of deceits that was my father's life. I couldn't tell what he was saying to her, what he was hoping to achieve or gain with his wooing ways. I don't know what words he used or what she said in reply. Not that it matters; nor does it matter that my mother may have given in on certain points—which, according to her, she did. What I could see, what was being played out before me, was not just my mother's refusal to agree to my father's concrete proposal, but a much wider-reaching refusal aimed not only at my father, but principally at herself, a cessation and a renunciation, a radical break with the past that would be as damaging to her as to him. That afternoon when I skipped class provided me with the most potent confirmation and demonstration of everything I had noticed in the last two or three years since her return from Paris: her stubborn determination, her self-absorption, her decision to reduce her world down to just her and me, her solitude, which, unlike mine, was chosen, not imposed from without.

And yet, in the midst of that certainty, doubt remained, and I was suddenly filled with the conviction that there were things I still did not know about or fully understand—Paris, for example, and the two men who had one day come to our apartment.

It happened when my mother had gotten up to go to the restroom, leaving on the table her leather purse—brown to match the tights she was wearing, her turtleneck sweater, and her shoes—and my father, like a newly-released spring, immediately snatched it up and rummaged around inside for something I could not see but at which I could easily guess. However, it wasn't this unexpected action on his part that I found most revealing, even though it was the first time I'd seen him do such a thing, the first time I'd seen actual evidence of what, until then, I had known only through the consequences for my mother and myself of similar actions and through the partial and slightly rose-tinted accounts that my mother was just beginning to give me. For when I saw my father grab the bag, open it, and start rifling through its contents, I happened to look up to see where my mother had gone, and there she was, standing in the middle of the room. She had presumably failed to find the restroom and was coming back to ask for my father's help, and so she had seen him do something that she was not supposed to see, and instead of alerting him to this from afar and coming back to the table to confront him or making some sound that would cause him to glance up and perhaps concoct some excuse while there was still time, she allowed him to carry on and stood quite still while my impeccably dressed father, so focused on what he was doing, so completely unaware that he had been found out, continued his rummagings without raising his eyes from the bag he was holding.

It was only a matter of seconds. Then, as if she had seen nothing, she turned and set off again in search of the restroom, thus preventing my father from discovering her there and realizing that he had been discovered and having to come up with some even less credible excuse than the one he would have concocted had he been interrupted moments before, because he had taken her money now and was putting it in his jacket pocket. It was only a matter of seconds, but during those seconds—as my mother watched intently, with a look on her face that expressed neither surprise nor anger, nor even weariness, but infinite understanding, as she watched him rifling through her bag and taking the money, which I did not see but she must have seen, and as I watched, too, through the window, as if this were a scene from a silent movie, with no means of intervening, so near and yet so far, artificially detached from a situation of which I could only be a spectator because neither of the two actors, neither my mother nor my father, was thinking about me—in those few seconds, what took shape in my mind was the evidence of a bond that did not include me, a bond that was no stronger than the one binding my mother to me, but different, a bond that had undergone its own evolution, independent of me and my significance, that had been born before I was born and had survived over time without me, a bond ruled by different codes of conduct, different criteria, and subject to different demands. What would my mother not have done to maintain that bond? What sacrifices, apart from her blind perseverance, would she have been prepared to make?

On that rainy afternoon when I had left school early, or had perhaps delayed going home for rather longer than usual, my mother returned from the restroom, but her expression and attitude were no different, no harder or sterner, than when she had left the table. She slowly made her way through the tightly-packed tables, reached the one she had left only shortly before, and sat down on her chair without saying a word, holding my father's gaze, for he, pathetic in his miserable little victory and unaware of his own tragic futility, was looking at her and smiling. That rainy afternoon, on her way back from the restroom, my mother gave no hint that she, like me on the other side of the window, had witnessed what he had done. She remained seated, answering my father's questions ever more languidly, as if nothing were keeping her there now and she were simply waiting for the right moment to leave. She did not stay much longer, just long enough for a brief exchange of words, whose sole intention was that this encounter, which they both knew was drawing to a close, would at least end elegantly; he, I assume, was anxious not to burn his last bridges in a battle he knew was lost, and she, I suppose, did not want to open any unnecessary wounds. When my father had made one final joke and they had both fallen silent again, my mother got up, took her raincoat, and, without bending down to kiss him, said something along the lines of *All right, I have to go now* or *See you around*, then turned and walked toward the exit. When, seconds later, she came out onto the street, the café doors swinging shut behind her, I saw no tears in her eyes, no sadness or anguish, only a desire to escape and get away from there as quickly as possible.

# XXV

My mother's face now is completely inexpressive, inscrutable, it doesn't and never will say what she feels, whether there is sorrow, anguish, or a desire to escape in the way she leans back against her pillow or blinks when they bring her meals. In order to feel sorrow or anguish, in order for others to be able to deduce from our exterior a tiny part of what we would not dare put into words, we need the faculty of memory, which my mother does not have. My mother gets angry, shouts, and weeps, but she does so mechanically. There's no point asking her about the present—or about the past. She doesn't think, she doesn't recognize me, her face cannot show me anything I don't know already.

Once my mother had left the café, it wasn't certainty or a lack of certainty that made me stay in the same spot from which I'd observed her furtive encounter with my father. If certainty, or a desire for it, had been important to me, I would probably have followed her, anxious to question her and find answers, even though in doing so, I would have to confess that I had spied on them. Instead, I remained huddled on the sidewalk, watching her vanish around the same corner where, half an hour earlier, the blind man and his dog had vanished just moments before my father emerged from the uncertain past to reinstall himself in the present, when all I was thinking about was the bus that would take me home to my mother's company, to her unconditional love, to my own unpredictable outbursts of stifled anger, compensated, after repentance, by equally violent outbursts of devotion and affection. To say that I was confused would not fully describe the state I was in. It's true that I was bewildered and didn't know quite what to think or do, but the chaos of contradictory feelings into which I was plunged was not enough to make me distrust my fledgling intuition, which I was already beginning to trust in as if it were some long-known fact. However much I would have liked to deny it, however hesitant I was about seeking certainty, however much I lacked any conclusive proof, and however many excuses I came up with for that lack—purely in order to continue ignoring the evidence and thus avoid having to change the past by imposing on it images quite different from those I had imagined up until then—a new and doubtless irreversible intuition was nonetheless taking root in me. I remained quite still and unresponsive, but this was due more to a kind of artificial calm than to mere passivity or the inability to behave otherwise, rather like when someone slaps us across the face and we choose not to return the blow, knowing that such a response contains far more scorn, force, and violence than if we had allowed ourselves to be swept along by what our mind was urging us to do.

So I stayed where I was, and after a few minutes, when I saw my father exit onto the narrow, drenched street, I followed him unthinkingly. Getting up and heading off on his trail, tracing the steps of his route, which, as I would soon find out, was completely anarchic, must have seemed to me a way of prolonging the state I was in, a way of keeping a cool head without neglecting my overriding need to think, of remaining in touch with what had just been revealed to me but without having to give myself away or risk my own freedom—so necessary now that I had only myself to confide in—a way of moving in the shadows, of seeing and hearing without being seen or heard. I had watched him leave the table and pay with one of the bills taken from my mother's purse; I had watched him go over to the door, open it, turn up his jacket collar, and, still without opening the black umbrella he was carrying, set off at a brisk pace in the opposite direction as my mother. I didn't wait until he'd turned a corner or reached the next block. I crossed the street and, leaving a margin between us of about fifteen yards, allowed myself to be guided by him. This was a risky enterprise, but because he was walking along looking straight ahead, with the tense, absorbed appearance of someone deep in thought, I was able to remain hidden. I may be wrong, of course, and this could be an entirely erroneous impression, influenced by the memory of the scene I had just witnessed through the café window and by the very different attitudes I had noticed in him and my mother, by his pathetically triumphant smile when he returned the purse to its place on the table, having first removed the money, completely unaware that she had paused and turned on her way to the restroom and witnessed what he was doing—this was, after all, the first time I'd seen him alone in the street— but watching him as he walked ahead of me, it occurred to me that he had lost some of the aplomb and distinction I'd attributed to him in the past. He still had that same peculiar elegance and walked with his back very erect, but he had about him an air of defeat. Beneath the still-falling rain, he seemed faltering and fragile, vulnerable in comparison with the other passers-by.

For the first five minutes, I was troubled, because I didn't know quite where we were going. We were walking aimlessly. We were as likely to go down one street, then head off along another, only to return in a circular fashion to the first street, as we were to walk whole blocks in a completely straight line. Even the pace was not constant, and more frequently than I would have liked, my father would slow down to peer in through the windows of the bars we passed. On empty stretches devoid of cafés or shops or even people, he would almost break into a run. Not bothering to protect himself from the rain, which, though bothersome, was too fine to really drench us, he walked down the middle of the sidewalk, head up, never seeking the shelter of the buildings, but concentrating exclusively on what lay before him. After a certain point, the initially broad and open streets became narrower, with no nooks or doorways to hide in. This meant that I had to keep a greater distance between us, and there were times when I nearly lost him. Nevertheless, I noticed him look at his watch on a couple of occasions, and whenever he did this, he would suddenly put on a spurt, as if he only had a certain amount of time in which to complete this route and had to recoup lost seconds. Were it not for the chaotic, entirely illogical path he took, you might easily have thought he was looking for someone. I couldn't understand what mysterious law governed all those to-ings and fro-ings, all those swerves and loops, all that peering into the windows of shops and bars only to shoot off afterward as if he were late for an appointment. There was no sense in it, unless whoever he was looking for was subject to the same lack of logic. It didn't have to be a particular person. It could be people who weren't even expecting him but whom he had reason to believe would be in specific places at specific times. He might have been hoping to surprise them by making minor detours from an otherwise carefully planned route.

This situation, full of sudden retreats and alarms on my part, lasted about thirty minutes, until, turning a corner and going down some steep steps, we reached the Calle Princesa. After another glance at his watch and a few seconds during which he seemed unsure as to which direction to take and I feared he might hail a cab, we instead headed off toward the Plaza de España. His trajectory became slightly more linear, and his pace, like my fear of being discovered, diminished. I wasn't thinking about anything, I simply followed behind, my hands in the pockets of my red parka and my folder firmly clasped beneath one arm. We reached the Plaza de España, walked across it on the park side, went up the Gran Vía, and reached Callao with no further detours or abrupt changes, stopping only at the traffic lights. At this point, my father followed the traffic circle toward the right and took the Calle Preciados at a slightly slower pace. Halfway down, he stopped next to the three-wheeled vehicle of a crippled man selling lottery tickets and cigarettes. I didn't manage to see what he bought, but when he received his change, instead of putting it in his pocket and continuing on his way, he stood to one side and stayed where he was. I was at the top of the street, ready to duck around the corner as soon as he gave the slightest indication that he was about to walk back up, and was reassured to see that he was pondering whether to enter a bar on his left. He again looked at his watch and only then decided to go in. I realized that this was not a place he often frequented, because he stopped by the door and did not go in until he'd scrutinized the interior, like someone gauging the quality of an establishment merely from its appearance. I looked around me, but couldn't see a single hiding place from which I could, without risk of being discovered, observe what he was doing inside. Since I couldn't follow him, I had to content myself with glancing in as I passed, but all I could see was him standing with his back to me, staring at the flickering images on a TV sitting on a shelf affixed high up on one wall by two large, metal brackets. Only just managing to resist the temptation to stop and wait outside the bar, I continued on down the street and, when I reached the next corner, took refuge behind a roll-off container overflowing with rubble and junk metal. I waited ten or fifteen minutes, ten or fifteen minutes during which the rain grew heavier and I had to stand with my back pressed to the wall so that the water would not transform my hair into something resembling a sodden, dripping piece of cloth. After that very brief, or very long, period of time, which I allowed to pass with my mind almost a blank, my father reemerged from the bar, this time opening his black umbrella while still standing in the doorway, before setting off toward the very place where I was waiting. I saw him pass by the container, behind which I had hurriedly concealed myself, and continue on toward the Puerta del Sol. It was beginning to grow dark, and when I felt it was safe, I rushed after him, fearful that I might lose him if the distance between us grew too great. We rapidly covered the last stretch of street, and, just before it ended, I stopped to see which part of the square he would head for. I had given up trying to make any sense of his itinerary, my clothes were starting to grow damp, and I had a vague presentiment that I was about to cross a definitive line. I knew that I was now nearly an hour late getting home and knew, too, that my mother would be worrying, and yet still I could not stop, and this obsession of mine was all the stranger given that I was clearly not expecting to gain anything from this pursuit of my father. Approaching my father in search of an answer to my questions was quite unthinkable, and trying, on the other hand, to find out through him what had happened to make my mother lose all patience was utterly crazy. My determination to carry on made no sense. It could have been simple curiosity, but the truth is that seeing my father wandering the streets like a vagabond left me completely cold and revealed nothing to me that I did not already know. I felt no sorrow, no tenderness, nor even an absence of both those feelings. It was something more complex, something I can only identify now that the years have passed and nothing matters any more. It was my mother I was looking for, it was my mother I was pursuing through the city, it was her image I was trying to capture through my father, it was those months I had never previously felt or imagined as they really were and that now appeared clearly before me, months I now wanted to make my own, it was my need for some reference point that would help me judge precisely what that time had meant to her, what kind of life she had led, what she had done and possibly suffered, what she'd had to endure, and the nature of the thing or person for which she had swapped me or momentarily given me up. Seeing my father walking ahead of me, observing his absurd wanderings through the city, what I was really seeing was my mother, or, rather, my mother in the company of my father, as I walked the unknown streets of Paris, all the while thinking I was walking the streets of Madrid.

Perhaps because it was my mother and not my father I was following on that rain-drenched evening that was fast becoming night—perhaps that's why I ended up forgetting about time and never for a moment considered giving up or abandoning my pursuit, until darkness overtook the streets and my father's trail through the steadily depopulating city became ever more difficult to fathom, with ever-longer stops in the bars he went into, ever-longer periods of time that I had to spend outside in the elements, with his search for something he could not find but that kept drawing him on becoming ever more complex and urgent, my feelings for him ever more detached and distant, the gulf of understanding separating me from my mother ever wider, and my unconfessed desire for all my theories about Paris to be true ever more pressing.

But before that happened and before I finally went home, there was a moment when I grew confused, and it was no longer the distorted image of my parents but my own image that I found myself escorting through the deserted streets. I think this occurred at a moment when the rain had grown still heavier, or perhaps when I had become more aware of it, and we were walking down from the Plaza de Antón Martín toward the more recondite and, for me, unfamiliar Plaza de Lavapiés. I had, I think, begun to shiver by then, and due to the steep slope or to having had one too many drinks during his repeated stops en route, my father was stumbling along many yards ahead of me. It must have been a moment when he had tripped or lurched violently and, without my noticing, come to a full stop, intending to rest or catch his breath, or simply wondering where to go next. I was walking along, head down and hood up in a vain attempt to protect my already dripping hair, scored on either side by two rivulets of rain water, and if I hadn't chanced to look up when I was five or ten yards away from him and seen him standing in the middle of the street, I would probably have run straight into him, so distracted was I, so immersed in thoughts that I can now no longer rescue from oblivion. Even today, when so much time has passed, I still start at the sudden fear that filled me then, thinking that perhaps he had discovered my presence and was waiting patiently for me to reach his side. Even though I realized at once that I was mistaken and that my father was simply lingering there, looking straight ahead, his umbrella open, with the same hieratic calm the wives of miners or sailors must feel after a catastrophe, standing by the mine shaft or on the pier, waiting for confirmation of what they already know. As if he, too, were deep in thought or bent beneath the weight of some crushing fear, at no point did he turn his head. I came to an abrupt halt, and without retreating or seeking shelter in a doorway or behind a car, I stayed where my steps had stopped, incapable of moving or feeling, or, perhaps, bold and defiant. The distance between us was minimal, and only the insistent drumming of the water on the rough asphalt and on the many uneven paving stones kept us from hearing each other's breathing. The street curved downhill ahead of us, and there was no light on the horizon announcing the imminent promise of a bar. We were quite alone—my father unaware that I was so close, and me, motionless, watching for the slightest movement of his back. Then, suddenly, without knowing why, with no possible explanation, I felt an enormous desire for him to turn his head and see me, to find me there, for everything to end once and for all. For a few seconds, I saw myself in my father, and I needed for that figure, which was at once him and me, to become one with the figure that was only me, for him to come and meet me or for me to go and meet him. For a few seconds, while my father stood stock-still in the street, what I represented on the one hand and what he represented on the other became mixed up in my head. For a few seconds, there was no distinction between us. For a few seconds, we stopped being just me, or me and him, and became the two things together, indissolubly united, with nothing in between. This hallucination, the product of tiredness or the cold or both things at once, lasted only a few moments, but during those moments, before my father set off again, we not only formed part of one body but, thanks to that, I was able to imagine a life in which we had never been separated, and I found myself feeling that old, familiar solitude, the onliness of being an only son. Odd though it may seem, that onliness was still present when I put myself solely in my father's shoes. Being my father, thinking I was him, I experienced exactly the same enveloping emptiness, the same discontent, the same doubts, and the same rebelliousness and revolt that I experienced being myself. It wasn't that I understood my father better in those moments or felt an unexpected sense of pity for him. I didn't absolve him, that would have been impossible—one cannot absolve oneself. It was more that in removing myself from me and projecting myself onto him, the weight I was carrying and considered to be my own, most peculiar burden was still present inside me, inside the person I was then, and so, for a few seconds, it was also my father's. You might say that, during that time, I identified totally with him and we were one and the same. The hallucination began to fade as soon as he set off again, and, allowing him to get some distance ahead of me, I once more followed after him. My father very quickly recovered his lost impetus, and again I was alone with my intuition, alone following my father, alone struggling with thoughts of my mother, alone walking the streets of Paris, all the while thinking I was walking the streets of Madrid. Even so, something of that illusion must have remained, because during the minutes that followed, what did persist was a feeling that immediately replaced it and that I cannot help thinking was a consequence of it, because it happened automatically, almost as a continuation of that dying illusion. Once more walking behind my father, once more letting myself be guided by him—his route dictated, it seemed to me, by an obscure plan that he himself had drawn up—by steps that again seemed to me faltering and fragile beneath the rain that continued to fall and vulnerable to the darkness that surrounded us despite the occasional streetlamp, very slowly, I say, sheltered by the night and the distant figure of my father, I began to think about myself and was filled by a vague fear about my own future. The memory suddenly surfaced of that distant winter morning when my mother and I went to pick him up from the prison in Burgos, and some of the words that she had said to me so that I would not be alarmed and would better understand what she was about to tell me echoed obliquely in my mind, just as I remembered and set them down here some pages earlier: "The fact that I haven't fallen doesn't mean that I won't one day. No one is immune, not even me and not even you, although I hope, of course, that you never find yourself in such dire need and never feel you have no other way out." I felt afraid and helpless, too, and while my strength was beginning to fade and my father was getting further ahead of me, I couldn't help but wonder, *Will I be immune? What will become of me when my mother is no longer here? Will there be someone to help me when I need it? Or will there be children and wives who will turn their backs on me, whose patience will run out?*

I didn't follow my father for very much longer through the rain-filled streets. I remember that we walked for a few more minutes, past bars that had already closed, that we arrived eventually at one with iron grilles on the windows that was strangely crowded at that late hour, and that after a long wait during which I had to content myself with waiting outside, without peering in through the closed windows or through the door—a heavy, wooden affair guarded by a bouncer—I decided to give up.

When I returned home some time later on that evening that was now black night, my throat burning and the book and the folder I'd been carrying under my arm as soaked as I was, my mother opened the door before I had even put the key in the lock, as if she had been watching from the balcony for me to arrive. She was still dressed, and very agitated, and the look on her face, while wanting to appear stern and challenging, gave way nevertheless to her overwhelming sense of relief.

"What on earth have you been up to? Where have you been?" she asked, without standing aside or bending down to kiss me, her voice breaking slightly.

". . ."

And almost seamlessly, trying to recover her censorious tone, when she finally stepped aside and allowed me to cross the threshold despite my dumb, inexpressive face, "Don't you ever do that to me again. I've been waiting for you all evening. I was very worried."

". . ."

And then, still without waiting for any response, touching my dripping hair, "Look at you, you're absolutely soaked. You'll catch pneumonia. Go and get changed this minute."

". . ."

And immediately afterward, when she saw me heading for my room, either obediently or sulkily, "You don't have an ounce of sense in you, do you? I have to watch you all the time. I don't know what will become of you if you carry on like this."

On that evening that was now black night, I said nothing, either not answering at all or else answering my mother's questions with vague excuses while I obeyed her every order and she ran to the bathroom to fill the tub and returned to dry my hair and body, rubbing me down with towels, and then, placing her hands on my shoulders, propelling me out of my bedroom, down the hallway, and into the scalding water. On that evening that was now black night, while I was taking a bath and my mother was watching me with disapproving eyes, while I got out of the tub and she wrapped me in fresh towels and again rubbed me vigorously dry and led me back to my room and held out a pair of clean pajamas, while she went to prepare dinner for me and talked to me from the kitchen and brought food on a tray to my bedside, while she sat down to wait and put an aspirin in my mouth and, holding my chin, made me swallow it down with the glass of water she placed between my dry lips, while she was turning on a heater and turning out the light and telling me that we would talk tomorrow and taking away the tray and closing the door so as to keep the heat in, on that evening that was now black night, I said nothing to her about where I'd been and why I was late, and she told me nothing, either—nothing about my father or about her meeting with him, the meeting I had witnessed. I heard her moving around the house, making phone calls, and, when she thought I was asleep, opening my bedroom door to leave it slightly ajar.

# XXVI

I remember the days that followed in the confused and disorderly way in which we always remember past events that time has done nothing to clarify. How else can I judge them except under the influence of the profound feeling of disquiet that filled me and kept me hovering between suspicion and trust, between sudden anger and tormented remorse, between an urgent, searing need to know and a proud refusal to ask the one person who had the answers to my questions, between rage at my own ensuing sense of impotence and complete sympathy for my mother's situation, regardless of what she might have done, and regardless of whether she had or had not been honest when she told me about it later on? Despite her admonishing words to me on the night I arrived home drenched to the skin, which had led me to believe that we would talk about it all the next day, she made not the slightest reference to her furtive encounter with my father, either that day or on any other. She said nothing about the matter, and as the silence grew and grew and my need to know the truth about her time in Paris also grew, my conviction that what I *thought* had happened really *had* happened and was not just a figment of my imagination became still stronger and plunged me into a state of nervous delirium. Her clandestine meeting with my father and the months we had spent apart became linked in my mind, and not only did I begin to believe that an explanation of the latter would inevitably bring with it an explanation of the former but in some way, I stopped distinguishing between them. The two events, the known and the imagined, became fused into one, and I felt unable to extricate myself from the anxiety and the contradictory impulses triggered by my mother's inexplicable silence. My mother did not talk about her meeting with my father, and I needed to know about the past, to confirm the suspicions that her silence only fostered. My mother did not talk about her meeting with my father, and just as I knew that I lacked the necessary coolness to ask her directly about her time in Paris, her failure to talk about that meeting made me distrust her sincerity, and so I confined myself to dropping the odd hint about what had happened. My mother did not talk about her meeting with my father, and although I felt sure that I would bring up the subject myself if her silence continued, I also felt quite incapable of doing so. I sensed that she would eventually offer me some explanation, but the longer her silence lasted, the stronger my belief that when the explanation finally came, it would only be a partial one. Not knowing what form that explanation would take, I could not know what my reaction would be if my hunch about Paris was right. On the one hand, although I did not confess as much to myself, I hoped I was right, that this final concession by my mother was what I imagined it to be, a concession I believed would change my view of her and of our relationship. On the other hand, though, I had to admit that it was precisely the feeling that I might be offended by some possible deception that egged me on. Consequently, while one moment I found my suspicions ridiculous and told myself that what mattered was the present, the next, I would be wallowing in the state of phony orphanhood to which I had been relegated by my mother's supposed treachery. One moment, I allowed myself to sink into melancholy and consider my mother a monster of hypocrisy, and the next, I felt moved by her situation and driven to absolve her by the mere thought of the vulnerable, fragile state to which she would be reduced if, as I presumed she might, she gave in to my father's designs. One moment, I considered myself utterly alone, with even fewer reference points as to how I should behave, and the next, I was filled by the liberating thought of the one thing that might redeem our wearisome solitude—namely, my mother's unconditional devotion.

In that overwhelming state of confusion, I did a lot of silly things, false steps for the most part, which, while I regret them, I can also understand and even forgive, even though time has passed and my mother and I are no longer the people we were then. The various energies bristling inside me, churning around in my mind, leapt out in disorderly fashion, prompting me to make strange remarks—ingenuous, frivolous, abrupt, and unexpected—which far from achieving their hidden aim, only contributed to increasing the tension between my mother and myself and widening the gulf between us. The day after the evening when I had followed my father through the deserted streets, I waited patiently to receive my mother's postponed reprimand for coming home so late, thinking that even though she had made no such promise, it would bring with it an explanation of their furtive meeting, but in the days that followed, when the reprimand still did not come and my hopes of an explanation gradually faded, alarm began to spread through my being, and my emotions quite simply exploded.

Even though I had few uncertainties about what the future held for me, even though I had witnessed through the café window my parents' definitive separation, my questions about what had really happened in the past burned inside me and drove me to rebel against a future that seemed about to be built on the shifting sands of pretense and lies. I doubted everything. I doubted my mother and the extent of her possible deceit. I doubted her reasons for going to Paris. I doubted what she had done there and even the months that preceded the moment when, on our arrival in La Coruña, she told me about her decision to leave, to put some physical distance, or so I understood it, between herself and the knowledge that her plans for a normal married life had once again been frustrated by a reality that refused to conform to her desires. I even wondered whether her deception had consisted purely of meeting up with my father in Paris after having found out he was there, or whether it went further back than that, to the time when he was still living with us and I had not yet discovered the package containing the fake ID and the business cards carefully hidden away beneath the table in what we called his office, in other words, whether my father's final departure had really been a surprise to my mother or whether, on the contrary, it had been the first step in a plan previously agreed upon between them, one that would imply a sudden refusal on my mother's part to continue battling for some hoped-for change in him and her surrender—whether or not it was total, I don't know, but it was certainly desperate—her blind surrender to whatever kind of irregular life he chose to impose on her. At the time, the image of my defeated mother, unable to bear my father's departure and temporarily giving me up in order to rejoin him in Paris, seemed to me as insane and unthinkable as the much colder and less innocent, albeit equally defeated image of her planning the whole adventure beforehand.

Needless to say, these thoughts emerged fueled by the suspicion and the profound confusion gripping me at the time, and because of that, not all of them were fair or in keeping with my mother's personality. Now, when so much time has passed, I can imagine her ceding defeat and, in despair at my father's absence, running off to find him wherever he was, intending to try yet again to bring him back to us. I can imagine her, too, going to rejoin him without any intention of making him come back, knowing that she could never get my father to submit to the kind of life she wanted but nevertheless unable to resist the impulse of her passion. While both possibilities, if true, would somewhat contradict the air of calm prudence she had always tried to project, they do not seem to me completely inconceivable. They would reflect only the part of herself she tried to hide—her fragility and vulnerability. What I find less easy to accept is that she could have been privy to his flight and to any preceding heist or swindle, if there was one. Something like that would be inconsistent with and unrealistic in view of her naturally prudent nature, her attempts to set my father on a path that would lead him away from the dangers that might easily land him back in prison, and equally inconsistent and unrealistic with respect to my father, with his love of secrecy and his determination not to admit his true nature to anyone. After all, even if my mother had known about his plans in advance and, instead of trying to dissuade him, had agreed to them, I doubt he would have admitted to having such plans, much less have allowed her to become part of them. He would have denied them regardless of the evidence stacked against him; he would have said it was a mistake and there was nothing to fear. It would have been quite a different matter, however, if after his abrupt departure, my mother had found out where he was and decided to go in search of him. Her acceptance, in that case, would have been implicit, and he would no longer have had to struggle to maintain an idea of himself that was at odds with reality.

But I only come up with these arguments now that passing time has largely extinguished the doubts I had then, and I certainly wouldn't claim that they're incontestable. Whatever the truth, whether I'm right or wrong, one thing is certain: I imagined and thought all kinds of things during those days when my mother continued to say nothing about her furtive meeting with my father and I was caught between conflicting emotions and did and said things that she, not knowing the reason behind my erratic behavior, could not possibly understand but accepted with her usual resignation. I was nervous and irascible. I didn't know what to do. My mother said nothing about her meeting with my father, and I would explode on the slightest pretext in an attempt to worry her, to trigger a crisis that would force her to explain herself. I spied on her. I went through her pockets. I listened in on her phone conversations and read her letters, hoping to find something that would either sanction or put an end to my fears. I was irritable and touchy. I was deliberately unfair and unpleasant, and while I regretted this, I lacked the necessary will to abandon my corrosive ways. And all the time this was going on and my anxiety was growing, she remained completely oblivious. As I discovered later on, other things were going on inside her head that either prevented her from noticing my nonsensical behavior or else forced her to postpone taking appropriate action.

I did a lot of silly things, but I don't consider all of them to have been false steps, nor do all of them prick my conscience, although it's true that none of them makes any sense except in the light of the anxieties eating away at me. I had no one to whom I could confess my thoughts, no one on whom I could offload my concerns, and I felt imprisoned by a renewed feeling of loneliness, not a loneliness filtered through or shared with my mother's loneliness, but a loneliness of the kind I had experienced on that far-off night when I decided, most uncharacteristically, not to tell her about finding the business cards and the false ID hidden under my father's table, a sense of being utterly alone in the world—similar to the feeling of desolation I'd sensed in my father on the night I followed him through the deserted streets of Madrid—a loneliness that prevented me from making a decision either to accept my mother's silence or, on the contrary, to bring it to an end by speaking out and thus forcing her to speak. When my constant vigilance failed to produce the desired effect, I sought refuge in the past and spent hours scouring my memory for forgotten events or events that were simply ambiguous or strange and which I hadn't known how to interpret when they happened. I thought about the days before and after my father's departure, I thought about our own early departure for La Coruña, I thought about my mother's departure for Paris, I thought about the months I had spent living with my aunt and uncle, and I thought, above all, about my mother's unexpected return. In some way, I was aware that the true origin of my suspicions lay in that sequence of events, in what I had seen and heard and felt while they were happening, in the premeditated way in which my mother delayed telling me of her sudden decision to leave Madrid, in the terse intensity of her letters and phone calls, in her frequent changes of hotel during her time abroad, and the cool reception given her by my uncle. But just as those suspicions had remained dormant and only taken shape as I watched my parents through the café window, none of those past events was enough, when recalled, to transform suspicion into certainty. If they were of any use at all, it was as a reference point, and in that respect, only the frosty way in which my aunt's husband had greeted my mother on her painful return to La Coruña gave me some room for maneuver. I was beginning to realize that my uncle did not like my father, and if, as I believed, my uncle's attitude and my mother's cowed behavior when she returned were due to her having been in Paris with my father, then a phone call to Delfina to tell her that my father was back and that my mother had even agreed to see him again could easily clear up my doubts and encourage her to speak openly to me.

When I think about it now, it seems like a completely crazy idea, and I find it hard to believe that I really thought my aunt would be so disloyal as to tell me about something that my mother had deliberately kept hidden from me. Surely I must have realized that she would probably say nothing—as was, in fact, the case—and, at the earliest opportunity, tell my mother that I had called her. After all, I only ever spoke to her when my mother was there, and I certainly never phoned her on my own account, and although my initial intention was to creep up on the subject and conceal my real reason for phoning by engaging her in a meandering and apparently banal conversation in which I would be content to interpret silences and telltale pauses rather than unearth any absolute certainties, I should have known that Delfina would only have to hear my voice to suspect that something was amiss. However, I would not go so far as to say that, simply because such a danger hung over my decision like a potential threat, phoning my aunt was an oblique way of alerting my mother to my feelings and provoking the longed-for explanation. That might have been my unconscious intention, or, more likely, I was poised between that wish and its opposite extreme—a total disregard, at once proud and troubled, for the consequences of such a gesture.

Anyway, I made the call, and although it's true that, as I feared, my aunt signally failed to clear up the doubt that had me in its grip, talking to her proved decisive in another sense: it precipitated events and set my mother on the path toward telling me what she had perhaps thought she would never have to tell me. I chose a moment when my mother had gone out to the store, on the Saturday afternoon following the meeting in the café where my unease had first begun. Fortunately, Delfina was at home and was the one who answered the phone. For a few minutes, I could hardly get a word in. When she heard my name, she embarked on a whole litany of trivial questions about my life and school, and not until she had exhausted every topic and given me all the advice she deemed relevant did she fall silent, waiting for me to tell her the reason for my call or put my mother on the phone. Feeling suddenly unable to take the step I had planned, I responded to her silence with more silence, and after a few embarrassing seconds, she went ahead and asked about my mother. I said that she wasn't at home, and my aunt asked in an alarmed voice, "Why? Has something happened?" I reassured her, telling her that my mother had just gone out to the store and would be back soon, and then, after a further pause, during which I rather regretted having phoned, I blurted out the news of my mother's meeting with my father in a near-incomprehensible babble, as if by piling word upon word there was a chance she might not understand or notice that this was the real reason for my call. My exact words, spoken with my heart racing, were: "I think my father is in Madrid and that Mom has seen him." Such was my uncertainty as to the effect my words might have on Delfina that what happened next inevitably took me completely by surprise. My aunt did not wait for this information to sink in before responding. She reacted at once, and instead of putting me off with some vague answer or saying what did it matter if my parents had seen each other, she did nothing to disguise her shock.

"What? What do you mean?" she asked with unusual urgency, with a directness and lack of caution that took me aback. I repeated what I'd said, and when I had, she launched three questions at me, in a tone of voice that sounded even more hysterical and demanding: "When? How do you know? Did you see him, too?"

"Yes," I said, still perplexed by her spontaneous, unrestrained response, "yes, I saw them both." And then, after a moment's hesitation, "That's how I know they met. But they don't know that I know. It was pure chance. I saw them when I was coming back home after school."

"Yes, but when?" she asked again.

"A few days ago," I said, "in the afternoon, it was a Monday or a Tuesday." I could have said more, I could have added that my mother had not mentioned the meeting since then, but I decided not to compromise myself and left my aunt to take the initiative.

As if she had read my mind, my aunt did not stay quiet for long. She took a deep breath, and as she exhaled, she asked me with renewed energy, "Did she tell you why she saw him? Have you spoken about it?" I replied in the negative to both questions, and she again fell silent. After a moment, she exclaimed, "This is horrible. She must be insane. I can't believe it. What on earth is she doing meeting up with him again?" And then, almost without pausing, "That imbecile is going to end up making a fool of her again. I don't know what your mother can be thinking. I really don't understand her. As if she hadn't had enough. As if—" My aunt did not finish her sentence. She left it incomplete, and I realized that, after her initial outburst, she had suddenly remembered who she was speaking to. I heard her breathe into the mouthpiece, and for a few seconds, she didn't say another word. I sensed that this was the end of the conversation and that all I could do now was to wait for what would happen when my mother found out. I was about to come up with some excuse in order to say goodbye, when I heard her shamefacedly ask my forgiveness. Her tone was quite different and reminded me of that other plea for forgiveness two or three years before, on the eve of my mother's return from La Coruña, on the afternoon when she had taken me to a café in order to lecture me about the future and I had burst into tears. On the other hand, unlike that other occasion, she did not withdraw her words. She apologized, and what she said was, "Look, don't you worry. It's probably nothing. They probably met by chance and she didn't think it necessary to tell you." And then, as if she found the words hard to say, "Just in case, though, don't say anything. Don't tell her that you've spoken to me. Wait until I've found out more."

That was the last thing my aunt said to me. I will never know if that was, indeed, the last thing she was intending to say to me or if she would have said more. After her advice to say nothing, which, I confess, troubled me as much as would a similar piece of advice directed at my mother and in which I, not she, was the person being kept out of the loop, she lowered her voice to an almost inaudible whisper and said that her husband, my uncle, had just come in and that she could say nothing more. She hung up without so much as a goodbye, and I was left holding the phone in my hand until I heard our own front door closing and my mother's voice calling from the hall, asking me to help her carry in the groceries. I cannot, therefore, know if that was or wasn't the last thing my aunt was going to say to me, just as I cannot know what would have happened if I had decided not to phone her that afternoon, if my mother would ever have told me about Paris or if I would still be assailed by the same doubts, if I would have needed to put those doubts down in writing as I am doing now, or if I would have allowed it all simply to slide into oblivion. Of one thing I'm sure: it was thanks to that phone call that other, unimagined secrets finally surfaced and allowed me to understand both how very alone my mother was and the opposition she must have met with in order to do what I feared she had done but still don't know if she did.

# XXVII

I believed I had witnessed the definitive separation of my parents on that day when I spied on them through the café window, and yet I said nothing about that to my aunt during our phone conversation. I deliberately kept silent, not out of forgetfulness, but for the simple reason that my doubts were focused not on the future but on the past, and I would have achieved nothing by assuaging my aunt's fears at the news of my father's reappearance. Yes, I deliberately kept silent, although not out of forgetfulness, just as my mother had kept silent about her meeting with my father and just as my aunt would rather her husband didn't know about my phone call to her, or, as now seems likely, just as she, over the years, had abstained from telling me things about my mother's life of which I knew nothing. None of the three of us—my mother, my aunt, or me—was innocent, and seeing the past in this light lends my memories a slightly risible edge that rather undermines their seriousness but does not particularly bother me, for it's far from reflecting my state of mind at the time. It's one thing being able to distinguish the different interwoven elements of a past event in retrospect, but the mark left on our memory by that event is quite another matter. My mother concealed things from me and my aunt, I concealed things from them both, and my aunt concealed things from me and her husband;

but if I was aware then of that trinity of parallel concealments, the truth is that it did not give me food for thought, nor did it make my need to know any less urgent. I only had eyes for what affected me directly. All that mattered to me was finding out if my mother had deceived me.

In that situation, phoning my aunt was a bold idea that left a bittersweet aftertaste; while on the one hand it served to confirm both her scant regard for my father and her equally scant, not to say non-existent confidence in my mother's strength of will were she to be confronted by him unexpectedly, on the other, it neither confirmed nor settled the matter that had driven me to phone her, and it also irreversibly blocked any room for maneuver on my part. Delfina had asked me to say nothing to my mother, but I knew that the information I'd given her would inevitably have consequences and that my mother would, in the end, find out about my intervention. Before taking that step, I had abandoned myself to chance, not caring what consequences it might have for me, but having witnessed Delfina's displeasure when she learned of my father's reappearance, I could not ignore the fact that, whatever she had said in the heat of the moment, it would be very difficult for her to get the truth out of my mother without revealing the role I had played. It never occurred to me that she would actually come to Madrid, but from the moment I hung up, I knew that, sooner or later, my mother would find out, and that it was only a question of days, possibly hours, before she gave me an explanation, before she discovered, one way or another, that I had betrayed her.

This realization was like a short, sharp shock, which far from stopping me in my tracks, only exacerbated my need to know. I guessed that my mother would not stay silent, that she would not respond with indifference to my unexpected knowledge of something she would have preferred to keep secret. She would be sure to try and restore trust between us as quickly as possible, to quiet the distress that her silence had caused me. I was sure that she would speak and that when she did, she would not make do with a belated explanation of what I already knew or with justifying in some way her unusual decision not to tell me about her meeting with my father. She would probably want to talk, and talk at length, to clarify my doubts, to reestablish the pact we had sealed on that far-off morning on our way to Burgos, a pact of honesty and openness. If I had felt sure that, during our conversation, she would actually touch on the topic that most concerned me, I would have happily sat and waited for it to happen. The problem was that her explanation would almost certainly deal only with that clandestine meeting with my father and would not provide a parallel explanation for what really interested me: the time she had spent in Paris. If I wanted to learn anything about that, I would have to force it out of her, but to do so, if I didn't simply want to make a stab in the dark, I needed something more solid than the feeble, disconnected intuitions on which my suspicions were built. Yes, I needed something more than that, and I needed it quickly, because if, when the time came, I had no alternative version to offer about the months we were apart, if I could not confront my mother with some pertinent comment that would catch her off-guard and compel her to come up with a more radical and more profound confession than the one she had been forced into, then later, after that conversation, it would be impossible for me to find another such opportunity to get her to talk. Confessions are not given in stages, because that would do away with the whole idea of wiping the slate clean, which, after all, is what confession is all about. Making a second confession would be tantamount to admitting that we hadn't been quite as open and honest the first time as we might have been, and to admit *that* is tantamount to saying that this second time might not be definitive, either. That's why, just as no one risks confessing twice, no one who has been less than frank at some earlier date would be so imprudent as to leave any loose ends, and my meticulous mother would be no exception. After speaking to me, she would almost certainly refuse to consider any new enquiry and would erase or try to nullify the evidence of any other concealments or infidelities she had left behind her.

If I wanted to get any real results, I would, therefore, have to act before my mother found out, I would have to be prepared for the moment when, once my aunt's foreseeable intervention had taken effect, my mother would finally have to decide to face up to making reparation for her faults. Right from the start, I saw clearly, albeit in a disorderly, impulsive, and rather less considered manner than you might think from what I've said, that I would have to anticipate my mother; of that, during the torments that gripped me following my reckless phone call to my aunt, I had no doubt. What I was less clear about—either then or in the two days that passed before my aunt's sudden arrival in Madrid and the no less surprising and unexpected outcome that emerged from it— was how to do it, how to resolve my burning desire to find out or what to include in that "something more" I needed to know. Of course, I wanted to know if there had been any kind of deceit involved in my mother's trip to Paris, but the answer to that question was so closely bound up with other enigmas, fears, and griefs—possibly unconscious and unacknowledged but nonetheless pressing and troubling ones—that it would be ingenuous to argue that it was the sole or most important question. Too many things inside me depended on the answer to that question for me not to wonder if it was in fact an excuse that concealed other controversies. Too many things were too closely bound up with each other for me to expect that one answer could resolve them all. There was my mother and everything related to her: What did she want? What had she done? Was she really the cool, persistent person who, almost to the point of exaggeration, carefully weighed up any matter directly affecting me, or was she the gullible fool capable of stumbling again and again over the same obstacles and errors or endangering herself and me by pursuing some unachievable dream? Then there was me and the various ways of interpreting my situation according to the answers given to each of the preceding questions: Should I be grateful or reproachful? Could I free myself from the great weight I felt, or should I, on the contrary, remain tied to my mother, eternally indebted to her unconditional love and devotion? There was my father, too, and his incorrigible egotism, which might come to be seen in a new light, depending on how my mother had behaved: Was he the only guilty person, or was he only partly to blame? Had he himself been deceived or betrayed in some way? But alongside these unknowns, which I converted into stark dichotomies when there was really no reason why they should rule each other out, there were other dilemmas that I found equally worrying and that also referred to a past I knew nothing of, but that would probably have continued to bother me even had there been no deceit, either real or suspected: What to make, for example, of my mother and the childhood she never mentioned? What to think of myself or my father, of the fragility I had sensed in him as I trailed after him through the Madrid streets? Where did my parents end, and where did I begin? Should my view of them depend on their view of me? Was I free to decide on things that had to do with me alone, or was I conditioned by things I knew nothing about? Did I really have the right to use their behavior as the yardstick by which to judge them?

I did not, of course, think any of this so literally; these are speculations that arise from recalling my confused state at the time, suppositions that I can't even be sure existed but that I must, nevertheless, set down and accept as real in the light of a feeling that appeared unexpectedly in the days following that conversation with my aunt, while I was still scrambling vainly around for a way to come up with new evidence that would help prepare me for the moment when my mother did finally decide to talk to me. It was, I suppose, a feeling of irrepressible filial solidarity after my aunt's harsh words about my father, as well as a delayed bonding reflex that, on the rainy evening I'd spent following him, I had felt spring up between us under the cover of the darkness and the overwhelming weariness clouding my mind. Whatever it was, the fact is that, almost unwittingly, I found myself thinking about my father, and I felt an irresistible need to justify and even absolve him, despite all the rancorous feelings that had been quietly accumulating in the two or three years that had passed since his sudden disappearance. I don't mean that I began to judge him differently or that I suddenly began to endow him with new qualities. After his sudden departure from our lives, I had placed him outside the field of my preoccupations, and that is how it has continued to this day. I mean only that in the face of Delfina's scornful comments, I allowed myself to be swept away by anger and was, for the first time, capable of thinking about him independently from what he meant for my mother or for me, and I was filled by a kind of proud acceptance of what he was. In the face of all the conventionalisms and external considerations urging me to condemn his behavior, to understand it as an illness or an oddity that threatened the normal order of things, I was seized with unusual force by the contrary impulse, namely, an involuntary admiration and respect that, in the light of my own rebellion, I felt he deserved because he had broken certain social rules and regulations which, ever since my prolonged stay in La Coruña, I tended to associate with my Aunt Delfina and her husband, with their rigid way of life, their cold way of relating to each other and the world around them.

That same unthinking estimation of him, which sprang unbidden from my deepest memories, that same, sudden fellow feeling for what my father represented, and onto which I spontaneously projected my own latent dissatisfaction and resentment at the hostility shown him by my aunt and uncle, extended to my mother, as well, and to the inexplicable tenacity with which she had tried for years, despite everything, to bind her fate to his; while it's true that I knew of the urgent, desperate hopes for change she had nurtured all that time, I knew, too, ever since our conversation on the way to Burgos, that those hopes did not, as they did in my aunt and uncle, have their roots in an explicit condemnation of my father's personality, but in the mere impossibility, for as long as he continued to go off the rails, of their having a life in common, a desire that was as natural in her as the obstacles that planted themselves in her way were inevitable. You could say that, without admitting as much to myself, I sympathized with my mother, and the earlier incomprehension with which I once viewed her insistence on putting her trust in my father over and over again was replaced by a greater understanding, one that allowed me to see how generous and rare and bold she had been in making that choice.

A product of my subterranean reconciliation with my parents' attitude—in opposition to the gray, hypocritical normality I was beginning to associate with my aunt and uncle as well as with the world of absolute certainties surrounding me at school and among my friends and acquaintances—was the inclusion, in my urgent need to know, of questions that went beyond my understandable eagerness to find out what had really happened in Paris, the extra worry of trying to work out the reasons for my parents' behavior, above and beyond its concrete manifestations. Shortly after I first became aware that being an only child made me different, I became aware that my parents were different, too, and a need to compare myself with them emerged quite naturally, a need to contrast what was innate and what was inherited, what was mine because that is how I would have ended up anyway and what was, on the contrary, the product of circumstances and of decisions not made by me. It wasn't just a matter of finding out once and for all if they had been together in Paris and, if they had, what they had done there, but finding out, too, what had led them there, what it was they lacked, what they secretly longed for or desired, if they felt alone or were perfectly content, what they thought, what they hoped for, what their childhoods had been like, if they resembled me or were completely different, if Paris had been what separated them or if they would have separated anyway.

It was thanks to this involuntary process that the day after I phoned Delfina, and while I was still despairing of finding a means of preempting my mother's intervention by confirming beforehand what had only been mere suspicions up until then, I began working on a plan I first rejected as absurd but that, in the end, presented itself to me as the only possible way forward, the most accessible, the one least likely to be discovered by my mother or to leave any clues, the one most likely to remain hidden, clandestine.

Despite my feelings of solidarity with my mother, and a kind of natural though unconfessed prejudice against my father dating from the time when he lived with us after leaving prison in Burgos, I had watched with veiled interest, and a certain degree of admiration and respect, everything to do with my father's forbidden world. I had not forgotten things like that chance encounter on our way back from Toledo with the former convict who had addressed him as "Professor," or the phone calls from people wanting to know where he was, or the strange visit, one or two years before, by those two men who came looking for him, in order, perhaps, to call him to account for some past act of treachery or a failed business deal in which he'd been embroiled, and it's not so very odd, then—in the circumstances I've described, in which I was assailed by a new need to reinterpret everything having to do with my parents—that those encounters and phone calls, along with other memories, should resurface and monopolize much of my thinking. Of all those memories, the one that struck me most was the visit by the two strangers, the bossy young man who did all the talking and the older man, more flexible, or less involved, who accompanied him and, either out of kindness or so that I would know where to find him if my father turned up, had given me the card bearing the name of a bar on the Calle Bravo Murillo, of which he had said very proudly that he was the owner. Not knowing quite why, perhaps out of superstition or because he inspired confidence and I thought it might be useful to stay in touch with him, I had taken the card and put it away in a safe place, even then, when it was still too early to connect my mother's recent Paris adventure with the younger man's more or less explicit allusions to his alleged meeting with my father in a place that was not Madrid and at a time when, even though my father had plenty of money at his disposal, he had been obliged to withdraw from circulation and abandon the territory he normally inhabited.

However, the day after my phone call to my aunt, I had already made the easy connection between the two facts—my mother's definite sojourn in Paris and my father's probable adventure in a mysterious city that was not Madrid. Several times during my bumbling search for facts to support the suspicion that had arisen following that furtive meeting in the café, it had occurred to me that perhaps the two cities were one and the same, and the only new thing to happen during that brief period when I was trying to preempt my mother's impending explanation was my sudden recollection of that business card and, for the first time, a distinct desire to use it. As I said before, the idea initially struck me as absurd, and I was tempted to reject it. Too much time had passed since those two men had turned up at our apartment, and if the older man was still running the bar, he probably wouldn't remember or wouldn't want to dig up such old business. Quite apart from the fact that it had been the younger man who had admitted to knowing my father in the city behind which, I thought, lurked the shadow of Paris, it was highly unlikely, even if he did remember, that he would know if my father had been alone or with my mother at the time he began his dealings with his friend. If, despite that, I ended up giving in to temptation, it wasn't because I had changed my mind or because I suddenly began to think that he really could provide me with trustworthy information that would help me resolve the dilemma and, one way or another, put an end to the suspicion that was plaguing me. I suppose the truth is—and this is further proof of my confusion, of my uncertainty and madness at the time—that I didn't mind if talking to him served no purpose. There were so many unknowns springing up all around me, and the unanswered questions about my parents were so numerous and so intertwined, that not getting an answer to one of them, even if it was the main one, was not enough in itself to dissuade me from my plan.

I did nothing that day, which was the third day following my parents' meeting in the café and the first, therefore, after making the phone call to my aunt. But the following day, which was a Monday—during which my mother maintained her discouraging silence and gave no sign of nervousness or doubt, which would have been a sure indication that my aunt had, as I feared, been in touch with her—on that morning, then, instead of getting on the bus I usually took to school, I went to the nearest subway station and caught a train to Bravo Murillo. After reaching my destination, it was easy enough to find the bar, even though I hadn't quite worked out the street numbers and had to walk quite a way. It was a perfectly ordinary bar, with the TV on at all hours and the floor strewn with cigarette butts and crumpled paper napkins, and olive stones or even larger remnants of food—the gray shells of snails and the black shells of mussels—scattered about among the other detritus. After much thought, after various turns around the block, several bold attempts to enter, followed by several equally bold retreats, several almost definite decisions to abandon my plan altogether, decisions which I swiftly rejected, I finally went in through the door, and the first thing I noticed was that the numerous and vociferous clientele was entirely male, which was still more striking given that the only person visible behind the narrow bar with its long, rectangular food display cases containing an unappetizing selection of pork rinds and potato chips was a fat woman with her hair and eyebrows dyed blood-red. It hadn't occurred to me until then that I would see anyone else behind the bar apart from the one person I was looking for, and such was my disappointment that I would have left immediately had it not been for the deathly silence that fell as soon as I entered, and I would have found it impossibly embarrassing to turn tail and leave for no apparent reason when I was only a few yards away from the woman at the bar. I didn't spot the man I was looking for until I had reached the bar and ordered a Coke, all the while glancing timidly over my shoulder, and the voices and sounds gradually regrouped to form the animated murmur my entrance had interrupted. He was leaning at the end of the bar where the thick, zinc counter formed a right-angle with the wall, immediately next to the section of countertop that lifted up to allow access to the area behind the bar where the woman was working away wearily and reluctantly. The man was shorter than I remembered, and he seemed less like the owner of a very ordinary bar than the manager or maître d' of some large restaurant, who, although always ready to engage in occasional, ephemeral tasks such as bringing a plate to a table or removing an ashtray, prefers to adopt, for his benefit and that of other people, the detached, relaxed pose of someone controlling things from the shadows, ruling from afar. He was speaking in a rather desultory fashion to another man who was sitting at a nearby table with his back to me, and although I noticed him turn his head to look at me, I realized that this was out of idle curiosity, not because he had recognized me. Since, apart from a few vague, febrile plans hatched on my way there, I hadn't come up with any real strategy as to how to make my approach, I breathed a sigh of relief and looked from side to side, at the same time trying and doubtless failing to feign an ease and command of the situation I did not feel. However hard I tried, it was inevitable that my beardless face, my scruffy school uniform would be completely out of place there, even though, as I soon found out, the other customers were far more diverse than I had first thought. They all seemed to know each other, and sitting in their various groups, talking at the bar, playing cards around a table, or distractedly watching TV, they could have been members of a supporters' group, a confraternity, or some village society or dining club, such was the air of fellow feeling and grave dignity that surrounded them. But beneath that secret, almost tribal camaraderie binding them together, I could nonetheless spot notable differences between them, contrasts in clothes and manners, which made their palpable complicity, their harmonious coexistence beneath the same roof, incomprehensible, or at the very least enigmatic. The range was very wide. From the almost destitute, complete with their sinister gestures and accents, to apparently modest representatives of the most humble trades; from harmless old men to besuited cigar-smokers, all gold rings and lighters and tie pins, to two individuals with alert faces who were dressed more informally, more fashionably, in leather jackets, jeans,

241

neck scarves, and ostentatious sports watches and seemed to be the main focus of the admiring or indulgent attention of their companions. It really was a very striking group of people, simultaneously disparate and similar, bound together by secrecy, by mutual dependence, by indecipherable codes of loyalty, by the knowledge, one might say, that each had something of the others' sins. Now that I think about it, they could have been gambling addicts or practitioners of some kind of perversion that was either frowned upon or actually criminal. They could have been normal citizens who happened to be unemployed and, thanks to a chance coincidence of tastes when choosing a place to spend the long, tedious hours, had acquired an invisible shared aura. It could have been anything, and yet what I thought, after that brief glance over my shoulder before I turned back to my as yet untouched Coke, is that they belonged to the same profession as my father, a profession in which the distance between success and failure is measured by a fate as ephemeral and fragile in its kindness as it is unavoidable when it turns against you. This, of course, was a purely subjective impression, predetermined before I even entered the bar, and to which, for that same reason, I give no particular value, even though it still persists. Whatever the truth of the matter, and precisely because I was aware it could not be trusted, that impression had no influence on the feeling which—imperceptibly at first, and then conclusively and emphatically—began to take hold of me only moments after I picked up my glass of Coke and took one tiny sip, meanwhile sneaking another furtive glance at the old man. I still had no idea how to proceed. My one quick look around the bar had not helped me to decide, and I didn't know how to begin that sought-after conversation, how to justify my presence there, or what attitude to adopt regarding my father. I felt uncomfortable, intimidated, and fearful, like someone, I suppose, who having gotten himself nominated to a post or for a prize using only the weapons of intrigue and demagogy, finally faces the challenge of making good his promises with deeds. I didn't know what to do and felt increasingly oppressed by my indecision. I looked at the old man, who had stopped talking now and was immersed in studying some advertising flyers piled up on the bar; I looked at my glass of Coke, telling myself that however slowly I drank it, I was bound to finish it eventually or, even worse, draw attention to myself by taking too long, and however hard I tried, I couldn't come to a decision. Then, at a certain point, as if touched by a sudden breath of clear-sightedness, I suddenly knew that I would do nothing, that I would leave just as I had arrived, and far from feeling frustrated or trying to deceive myself by saying that I would come back another time, I experienced an intense, unexpected sense of well-being, a feeling so in keeping with my newly accepted powerlessness that it felt more like an unequivocal acceptance of that decision than the weary resignation or the logical relief one might feel after a burden has been lifted from one's shoulders, as if the fear that had stopped me taking that step up until then had merely concealed a far greater fear of the possible consequences. At the same time, the feeling of oppression also lifted, and with it, the feeling of discomfort, of being observed. The awkwardness I'd felt ever since entering that place also disappeared, and I was able to shift my position slightly and thus gain a more panoramic, detailed view of those men with their evasive, smug, or defiant faces, faces that contained the very essence of my father. I observed them slowly, and slowly observed myself in that strange setting, and while I was looking from one man to the next, while I was noticing their ways of speaking and moving, while I was absorbed in the sound of laughter and overheard comments, and although the memory of my mother with my father, of my mother alone, and of my mother with me did not abandon me but hovered above my thoughts and before my eyes like an invisible film, blurring my vision, distorting and transforming the whole scene, filling it with irrelevant meanings, slowly, inevitably, like a great rush of warm water come to rescue me from the sharp sting of an icy sea, I noticed that between me and them, between myself and everything that the bar and even my parents meant, an extraordinary wall of distance was growing.

# XXVIII

My aunt arrived the following day on the morning train, but I didn't find this out until the afternoon, on my return from school, when, as soon as I'd closed the front door and was about to walk down the hallway leading to the living room, I heard my mother's voice and, shortly afterward, that of my aunt energetically interrupting her. Despite my surprise at how fast things had happened, I noticed that although they were both trying hard not to raise their voices, they were not talking but arguing. I was so taken aback that I couldn't absorb what they were saying, but it took only a few seconds for me to realize that the bomb had finally exploded and that all my attempts to anticipate events had been in vain. My first impulse was to turn around and run away, and, given that they hadn't heard me come in, to go out into the street again and only come back when they had calmed down, or at least when I felt more able to cope with a three-way conversation for which, naïvely, I had not prepared myself. I was afraid to confront them from a position of weakness, without knowing exactly what each of them knew, what the fight was all about, or how long it had been going on. Soon, however, my need to know won out over my need to escape, and I continued on down the hall, taking care not to make any noise and, at the same time, pricking up my ears, which received, quite clearly, these words from my aunt: "I don't care. You simply can't do it. It doesn't belong to him." I was walking deliberately slowly and wasn't even halfway down the hall when I heard my mother answer, "Yes it is. It's his. He paid for half of it." And then I heard my aunt cutting in, "No, it isn't. It may have been his years ago, but that doesn't matter. Now it belongs to you and to your son." I was, by then, standing right next to the door leading into the living room, where they were sitting; I stood there with my back pressed against the wall, my ears straining to catch every word they said, but I was ready, too, to flee back down the hallway should there be the slightest risk of them discovering me; I could then pretend to be an entirely innocent new-arrival. That was almost all I had time to do. While I was thinking about what I had already heard and wondering in amazement at its possible meaning, and after a rhetorical pause or an explicit refusal to reply on the part of my mother, my aunt spoke again, adding emphatically, "It's your son's inheritance. You can't just throw it away. You have to compensate him in some way." Immediately after this, I heard footsteps, but before I realized the threat they represented, my Aunt Delfina had appeared in the doorway and, after a startled glance in my direction, she stopped on the very threshold and stood looking at me. For a few very long seconds, I could hear all three of us breathing. I was looking at my aunt; my aunt was looking at me; my mother, as yet unaware of my presence, was waiting for her sister. I think she said "What's wrong? What are you doing?" but I'm not sure, because my memory is filled by what happened next. In response to these questions, or possibly spontaneously, my aunt leaned back in the doorway, immediately across from where I was hiding, and without saying hello or smiling, she turned toward my mother and said dryly, "Tell your son, go on, tell him you're going to sell the apartment and give his father half the money. Go on, tell him, and see if he understands." Having said this, she again turned to look at me, then leaned back further against the doorframe and, giving a theatrical wave of the hand as if to usher me in, waited for my mother's reaction. I didn't move, feeling both terribly embarrassed and, at the same time, struggling to take in this news; then, when I heard a dull thud like the sound made by someone stamping hard on the ground, I sidled into the living room, my back against the wall, at the very moment when my mother, a look of alarm on her face and both hands resting on the arms of the chair facing the door, seemed about to get up and come over to me. "Go on, ask her to tell you. See if she can," I heard my aunt saying to me as if from the depths of a very deep sleep.

I need hardly describe the state of embarrassment and extreme distress in which I waited for what my mother might say. My amazement at her plans for the apartment, my unease because I still didn't know if Delfina had told her about our conversation, and my awareness that she must realize that my aunt had not just happened upon me right then in the hallway but had caught me eavesdropping, as well as my continuing suspicions about her time in Paris all conspired to keep me on the back foot, rendering me incapable of uttering a single word of excuse in all the seemingly endless time during which, after my aunt's last words, my mother fell back again into her armchair and looked at me in silence. I had been so preoccupied and caught up in the past, trying to make plans in order to get to the bottom of it, that I had completely lost sight of the present, and now, when it came to meet me, I had no answers, no idea how to face it. My situation then was a kind of preparation for what would come afterward, not on that particular day, which was already drawing to a close, but on the following day, when, suddenly, in a truly rare and radical way, I would have to reconsider my whole life up until then. Nevertheless, perhaps because the echo of that more powerful experience cancels it out, the image of those seconds in which my mother looked at me without speaking is somewhat vague in my memory. I know that I stood stock-still, caught in the grip of a noisy confusion of fears, but it's also true that memory imposes order and hierarchy, and now, when I look back, I cannot imagine the episode with all the intensity I imagine it must have had. Compared with what would happen twenty-four hours later, my feeling is that it did not last long. It passed quickly, or so it seemed to me. Between the instant when our eyes met and the moment when my mother broke her silence, almost nothing survives—it's a void that immediately begins to fill up, and I can see her blinking and, still looking me straight in the eye, saying to my aunt, "I'm sure he'll agree with me, not that it's any of your business, anyway. That's something he and I will have to work out."

I remember the ensuing silence, like a kind of truce, during which, since I was momentarily not the focus of attention, I had time to review all the hasty decisions that had arisen from my witnessing that clandestine meeting in the café. But apart from that succession of fleeting images that sent me back to the first appearance of a suspicion that was, it turned out, perfectly capable of being cleared up, and, therefore perfectly measurable, what I remember during the cascade of seconds after my mother spoke was the growing sensation that I was about to enter an unknown and even unimaginable reality, unlike the one inhabited by the doubts and fears that had plagued me during the past few days. I felt the terrible coldness with which my mother had answered my aunt, as well as the frank and equally chilly way in which Delfina had spoken to her earlier. I had never been present at such a serious quarrel between the two sisters, nor had I imagined they could possibly clash in this way. I knew they were very different in temperament and in the ways they judged and dealt with the superficial aspects of life, but I had never thought there could be any insuperable differences between them. I was, then, entering unexplored territory, compared with which any explanation for the motives behind the meeting between my parents paled into insignificance. The fact that my mother was preparing to sell the apartment, whether on her own initiative or under pressure from my father, was as nothing compared with what was about to rain down upon me. To tell the truth, I still don't know how it happened, I don't know why my mother didn't stop my aunt, why she didn't interrupt the conversation but instead set off along the path opened up by Aunt Delfina, apparently oblivious to the fact that I was there listening intently to every insinuation, every hesitation, every assertion. I can only think that she wanted this to happen, to thus create the right conditions for our conversation the following day, the moment I had so longed for and that, in the end, came about in the most unexpected manner. As for me, what can I say except that I listened with growing incredulity, still pressed up against the wall by the door, making no noise, not moving a muscle, trying to appear invisible, not wanting to remind them in any way of my presence, and not wanting them not to stop, either, but to go on talking. Then Aunt Delfina, on hearing my mother's defiant words, stepped back into the living room and retorted, "That's where you're wrong. It *is* my business. Of course it is. I can't allow you to go on ruining your life and his. You've gone wrong too many times already."

"How can you say that? Ruin my life? I think I've managed pretty well. There may be things I wish I could have done, but basically I've lived the life I wanted to live."

My mother had spoken very curtly, without looking at me, and Delfina—who, for a moment, seemed about to sit down again in the same armchair she had left just before discovering me in my hiding place—remained standing and merely rested one hand on the back of the chair, slightly surprised, perhaps, that my mother was still fighting.

"Don't talk nonsense," she said firmly, turning to look at me. "How can you possibly have wanted the insecurity, the fear, the loneliness, and the anxiety you've had to live with? Are you going to tell me that you foresaw all that?"

"No, I didn't. But it happened, and that's all there is to it. Besides, it ended ages ago."

"You say that now, but what will happen next month?"

Delfina's question was like a whiplash cutting through the air and leaving me feeling simultaneously frozen, afraid, and grateful for what I was witnessing. My mother was speaking more slowly now, more emphatically, and my aunt had tried to compensate for this with a speedy response.

"You know very well that nothing will happen. I've never deceived you. I've never told you that I was going to do something I had no intention of doing. It's over. There will be nothing more. Why can't you accept that?"

"Yes, but meanwhile, you're going to sell your apartment to give him some money, and who knows how long that will last him. A week, maybe two at most."

Delfina glanced at me again, while my mother, who hadn't looked at me since my forced entrance into the room, raised her head and studied me long and hard. For the first time, a silence fell, and I knew then that nothing would stop her. I saw concern on her face, but not anxiety or doubt. Sitting across from me, she gave a long sigh, as if summoning up all her patience, then turned back to my aunt, "I'm giving him the money because that is the best possible proof that this is the end. Now that it's over, it's only fair that we go back to the beginning, him with his money and me with mine. It's the only thing we bought together. He needs the money, and I'm not going to leave him in the lurch. If he asks for more, I won't be able to help him. What's left will be mine, and I'll look after it, don't worry. But since half of this apartment is still his, I'm not going to deny it to him if he's in trouble."

"Don't be so naïve," Delfina said quickly, still looking at me out of the corner of her eye, unable to disguise her discomfort at my mother's unwonted rebellion. "You know as well as I do that he'll always be in trouble, that the money you're so happily proposing to give him is very little in comparison to everything you've had to put up with. The problem is that you're as irresponsible as you always were, the same adolescent girl ready to go wherever your first impulse takes you, without thinking about the pain you might cause. You never learn . . ."

"Don't go any further, Delfina. Don't lecture me. It's so easy to do that. Besides, when have I caused pain? When have I allowed myself to act on impulse?"

"You know very well what I mean."

"No, I don't, I really don't. Tell me."

Delfina fixed her eyes on my mother, and my mother, who was sitting bent forward in a position of false submissiveness, legs crossed and hands clasped, suddenly leaned back in her chair like a creature bracing itself to face some unexpected danger.

"I can't believe it's what I think it is. Is it, Delfina? Is it what I think it is?"

"It doesn't matter. It was just a manner of speaking . . ."

"All right, don't say it. I will. You were referring to my big mistake. No, not to my big mistake, because it would seem that my whole life has been one long mistake. You were referring to my *first* mistake, to the origin of all the insecurity, fear, and loneliness I've lived my life in . . ."

"Oh, please, don't get sarcastic. I wasn't speaking of anything in particular, but yes, now that you mention it, you're right. That's how it was. Bad beginnings breed bad endings."

I noticed that Delfina had drawn back now and was struggling to control herself.

"I can't believe it. It's just incredible that after sixteen years, and after Dad's death, that idea is still going around in your head."

"It's not going around in my head. It's just further proof of the irresponsible way you behave sometimes. Once you're set on doing something, you won't listen to anyone, there's no way of making you change your mind."

"I had to leave, Delfina. I can't believe you're still saying this. I had to leave. I had no alternative. Believe me."

My mother had altered her tone of voice again, and it sounded dull now, almost doleful. Her outward show of aggression had disappeared, and it was as if she were talking to herself. Then, however, she changed. She remained silent for a few seconds, as if she needed time to climb the walls of the imaginary hole into which she had fallen, then, fixing her eyes determinedly on my aunt, she recovered her composure. At no point did she look at me, at no point did she seem to stop to consider what I might be thinking.

"That's rich, *you* reproaching *me* for leaving home, Delfina. Have you never thought that you might have played some role in that, that it might have been your fault in a way? No, you've obviously never even considered the possibility. You've always been so clear about everything. First this one thing happens and then this other one, first this, then that, but you probably had some influence—how could you not? I'm your sister. I lived with you. We were together when Mom died."

"That's ridiculous! Don't be so unfair. I've always respected your decisions, even that one. I'm only saying that you could have done things differently and not just left home the way you did. Your life might have been different, and besides, it's not true that I made you do it. You did it because you wanted to. You were an adult by then."

Delfina, who had grown quieter since our surprise meeting in the doorway, had spoken in a weary but cutting voice, as if she weren't sure how appropriate it was to continue this argument, but at the same time unwilling to give anything up. She wasn't gesticulating now.

"Yes, I was eighteen. But speaking of feelings, do you have any idea how alone I was? Do you have any idea how alien I felt living in that house that used to be ours, living under the rules imposed by Dad's new wife? You can't know, because you weren't there. You had already left."

"Oh come on, don't exaggerate. It wasn't that bad. That kind of thing happens in all families and people get over it, so don't use it as an excuse for your future misfortunes."

"Of course these things happen," answered my mother. "I'm not using it as an excuse. It hasn't marked my life. But that doesn't mean there wasn't a time when it did matter to me, when I felt really vulnerable. Do you understand? Maybe older sisters don't feel vulnerable. Since you don't have anyone above you, you haven't grown up thinking that there'll always be someone to replace your parents when they die."

"Oh, really. Do you honestly think it didn't affect me, as well? Look, don't go on, there's no point."

"OK, you're right. I agree. You probably do know what it feels like to be vulnerable, and maybe it's worse being the older sister. But I was the younger sister. When I was born, you were already there, you were my reference point, my second line of defense. I couldn't help feeling that I had two walls around me. You were one and they were the other. I'm sure that your world collapsed, too, when Mom died and Dad began to betray us, as if he had never shed a single tear and never sworn that the three of us would always stick together. I'm sure that's true. I don't doubt it. But you felt that only once, and I felt it twice. Once, at the same time as you did, and again, when you went to live in La Coruña."

My mother still did not look at me, and Delfina, who until then had looked at me every time she spoke, now forgot to do so, temporarily overcome by the urgent need to respond.

"But I didn't abandon you. It was my life! I had to get out of there. You know I did my best to stand up to her, but I lost the battle. I objected right from the start, as soon as she started demolishing everything that had to do with Mom, as soon as the first photo was taken down and we began to discover that we couldn't do or say things that we had considered perfectly normal before, as soon as she began to deny Mom's whole existence, not only at home but in our lives as well, and Dad let her do as she pleased, even things he shouldn't have let her do. You know how I stood up to her. I'm not to blame for our father's passivity or for her piling on the pressure all the time.

I was young, too. I lost the battle. I couldn't stand it, and so I escaped. That's all."

"That's exactly my point. That's what I mean. You escaped."

"But I didn't abandon you. After I got married, I was always there for you. For all these years, you've always been able to come to me. Who listened to your fears? Who gave you refuge? I was even your accomplice . . . You can't accuse me of having neglected my obligations to you. It's just that I can't accept this latest thing, you simply can't—"

"I know you were always there for me. I know how hard you fought. I know how much you've had to keep silent about. I know how much you've done to help. And believe me, I'm grateful. Even though I did the opposite of what you advised, even though I'm about to ignore your advice yet again, you've always helped me and you still do. I mean, even your coming to Madrid to try and make me change my mind is helpful . . . But I'm not talking about how you've behaved over the years. I'm not even talking about what I thought about your getting married or about the two years you virtually disappeared. As you say, it was your life. As you say, you had to leave. I'm not talking about what I *thought* of it at the time. What I'm talking about is how I *felt*. I'm saying that everything, absolutely everything, affects us. I'm saying that an event, however seemingly trivial, like your sister leaving home, can affect you. That's what I'm saying, and it just so happens that it did affect me. I'm not saying whether or not I was right to feel abandoned. Who am I to say!"

I noticed a touch of reluctance and artificial coolness in the condescending thoroughness with which my mother had spelled out her motives for complaint. She had uncrossed her legs now and was sitting leaning slightly forward, arms resting casually on her knees in marked contrast with the stern look on her face.

"And yet you talk as if it still affected you. You say you're not reproaching me, but you are. You're contradicting yourself . . ."

"Of course it affects me. I think about my situation then, and I still feel like crying. My whole world collapsed. Suddenly, almost without being aware of it, I went from feeling safe and secure in a solid family of four to only having a father I could barely recognize. To tell you the truth, it still affects me. But it's something I can't control. Thinking and feeling are two different things. Feeling influences thinking and both are part of us, but they're different."

"But you called me selfish. You said that you did what you did because I left home."

"All I said was please don't talk to me about selfishness, because you're still convinced that I did what I did for frivolous reasons, and that's not true, Delfina. You don't seem to realize that I did nothing you wouldn't have done yourself. You couldn't stand the situation at home and you escaped. Well, so did I. I only said that you forced me to do that in order to make you aware that, just as your choice of exit strategy was influenced by your desire to escape, so the decisions I took were influenced by my feelings of abandonment after you left."

"But you can't compare the two! When I left home, I didn't go crazy. I didn't just vanish . . ."

From where she was standing, my aunt turned toward me, perhaps regretting the vehemence of her last words or perhaps wanting to see their effect on me, and before my mother could respond and before she braced herself for my mother's riposte, she withdrew her hand from the back of the armchair, moved a little closer, and nervously leaned her whole body against it.

"So what if I did, Delfina? What does it matter? Was that really so inconsiderate of me? I don't think it would have changed anything if I'd done as you did. I don't know why you keep harping on about it."

"Look, there's no point in continuing this discussion. You mix everything up. I don't want to talk about the past, it's of no interest to me. I mentioned your leaving Dad's house, but that was only because that was the most obvious example, and everything else was just more of the same. That's all. Let's just drop the subject. There's no point talking about it."

Delfina drew back again from the armchair and began slowly to move away, only to immediately stop and remain where she was, although this time without resting her hand on the chair back for support.

"No, I don't want to drop the subject, not until you recognize that you can't judge my life that easily. Everything I've done, I did because I thought it was for the best."

Although my aunt's suggestion that they bring the discussion to a close had been more rhetorical than sincere, my mother's instant rejection of her words visibly upset her. She made as if to answer, but at the last moment she seemed to think better of it and waited a moment before saying anything more. My mother was sitting very erect, hands gripping the arms of the chair, her head turned toward my aunt.

"Of course. I've never said otherwise. I've always thought you were acting for the best, but if you had stopped to think, as I'm asking you to do now, perhaps things would have turned out differently."

"Don't you see, Delfina, it's not a matter of thinking. I'm very happy with the decisions I made. Everything you think of as a mistake, everything you think I could have avoided in order to not end up in the situation I'm in now, I would do again. I don't regret anything. I'm quite sure that I did what I should have done, that I did what seemed right to me, or what I had no other choice but to do."

"Don't be absurd! It wasn't the best thing or the right thing for you to leave home. Neither was going off to Paris. Or putting up with what you've had to put up with. Of course you had other options. You could have saved yourself a lot of disappointment and a lot of loneliness. Why did you have to wait so long? It's much too easy and too irresponsible to excuse everything by saying that you had no alternative."

"Don't simplify matters. They're two different things. I didn't say it was *always* because I had no alternative. I had my own reasons, too . . ."

"*And* you had no alternative . . ."

"Yes, when I left home, which you seem to think was so very important, I really didn't have any other choice. Since then, I've always done what I thought was for the best."

"Forgive me for insisting, but I see no sign of that in your subsequent decisions, nor do I understand what you mean when you say you had no choice but to leave home. Why? Why did you need to leave home, considering all the anxiety and pain you caused? Couldn't you have just done what everyone else does, what I did?"

The pace and tone of Delfina's responses to my mother changed according to rules I found hard to predict; having started out by trying to strike a conciliatory note, she had, as she spoke, grown gradually more agitated, so that her last question emerged rather abruptly. She was still standing in the same place, although now she was resting all her weight on her

258

left leg and had her right leg stretched out and balanced on the heel of her shoe, pointing toward me.

"Oh, please, not again. Not appearances again. Why are they so important?"

"It's not a matter of appearances, it's a matter of respecting other people. You left without warning, without telling anyone."

"Yes, you're right, I did, but you don't know why. How could you?"

"Apparently it was my fault, because I got married and left you all alone . . ."

"Please don't make fun of me. I said earlier that your absence was a contributory factor, I didn't say it was the only reason I left. No, that was because of something that happened before. But forget it . . . You're right, these conversations are pointless and absurd, we just end up saying things we shouldn't. Really, let's drop it."

My mother, who hadn't smoked once since I entered the room, glanced around as if searching for some lost pack of cigarettes. She failed to find it, and before looking back at Delfina, she suddenly met my gaze. As she said those last words, her voice had grown softer, taken on an imploring tone, but her eyes, in the brief moment they met mine, seemed utterly serene.

"What's wrong with you? You can't just leave it like that. I need to know what you're accusing me of. I don't remember having done anything wrong."

"No, Delfina, of course not. You didn't do anything wrong. It was me . . . But forget it. There's no point talking about it. It's not your fault, so don't worry. You can't understand, because you don't know. You don't know, and you're not going to . . ."

"Speak to me. Tell me. Don't just say nothing. I'm your sister. I can at least try to understand. I've been very harsh and said things I shouldn't have, but I do know what you've been through."

"No, Delfina, you don't. The truth is that you have no idea what my life was like after you left. You don't know what I talked to them about. You don't know what we ate. You don't know where we went or who we saw. You don't know when we got up and when we went to bed. You don't know what we did every hour, every day. Do you? Answer me, Delfina. Do you?"

"No, I don't, you're right."

My mother had become visibly distressed, and I saw a look of alarm in Delfina's eyes.

"You don't know anything. You don't know the extent of my despair. You don't know how lost I felt or what I came to long for. You don't know how unbalanced I became. You don't know how powerless I felt in the face of that woman's meticulous destruction of the past. You don't know how much I hated her or that I came to hate him even more. You don't know how much anger I stored up against him. You don't know the lies I told myself so as not to have to accept that his indifference was actually sheer cowardice, that he actually did care what I thought, but that he didn't rebel because these were forces against which he was not prepared to fight. You don't know how discouraged and bewildered I became. You don't know how helpless I felt to see him so humiliated, so silent and sad. You don't know that sometimes he didn't dare to look at me, you don't know about the knot that formed in his throat when she did or said something intolerable and he would lower his eyes so as not to meet mine. You don't know how torn apart I felt. You don't know that I would sometimes have preferred to think that he really was the heartless person we believed him to be, anything rather than see him like that, incapable of doing what his conscience cried out for him to do. You don't know that at the same time as I despised him, I couldn't help but feel sorry for him. You don't know the extent of my rancor or my understanding or my devotion. You don't know that sometimes I thought I was the victim, the one who had the right to complain, or that at others I felt responsible and thought he was the one who suffered most. You don't know that it often seemed to me that he really missed Mom or that sometimes I would have liked to be her in order to comfort him and make up for the things his wife did. I thought that Mom, wherever she was, would approve, that her union with Dad, though no longer an earthly one, was more important than any other. You don't know that I came to believe I was the link between them. You don't know that I sometimes thought I was Mom and that sometimes Dad really wanted me to be her, too . . . You don't know how crazy things got."

"Stop, stop. Please stop. Don't go on. There's no need. It's pointless . . ."

"You see how impossible it is for you to understand? You see how much you don't know and don't even want to know?"

"You're not making any sense. You're hysterical . . ."

"No, you're wrong. I'm not hysterical. I know perfectly well what I'm saying. I know perfectly well that there are three of us here, and I know perfectly well why you've come." My mother paused and looked at me for a moment, as if to emphasize that even though she was talking to Delfina, the conversation was meant for me as well. "I know that by selling the apartment, I am, according to you, committing yet another act of craziness. But I can't allow you to continue to think so poorly of me. Your irresponsible, impulsive, feather-brained sister who always does the wrong thing, the one who ran away from home, the one who's always in need of advice. Things happened, Delfina, for which there are no words. Things you cannot even suspect . . ."

"But you're distorting everything," said Delfina. "It can't have been the way you describe it . . ."

For the first time since my mother had searched in vain for that pack of cigarettes, Delfina gave me a fleeting glance before answering. They had swapped roles, and now she was the one who sounded pained and almost imploring. Clearly undecided as to what to do or think, she had put her hands in the tiny pockets of her jacket so that her elbows stuck out stiffly on either side, making her look a little like a penguin.

"Of course I'm distorting things, but what does that matter now? Acknowledging that in no way diminishes the depth of my feelings then. I had to leave. If you knew, if I could explain, then you would agree that I was right."

"Stop talking like that. I won't have it. You're tired and upset. These are just fantasies, just like the picture you paint of Dad. It wasn't like that. All right, Dad betrayed us, but what does it matter if he was also a coward or felt remorse? That doesn't excuse him. He wasn't a victim, unfortunately, he may have been heartless, but not a victim. Mom would not have approved. Mom would have despised him . . ."

"Delfina, it happened. Don't try to run away from it. It happened. I'm sorry, but what can I do? You're right, I was distorting the facts, and Dad's cowardice was no excuse. But it happened. You can deny it if you like, refuse to accept it, but at least give me your vote of confidence and believe me when I say that I had to leave, that I had no alternative, that it was not some silly, gratuitous act, that my life since then has not been, as you say, a continuation of the same thing, that the fear and the loneliness were my choice, my reward, if you like, that I did what I did out of love or conviction or desperation, and that I don't regret it."

There was a silence, and Delfina, who had been staring down at the floor for a while, looked up and fixed her gaze somewhere above my mother's head. I couldn't see her eyes, but I imagined them to be blank and lost. She kept fidgeting, caught between conflicting impulses. She had removed her hands from their uncomfortable refuge in her pockets and placed them, palms flat, on her thighs. She had changed the position of her feet several times, and they now formed a right angle, with one foot pointing at my mother and the other at me.

"But Mom didn't . . ."

"Leave Mom out of it, Delfina. That's another lie we created between us. Dad was an egotist who forgot about his guilt by hiding away inside his own cowardice. Grief doesn't last forever. I soon realized that. But I can tell you that the image we've cultivated of Mom over the years is just as false. Another distortion. We've always thought of Mom as some kind of storybook heroine and Dad as a bit of a fool, easy to manipulate, and whom she led along the path of righteousness until, alas, she died and that other woman arrived. Mom was the intelligent one, the sensitive one, the high-minded one, the one who had sacrificed herself for her sole weakness, a weakness, moreover, that only increased her stature: our father. The perfect wife. Superior in every way to her husband, but redeemed by the way she so lovingly gave herself to him. It wasn't like that, Delfina. Mom was just like Dad. She wasn't the archetype you and I have created between us. Mom was as normal as Dad, as worthy or not of criticism and as foolish or not as him. Oh, she was definitely the nobler of the two, but make no mistake—otherwise, she was as simple and straightforward as we remember. She always did exactly what she wanted and made no sacrifices at all. She lived according to her own idea of happiness. She had everything she could possibly want. As bad luck would have it, though, and as no one could have foreseen, she died far too young, but that's all. People don't sacrifice themselves. People usually do what they want to do, what suits them best, what fits their personality or brings in the most money. No one sacrifices themselves. I haven't, and neither have you. Even if you sometimes think you're like Mom and have some kind of duty to fulfill, the only duty you have is the one you owe to your own will."

"But who's saying I'm self-sacrificial, that I feel what Mom used to feel? Who's saying I do anything out of duty? Look, let's just stop this conversation right now. It's absurd."

"No one's saying that, Delfina, no one. It's just that sometimes I've imagined you at night, when you're lying in bed in the dark, and I've wondered if perhaps you ever fall into the temptation of thinking that. And I've wondered if, given that you, too, escaped from home, you might think the world you chose and from which you've never moved, La Coruña and all that, isn't really yours, isn't the world you were made for."

"But who says that? How can you even think . . .?"

Delfina's voice faltered, and her expression—which had passed through various states, from uncontrolled aggression to alarm tinged with sadness—took on a somber air. She was no longer looking at me and was once again resting one hand on the back of the armchair.

"No one, Delfina, no one. I'm just warning you, because if you ever do succumb to that temptation, you'll be lying to yourself. It would be a complete lie. You're not on the right path, you're on the path you chose and that you want to follow. You are that path. There's no great purpose behind your life in La Coruña. You haven't given up anything. You are what you do. Like everyone. Like Mom and Dad. Like me."

"I know. Of course my life is the way I want it to be. Have I ever said otherwise? Listen, we're both getting hysterical now. We've been talking for ages and we just keep going around and around in circles and all we do is talk nonsense and hurt each other. It's ridiculous, pointless. After all, we love each other. So let's just drop it, shall we?"

"Yes, let's. Don't worry, consider the subject dropped. I only said that because it seems to me sometimes that you might feel that way. I said it because sometimes I've felt like that when I've put myself in your shoes. I've been tempted to think that you don't have everything you deserve to have, that your life could have been different, more satisfying, rather than that of the resigned, perfect wife . . ."

'That's enough. Drop it, please. I can't take any more."

"But, Delfina, what's wrong. Don't cry, please. There's no point. I just wanted you to see that you, too, could, that I . . . oh, Delfina, it's OK. Don't cry, please . . . don't cry."

"I'm not crying, oh, now *you're* starting to cry. Why are *you* crying? Look, I was crying, but now I'm not. It was just a tear or two. It's because I'm tired."

"Don't worry. It was just a tear or two with me, as well. Aren't we silly? What's he going to think of his aunt and his mother?" My mother paused, lowered her head, wiped away her tears with her hands, then looked at me and said, "What a sappy pair, huh?"

My aunt turned to look at me, as well, and my mother, assuming the conversation was over, got up and walked over to her. I was too taken aback to answer and stood, unmoving, frozen against the wall where I had stood all the time they had been arguing. My mother kissed Delfina on both cheeks and, after briefly embracing her, came toward me. Carefully, so that she wouldn't notice, I removed my clenched fists from behind my back and stepped slightly away from the wall. "What a sappy pair," she murmured as she kissed me, before folding me in her arms and hugging me for rather longer than she had hugged Delfina. "What a sappy pair."

# XXIX

I don't know, although I can imagine, why it was that my mother decided to speak, why she wanted to tell me what she had never intended to tell me. I don't know, of course, but I'm sure that the argument I've just reproduced was not the reason behind her decision. It helped to precipitate it, helped her to find the right time and place, but it was not the only reason or what made it necessary. Indeed, I believe that if the idea of talking to me had not already been there in her mind, her confrontation with Delfina would never have happened in the way it did. How, otherwise, to explain her acceptance of my presence there or the fact that, far from stopping their quarrel as soon as she saw me enter the room, she did something that went entirely against her nature and took center stage. In all family disputes that result in a sharp exchange of reproaches, however bitter and stormy that dispute is, there is always a point at which you can decide either to back down and allow the other person to proceed alone along that rancorous path, or else to steam ahead, knowing full well that you will say things you'll regret later on. If my mother continued to speak despite having me there as a witness, it was because she wasn't exposing herself to any risk that she had not, in some way, already accepted. Whether or not she made the decision at that precise moment, she nevertheless took that risk, and I would go so far as to say that some of the things she said were intended not for my aunt's ears but for mine. It was not the argument itself that prompted her desire to speak but, rather, her desire to speak that prompted the argument. The question, therefore, is not *Would my mother have told me, had there been no argument?* The question is would she have done so if the cause of the dispute had not occurred, if she hadn't had to consider selling the apartment and there had been three and not two of us living there; that is, did she intend telling me?

Whatever the truth of the matter, it's a question to which probably not even she had a clear answer. And now no one does. I don't know why she went to Paris or the reason for her early return, or what terrible disappointment or insult finally forced her to accept defeat; I don't know what part of her past gave rise to the determination I saw in her tearless eyes the afternoon I watched her leave the café I had happened upon after lingering for no particular reason on my way home from school, nor do I know what arguments persuaded her to take the symbolic step—which so enraged my aunt—of selling the apartment. I don't know the answer to these unknowns, just as I don't know the details of my father's abrupt departure at a time when my mother had such high hopes that he would stay, or what he did with the business cards and the fake ID I found under the table in the room where he used to work during a period I can't even remember, or a whole multitude of other things that happened without my being there to witness them and of which I know nothing because no one told me and no strange coincidences placed them before my eyes.

I can't even be sure of things that happened only to me, and can't detach the memory of what happened *after* the argument with my aunt from the subsequent feeling of dread that filled my mind even *before* I had any real reason to fear anything. There are times when it seems we can predict what awaits us, and in a fraction of a second, that future appears before our eyes like a melody that suddenly springs to our lips, a melody sprung from some lost corner of time and that our lips spontaneously begin to whistle. These are only ever very brief moments, they tend to occur during times of extreme melancholy or exhaustion, and like those catchy tunes unexpectedly brought back to life, they are forgotten as soon as we become aware of them. It has to happen like that for the premonition to come true, because otherwise, the fear and dread it stirs up would be enough to destroy it. I knew that the conversation between my mother and my aunt would inevitably be continued in another conversation between my mother and myself. I knew this from the moment my aunt ordered me into the living room, from the look my mother gave me when, making as if to get up from the armchair in which she was sitting, she suddenly released her grip on the arms and sat down again. What I didn't know then, but sensed when the argument between them had finished and they started behaving as if they had never exchanged any reproachful remarks or shed any tears in my presence, was that there would be no room in what my mother would say to me for what happened during her time in Paris—which I would not mention, either—and that she would speak about other, entirely unimagined things.

That desolate, urgent certainty lends a phantasmagorical air to my memory and prevents me from painting a true picture of how we spent the rest of the evening, or even what we spoke about over breakfast the next morning. All real trace of what we did has vanished along with most of the gestures and words we exchanged from the moment my mother finally got up from her armchair, came over to where Delfina and I were standing, and gave each of us a kiss. My aunt did not travel back to La Coruña that night, but apart from that detail, the only impressions I can summon up are far too feeble and subjective. I seem to remember, for example—although I can't be sure that it isn't a vision retrospectively contaminated by what would come later—that Delfina seemed very nervous and was more silent than usual. I seem to remember her attempts to disguise her nervousness and to keep from sliding into the dark abyss of her thoughts, the meekness and theatrical stoicism with which she tried to regain her composure, and I seem to remember, too, the silences and the pauses in their hesitant attempts at conversation, as well as my own docility and the dumb fixity with which I waited, paralyzed and expectant, incapable of contributing anything more until what I knew would happen finally happened. I remember, or seem to remember, my mother's vigilant eyes and her tense posture, like some crazed illuminist, as she searched inside herself for the right words to use the following day, enjoying the kind of illusory truce experienced by a patient or a prisoner in the hours before hearing, from the doctor or the trial judge, their unpostponable sentence. I remember the look on her face, one of concentration and fear combined with a feeling of relief and confidence that her calvary was almost over, the beatific serenity of someone who prefers the certainty of knowing her fate to the torment of uncertainty. I seem to remember my overloaded brain buzzing while I repeated to myself whole segments of their still recent argument, and that on several occasions, I glanced from one to the other, trying to establish which of them had been more wrong, which of them had been weaker and more insincere. I seem to remember, or so it seems to me now, the great, suffocating weight of a past that was not mine and I did not accept as mine, and the fragile and far too dependent future that I represented. I remember their attentiveness, their efforts to reassure me and play down the importance of their argument; I remember their feigned cheerfulness, the anecdotes they insisted on dredging up from their reluctant memories in order to distract me; and I remember, too, how clearly I saw that this was an act they were putting on, and how differently they would have behaved had I not been there. I seem to remember my sporadic attempts, foiled before they even began, to dynamite the whole performance, to say, "Enough is enough," and I seem to remember my confusion, my touching ineptitude, my inability to take control of the situation. I remember all that, or so it seems to me, and I was, I believe, aware of my mother's unusual firmness—with her behaving for the first time more like mother than daughter—and aware, too, of my aunt's fatalism, resignation, and capitulation, and of the irreparable breach that had been opened up between them by the unspoken conviction, shared by all three of us, that nothing would stop my mother now, that she would do whatever she liked and had already made her decision. I think that, despite everything, a certain calm prevailed and that no one mentioned my father by name, not even when my mother and my aunt began spelling out to me, in hesitant detail, the chain of events that had led us to that situation: my aunt's phone call from La Coruña to ask about the furtive meeting in the café, my mother's confirmation of this, to which she innocently added the fact that she intended to sell the apartment, Delfina's fury and her hasty trip to Madrid . . . I think there was even a point when my aunt could not help going back in time and asking my mother, "But did he ask you to sell the apartment?" to which my mother, with no trace of anguish or grief, only weariness, answered, "No, he just asked me for money. I was the one who suggested selling the apartment. It seemed only fair." And I think that after a brief period of embarrassment following their earlier disagreement, and determined not to highlight their palpable dissent, they turned their respective gazes inwards, and my mother added, as if to herself, "I had to do it, the poor guy."

I'm not really sure about anything until the following morning, at breakfast, and even then the substance out of which my memories are built crumbles at the slightest touch. Were it not for the deceptive slowness with which those hours passed, I would say they were like a wandering mountain stream, as likely to disappear into the earth and travel long distances underground as to resurface later on and cascade over waterfalls—a burbling, sinuous torrent that one moment, divides, leaving behind it unexplored, barely glimpsed byways about which I can say nothing, and the next, swells and swirls deeper in pools and in the labyrinthine meanderings with which it cuts through valleys and riverbeds. Those hours were too dense and too exhausting, the frontier represented by their waters too choppy and full of rapids and whirlpools, its fords and shallows too uncertain, and too few and slippery the precariously improvised bridges and stepping stones providing a way across the chasm between the two banks, between what I had once wanted to know but, despite all my suspicions, never will and what is now fixed but of which I had no inkling then, no knowledge. It's almost dead time, neither irrelevant nor empty, but as impossible to separate off from the uncertain past that precedes it as from the experiences and thoughts that came afterward. Not only is there a marked contrast between my expectations of what was to come and the subsequent reality, there are still too many unknowns that resist its onslaught. There are still too many burdensome associations, too many persistent echoes of old rules and old ways, too many dilemmas arising out of that meeting in the café, and too much new and as yet unassimilated information emerging from the heat of that recently witnessed argument, too much dizzying anticipation at what I felt sure would be the imminent *denouement,* and the powerful, all-enveloping sense, projected onto it by the present, that something was about to end; the impression that grips me when I look back is that, afterward, nothing was the same, that everything ended and began again, that while certain stretches of the stream's course remained unaltered, both its final course and the map were irrevocably changed. No more father, either alone or in company. No more Paris. No more of my mother's incomprehensible stubbornness. No more only-child inquisitiveness. No more triangular relationships with me as the vertex. But the doubt would last forever. The weight and shock and grief and resentment would last forever. My mother and I would be together forever and forever apart. The need and affection would last forever, as would the threatening murmur of the dark night in which we turn in despair to the warm illusion of the person sleeping beside us.

It wasn't just my state of confusion and the speed with which things happened, it was simply that those hours represent too large a leap. Any questions I had about the reasons that triggered my mother's flight from her father's house began to surface only shortly before her own conclusive explanation. Since there was no room then for suspicion to be born and given due consideration, I cannot now fit it into some neat causal sequence, find some handhold that would allow me to cross the abyss, oblivious of the great void beneath my feet.

In fact, before the truth blazes forth, there is only one point when my paralyzing premonitions loosen their grip on me and something meaningful and reliable emerges in my memory. It happened the following morning, after breakfast. I had been particularly quick and was dressed and ready for the long day of respite that school would bring me. My mother and Delfina, whom I had heard come out of their respective bedrooms and say good morning to each other, were already in the kitchen when I arrived, although, unlike me, they were still in their nightclothes. Both of them looked at me (my mother was heating up the milk and making the toast, and my aunt was washing the dishes from the previous night's dinner), and before I sat down at the white, marble-topped table, both made some ironic comment about my unusual promptness. Both seemed tired, and there was a heavy atmosphere in the apartment, the sour smell of cold cigarette smoke and human warmth that impregnates and penetrates walls and books after you've spent a long time in a room and not taken the precaution of opening the windows. We had all gone to bed at the same time, and I had lain awake for more than an hour, listening for any noises that might suggest a clandestine meeting, but maybe their patience proved greater than mine and they ended up meeting in my mother's bedroom or in what used to be my father's room and was now being used by Delfina. They could have waited conspiratorially for me to be neutralized by sleep, or perhaps one of them, unable to sleep or waking in the middle of the night, had gone in search of the other. Perhaps they'd argued again or had been able to speak more calmly, without any intimidating witnesses or the distorting fury of the first shock of conflict. They could have reached an understanding and could, likewise, have dug down deeper into the tunnel of old resentments.

I thought about all this as they were discussing train schedules and tentative plans to have lunch together that were quickly scuppered by my aunt's determination to set off at once back to La Coruña, and when I had finished my breakfast, without either of them having sat down to share it with me, I returned to my room in search of the backpack that served as my schoolbag. My mother followed me, on her way to the bathroom, and before going in, gave me her usual fond kiss and asked if I would be coming straight home from school that afternoon. But that was not the significant moment, even though a slight tremor of her lips as she asked me the question told me that this was what she wanted me to do; nor was it the moment after I gave her the expected affirmative response and she reached out one hand to my face—at the same height as hers now—and gently stroked my chin. The significant moment, if I can use that adjective to qualify a piece of advice given quite hastily and shyly rather than after careful consideration, occurred when my aunt said goodbye to me in the entryway, where I found her waiting for me as I hurried down the hall. It was the first time we had been alone together since our phone conversation three days before, and although I could see that she was nervous, she nevertheless made no mention of that conversation or made any attempt to excuse her all-too-foreseeable betrayal. Like my mother, she stroked my chin and, after kissing me on both cheeks, told me that she wouldn't be there when I came home from school, and after a few words of conventional advice about my studies and my

275

taking proper care of my mother, she was about to close the front door when, trying to adopt a casual tone quite out of keeping with the whisper in which she now spoke, she said, as if it had just occurred to her or as if she didn't know what else to say as I walked over to the elevator, "Take no notice of your mother. She and I were both on edge yesterday and talked a lot of nonsense. Forget what you heard. She was very upset. Don't try to broach the subject with her, and if she mentions it, just let it go. It's not worth discussing."

Delfina kept the door ajar, standing half in and half out of the hallway, but rather than looking me in the eye, she was staring at some indeterminate point on my chest. When the elevator arrived, she waited in silence for me to slide open the grate, and just as I was about to enter, she, not convinced that I had understood, or, more likely, trying to tone down or disguise her words, which suddenly seemed too explicit and more of an encouragement than a deterrent, added, "Maybe she's right about the apartment."

My Aunt Delfina said nothing more that morning, which was the first time since that afternoon in La Coruña—the day before my mother was about to return from Paris—that she had tried to advise me on a subject on which I really didn't want any advice. This, however, was the last time. She never again alluded to a subject that was normally never mentioned; she never again alluded to that non-existent problem.

In contrast, just a few hours later, my mother would say to me, just as she had years before on our way to Burgos, "Pay attention and listen."

276

# XXX

As with the trip to Burgos, my memory grows confused, and I can't separate out what happened on that afternoon from all the ornaments and extras I've added over the years, whenever I try to remember or chance to think about it. However, unlike the morning when we picked up my father from prison, what I remember this time is not accompanied by any incidental details, I don't need additional information to find my way around it. We didn't take the car that we rarely used in the city, we didn't go to another place, and my mother didn't ask me to dress in any particular way. It didn't happen suddenly, it wasn't a surprise. I was prepared. I was expecting it, even though I didn't know precisely what form it would take.

I returned from school feeling simultaneously fearful and ready for anything, calm and frenetic, hatching unlikely stratagems and ambushes, ways of coaxing information out of my mother in imaginary dialectical duels. It was shortly after six when I entered the building, and from his niche, with its window that resembled a post-office counter, the doorman greeted me with the same old quip he made every day, and I went up the four flights of stairs, without waiting for the elevator or pausing to respond to the joke. Although the apartment was unusually dark and silent when I went in, it seemed to have shed the sour smell that had impregnated it that morning, doubtless thanks to the woman who came to clean and do the laundry in our absence. As I proceeded cautiously down the hallway, my mother came out of her bedroom, where she had been lying down or sleeping, as evidenced by the rumpled bedspread glimpsed in the brief moment I stopped to greet her, and then she followed me, as she usually did, from room to room, asking me the usual questions which I did my best to answer, telling her of my various comings and goings. I reciprocated by asking about her day, after which she abandoned her pursuit of me, and it wasn't until a while later, when she saw me pass by on my way back from the kitchen, that she called me into the living room. She was listening to a record and sitting in the armchair facing the door, just as she had the day before, lit this time by the feeble, grayish light coming in through the window behind her. She was thus half in darkness, in the shadow of the high-backed chair, where she sat with her legs up, her feet resting on the cushioned seat. Only the beige of her fitted sweater retained a little light, while her brown skirt and tights seemed to blend in with the darker brown of the upholstery. She had her hair pulled back in a bun, a style I liked but which, that evening, despite her youthful use of a pencil as hairpin, only seemed to emphasize the weary expression on her face. As I stood in the doorway, waiting uneasily for her to speak, I could, however, make out a slight smile on her lips.

"Sit down," she said.

Many years have passed since then, and my memories tend to overlap and nothing is as it was, but I can remember my mother's firm voice as clearly as I can remember the feeling of emptiness and disquiet that filled me when I heard it—like the time before an exam for which we are

278

ill prepared, when it's still so easy to think that, with a little luck, we'll scrape through, a time that ends far too soon and leaves us facing something that no longer depends on us alone, and reveals the hopes of success we had been nursing up until then to have been flimsy and unfounded. As with that morning in Burgos, my memory grows confused, as if it were some now nonexistent building whose shape we can clearly recall, but not where the windows were, or what materials it was made of, or what the decoration on the façade was like. Past and present merge into one, and it's the thoughts I had then, more than my mother's vague and only approximate words, that guide me and endure. "Sit down," I hear her say now, just as I heard her say then. "Sit down," she says in my memory, while I think what an unusual and, at the same time, foreseeable and desirable scene that is, and just as on that afternoon, I can only remember the final stages immediately before arriving here, the whole day spent at school and then my return home. She's still smiling, aware, perhaps, that, in her nervousness, she spoke somewhat brusquely, and she gestures with her hand to the other armchair, very close to hers. I see her looking rather doubtfully at the sofa, as if it had suddenly occurred to her that it might be a better backdrop for what she has in mind, but for some reason, she rejects the idea.

"Listen," she says now, just as she said then, after waiting in silence for me to make myself comfortable. She's leaning one elbow on the arm of her chair, and her other hand is resting on her bare feet. She's still smiling, and I'm not thinking, only waiting, conscious of my impatience. Her imperative was both a command and a pause she has given herself so as to put her ideas in order.

"A few things have happened lately that we need to talk about. They're not important, but they deserve an explanation."

My mother is nervous. I can tell, because, again, she stops speaking, as if she didn't know how to continue, then suddenly she straightens up and slides her legs to the floor and puts on the shoes that are lined up before her on the carpet. She bends over toward the coffee table in front of her and takes out a cigarette from the pack lying there on a pile of books, next to her lighter. She lights the cigarette and leans back, holding an ashtray in her left hand. This time she doesn't take off her shoes or sit with her legs up; she crosses one leg over the other and remains silent while she exhales the first puff of smoke, having first held it for some time in her lungs. The music stops, and for a moment, I can hear the dull buzz of the speakers, until the arm swings back to its rest and the platter stops spinning.

"We have to talk. That's the only way we can restore trust between us."

My mother speaks slowly and hesitantly, although she has now made an effort to soften the somewhat chilly tone of her first words and is smiling more broadly. She's holding the ashtray steady on the arm of her chair and gently swinging one foot as she starts to thread together the explanations that will help create the diaphanous cloth on which she will later embroider her whole argument. I haven't even opened my mouth, and she seems to prefer it like that. There's nothing I can say, she is the one doing the talking.

"I know how shocked you must have been by that meeting in the café and how confused you must have felt when I didn't even mention it to you. You must have been in quite a state if you felt driven to phone Delfina."

She is finding it difficult to begin, and perhaps that's why she's looking at me so hard, as if to make sure I'm following what she's saying. For a few seconds, she says nothing, and I think of the veiled reproach in her last words, which I know was entirely involuntary, and of the strange way she described that meeting. "That meeting in the café," she said, instead of saying what would have seemed easier, that meeting with your father. But we're only at the beginning, we have to go step by step.

"I'm not excusing myself," my mother says, after taking another puff of her cigarette, causing the coral and ivory bracelets on her wrist to slip down over her sleeve to her elbow then slip back up again once she has removed the cigarette from her lips. "I don't need to. I know you'll understand. I didn't intend to hide that from you. I wasn't sure what I was going to do, and until I'd made that decision, I didn't want to alarm you. Do you really think me capable of concealing something like that from you?"

These words are spoken without much conviction, and the question seems more rhetorical than anything else. She falls silent again, and before the silence grows too dangerously long, I utter an almost inaudible "No" to speed up the pace of her argument. "Of course not," I add more loudly. She seems grateful for this and smiles with spontaneous intensity. I can see the expression on her face, which, even in the dim light, looks terribly pale.

"He asked me for money, but you know that already. He phoned in the morning wanting to arrange a meeting."

*Again, that lack of a name*, I think. Again, that artificial void. Meanwhile, her smile has disappeared, as if, you might say, it had gone in search of the words with which to vanquish the shame and fear pursuing it.

"That's the only time I've seen him," she adds quickly, as if it were important to make this clear, because she thinks this is the main point of friction: seeing my father without telling me. She's right, although the emphasis is wrong. It isn't because of him, but because of her. *Like Paris*, I think, without being able to think beyond that because my mother continues to talk.

"At first, I refused, because we simply don't have that kind of money. But he seemed so defeated, and although he tried not to show it, I could see that he was really worried. He said it was some debt he'd run up, and that he needed to pay back the money as soon as possible."

My mother lists these facts, as if she were reciting a text learned by heart, and I tell myself it couldn't possibly have been that way. He hadn't seemed particularly defeated to me, so why did she say he was?

"I told him I couldn't give him the money, and the idea of selling the apartment only occurred to me after I'd left the café. I didn't want to tell you anything about it until I'd thought it through properly, but then you preempted that decision, and, well, what happened happened. I can quite understand why you did it. I would have done the same. My silence led you into deceit."

I hear her last words while I'm still thinking about my father, whom she doesn't refer to as my father, and about that lowness of spirits that I had failed to notice when I was watching them from my hiding place on the opposite sidewalk. I could, I realize, quite easily believe her version, but I don't really care, something stronger than her possible betrayal of me gets in the way. It isn't Paris, although Paris continues to preoccupy me and I still want to find out the truth about it, even though I'm beginning to think it's an insoluble enigma.

"I believe I made the right decision. Delfina can't understand it. She leaps to conclusions. She's too influenced by all those cocktail parties she goes to and the stuffy people she meets. Plus, she's never had children herself."

I don't know why she mentions children. I have the impression this isn't the first time she's used that lack to explain my aunt's behavior, along with those cocktail parties and that scornful reference to my uncle's world, but it's the first time I've really noticed it. She emphasized my aunt's lack of children, but given the absorbed way in which she said it, it was almost as if it came out unthinkingly, like one of those set phrases we often resort to and that, repeated ad nauseam, end up summarizing everything we think about a particular subject.

"Delfina doesn't understand. She worries about us too much and doesn't realize there are certain decisions that have to be made, even if they might prove prejudicial to us. We're all the family she has. I'm not saying she's not happy, she might well be. But she's too much alone. We represent the future for her. That's why she wants to protect us, and her desire to protect blinds her to other things."

I don't know what she means, but that doesn't matter, because I know it's purely incidental, coincidental, and I look away and see the little red light that tells me the record player is still on although it's no longer playing. "She's never had children herself," I repeat inwardly while my mother again pauses and takes a pull on her cigarette, gestures betrayed by the tip glowing more brightly in the darkness and by the bracelets that rattle their way up and down her arm.

"But you're not like Delfina. You're like me, and you know that this is a better way to do things. He paid half the cost of the apartment—well, his parents did—and it wouldn't be right to deny him what is his. It would be ignoble. After all, now that he no longer lives with us . . ."

My mother stops talking, as if she regretted what she'd said, or regretted not weighing her words more carefully. She doesn't hesitate exactly, it's merely a slight vacillation, just long enough for her to realize that to remain silent would be worse. She takes advantage of that pause to knock the ash off her cigarette and into the ashtray balanced on the arm of her chair. Despite the encroaching darkness, I can still see her pale, freckled face, from which all trace of a smile has gone. I think briefly about my father and tell myself that, this time, the void left by his unspoken name was more obvious, because, in her desire not to say it, she has had to replace it with a pronoun. She says, "He no longer lives with us and never will again, let's be quite clear about that."

She spoke quickly, as if speed would diminish the effort of saying something she finds difficult to say, and as if her difficulty might then pass unnoticed by me. That final phrase, although spoken more for her own benefit than for mine, sounded forced, unnatural. She hasn't said anything I don't already know, but hearing it put so bluntly troubles me, and I peer timidly into her eyes, two dark hollows barely visible in the steadily thickening mist covering them. The little light coming in through the window is in her favor, and noticing my look, she hurriedly adds, "I'm not saying anything you don't know, anything you haven't already guessed, I imagine."

She spoke as quickly as before, but I noticed the tension in her words, the door left open to the possible error represented by that fragile, hesitant "I imagine." I sense her overwhelming need as a mother for me to respond, and I nod affirmatively.

She doesn't sigh or smile, but conceals her relief by taking another deep pull on what little remains of her cigarette. She stubs it out with more tinkling of bracelets, then uncrosses her legs and leans forward to replace the ashtray on the table. Only after exhaling the last puff of smoke, as if she had regained her strength, does she say, "We've never spoken about it before, but we both know that's how it is. We know each other so well that sometimes we forget to speak. It's as if when we think something, we assume that the other must have thought it, too. 'I'm there in your eyes and you're there in mine,' you said to me once when you were very small. You won't remember. You were only about three. But I remember, because it sums up our relationship so very well. We live so closely, so dependent one on the other, without siblings or cousins, that we forget to speak. We're like an old married couple . . ."

My mother intends this as a joke. She's more relaxed now and is smiling again as she was at the beginning, but I can't do the same, I can't show her that I, too, have relaxed, because I can't stop thinking about what she said about cousins. She said "without siblings or cousins" without specifying whose, but it's obvious she meant mine. She has unconsciously brought my attention to the fact that I have no siblings or cousins. I have cousins on my father's side, but I never see them or have anything to do with them, and so it's as if I had no cousins. I don't have grandparents, either, and my only real aunt is Delfina, but she didn't mention that. There's something about her remark that shocks me, and even though it's perfectly true, it still troubles me to hear her say it, as if she had gotten inside my head or as if my mind were an open book. I don't know if she realizes this, but she carries on almost without stopping, "It's good that we should be so close, but it can be awkward at times and lead to misunderstandings and false impressions, because we don't talk enough, or because we assume that the other person already knows what we think because we've already thought it."

I'm listening intently despite my blushes, despite the darkness that's gradually filling the room but that my mother, so sunk in her own thoughts, appears not to notice. Nevertheless, I feel quite calm, and my thoughts emerge from somewhere deep inside, as if I were not the person sitting across from her but someone else watching and listening to myself; there's what my mother says, what the person with her is thinking, and then what I'm thinking. I know we haven't yet gotten beyond the preliminaries and that it will take a while to get to wherever it is she's heading, but my second me, the one accompanying her and whom I only see and hear in the distance, is not quite so calm and feels somewhat tense and irritated by my mother's slow way of speaking, by her feigned seriousness, by the absence of the name she still hasn't mentioned and yet is the one name that cries out to be spoken.

"I know it's my fault. I haven't deliberately kept silent, I just didn't notice that all the while time was passing, and so the two come to the same, in the end."

My mother, who raised her voice slightly as she spoke those final words, falls suddenly silent, reaches forward as if to get another cigarette, thinks better of it, and withdraws, glancing around her, as if she's only just noticed how dark the room is and is thinking that perhaps she should turn on a lamp; then she looks at me and says, "It can hardly be news to you. You knew he would never come back to live with us, even though we haven't actually spoken about it. You knew as well as I did . . ."

I see how difficult she is finding it to continue, and I understand, too, just how extreme that last statement is from the speed with which she corrects herself, "All right, not as well as me, the difference being that you were under no obligation to speak, whereas I was."

She's finding it hard to go on, I feel the care with which she weighs each word, and even though the darkness covering her face has thickened, I see her struggle and frown.

"I didn't want to think about it. I wanted to unconsciously delay something that brooked no delay, but meanwhile, time has passed and made the decision, because sometimes it's time that decides, not us."

She has gotten into her stride now, and the words emerge from her mouth fluently, but for a few moments, I stop listening and wonder what it was that brooked no delay. Her words are ambiguous. I can't understand her, just as I can no longer see her face, which is almost completely obscured now, just a pale, evanescent smudge against the earth-brown backdrop of the armchair and the mauve light of the window. What was it that brooked no delay—talking about it, or not wanting to think about it? It's true that we both knew, but *why* exactly does he no longer live with us, I ask myself. The fact that we both know doesn't explain anything, and only makes the need for an answer more urgent.

"The problem is that nothing in particular happened to prompt me to tell you. And it's difficult if there's nothing putting pressure on you to do something, if nothing happens and only time decides."

My mother falls silent and looks at me, then decides to pick up the cigarette she had previously rejected. She keeps her eyes fixed on me while she lights it and doesn't reply to what I'm thinking without saying but that she can doubtless sense. She's gone back to that same idea, that time decides. I don't know if it's true, but just supposing it is, *when* does time decide? What happens in between so that one day, we know what we didn't know or hadn't wanted to know before? There's no answer, only my mother's eyes fixed on me as she exhales the first puff of smoke and leans back again in her chair.

"Nothing happened, and yet we both know."

She's getting tangled up in her own thoughts and repeating herself, and it's that inability to progress that seems to me to confirm that she's lying, or at least not telling the whole truth. She's finding it hard to justify her inaction. This doesn't annoy me, it doesn't interrupt my thought process. I think about Paris and wish she would say something about that. Perhaps she's right and nothing did happen, but without knowing whether or not she was there with him, I can't believe it. That void will always be there. Like the void of the name she doesn't say out loud but is a constant presence. Why then and not now? Time helps only in some respects but is, by its very nature, too insubstantial, too slippery.

"There was no precise date. There was nothing that made any announcement or explanation necessary. I didn't get married again, and we haven't changed the way we live. There was no need. Just because something ends doesn't necessarily mean it has to be replaced by something else."

My mother falls silent again in order to observe the effect of her words. I hear the tinkle of her bracelets slipping down toward her elbow, and think that perhaps she's right. I myself have changed. Before, I felt no sense of oppression, and her constant, unconditional presence didn't weigh on me as it does now, but that change is invisible, it hasn't been replaced by anything, I haven't transferred my affections to someone else. I'm the only one who knows about that change. There's no outward sign of it. Or is there, I wonder, as her bracelets tinkle their way back down her arm and a cloud of smoke rises up above her head. Was the sudden attraction I felt for my father while I was pursuing him down those rainy streets, was that a real change? However momentary and troubling, was the brief sense of identity I felt as we stood there in the street, was that a way of replacing my mother, of confirming that she was no longer unique? I don't know. I think about it, and it worries me, but I have no answer. Anyway, if it was true, that still wouldn't resolve all the other unknowns or make what she's saying any more significant. It isn't that nothing has happened to make manifest or explicit what we both know without ever having spoken about it. It's that there's nothing to explain it. That's the problem: the fact that nothing has happened to justify it is not the same as the fact that nothing has happened to confirm it. It's the former that worries me, not the latter. I want to know what else there is apart from time passing. I want her to turn on the light so that I can see her vanishing face.

"Often, there's no need for any specific motive. Sometimes all it takes for us to stop liking some dish we used to like is a bout of food poisoning or indigestion, but mostly such desertions are spontaneous. Without knowing why, we suddenly can't abide a gesture made by the person we love most and that we used to find so amusing. Without knowing why, the friends we used to spend our leisure time with suddenly become boring, repetitive. I'm not saying this always happens, but often it's the simple passage of time that distances us from them."

My mother stops talking again, as if she didn't know how to go on, just at the moment when a tiny fragment of ash falls from her cigarette. I watch it glow in the air and burn out before it touches her skirt, and at the same time, I hear the tinkle of her bracelets as her free hand hurriedly brushes the potential danger away, and I feel, as if I could actually hear it, the flow of her thoughts choosing the words she's about to say.

"Maybe something like that has happened to us. Not only has no external factor urged us to speak about it, there weren't really any clear reasons to do so. Why then and not now?"

My mother says exactly what I said to myself a few minutes before, and hearing those words on her lips startles me and makes me feel at even more of a disadvantage. It's the second or third time that she's responded to something I was thinking, and this, I tell myself, is proof that she has been building up to this conversation for a long time. It can't be mere chance, she's clearly thought about it a lot, she's tried to have all the loose ends tied up before sitting down to talk to me. That's why I'm listening to her and not believing her, but not feeling irritated, either. I'm aware only of my own incredulity, and I suddenly seem to understand why she doesn't turn on the light, why she doesn't even mention doing so. We're sitting here in the near-darkness, and that's not normal. She can see me better than I can see her, because she has the fading glow of evening in her favor, but it's still not normal *not* to do something about that. She should want there to be light, she should get up and turn on the lamp. She doesn't, because she feels insecure, she fears that her reasons aren't convincing me. She's nervous; I can see what her strategy is, and beneath it, I can see what she's only thinking but not saying, the definitive void left by the person we don't name, even though he's there and he's the explanation for everything.

"I don't know why. I didn't set any limit—this far and no further. He didn't do anything he hadn't done before, and I didn't go against my own feelings as the result of some premeditated decision. I didn't get up one morning thinking he'd gone too far and that, purely as a matter of survival, I should stop allowing things to continue as they were."

*So why keep talking about it*, I wonder as I study the shadowy shape of her head, her hair pulled back, perfectly silhouetted against the darkness. Why not go straight to the thing she doesn't want to tell me about? Why linger for so long over what didn't happen? I'm listening to her and not believing her, because I don't know what I prefer, or what would best alleviate the suffocating effect of those unworldly words focused entirely on me. I'm listening to her and not believing her, because it pains me to not believe her and I prefer to regret being unfair to her to not having that as an option. I realize that I've stopped listening, and it's then that her voice, which was only a murmur, fades for a few seconds, giving her time to think about what she has said or perhaps to observe me, taking advantage of the darkness she has chosen. I can't help thinking that it's Paris she's talking about without talking about it. Paris lies behind it all. It doesn't matter if they were never there together and that it wasn't Paris that separated them. The point is that she knows I'm thinking about Paris, that I'm plagued by uncertainty, and still she doesn't mention it. She's not going to unless I do, and I have no proof of anything. I'm not sure. I'm in a constant state of doubt. As I was a moment ago. As I am right now, not knowing if she really does know that I'm thinking about Paris.

"I can't even say for sure that I was the only one who felt like that. Here I am trying to explain when or how I became aware that we would never live together again, when maybe he was the one who decided. He probably preempted any decision I might have made and has continued to act accordingly. Not that it makes much difference."

I hear the unspoken bitterness in those last words, the first time I've heard her speak reproachfully of my father in my presence, and I'm not surprised. I consider it further confirmation of the definitive nature of this conversation, which will be the last of its kind once it's over, there will be no others; whatever we do or whatever we become in the future will be built on what she tells me today, whatever she doesn't tell me today, she will never tell me, because it would be suicidal to recant. I would never believe her again. This moment is too serious. She remains silent and, with a resolute movement, stubs out her cigarette and places the ashtray on the table while I ponder her words and, thanks to the pause, discover something I hadn't noticed. Up until now, she has spoken in the first person, taking it as read that she was responsible for the breakup; she hadn't previously left open the possibility that the breakup was initiated by him, and her silence on the matter betrays her, allows for such a possibility to exist. Otherwise, she would have been vaguer.

"But whether or not he did preempt my decision, the truth is that he never did anything to disillusion me, because I never had any illusions about him. Delfina thinks I did, because she can't imagine any more powerful mandate than that of our instinct telling us not to take any risks in life that might lead to disaster. That's the way she is, but not me. I knowingly chose that path; I knew all the obstacles awaiting me. It didn't occur to me to think there might be no hope, because I knew from the start that there wasn't. It's just that everything has an end, and I suppose I've reached that end, but I've reached it without anything having happened that required it to end. That's how it usually is. We may not always want to accept the fact, but we're in constant motion. No one can guarantee anyone their unconditional love. Only the love between parents and their children is unconditional, and perhaps not even then. We mothers are very egotistical and would like to think that love between mother and child is unconditional, but it isn't. We are clear proof that nothing lasts. There is no loyalty like that of a mother's loyalty to her child, and yet all mothers know there will come a time when that child will break free and create his or her own bonds. However, that certainty, which I accept, that future lack of reciprocity, neither erases nor diminishes a mother's love. It's the same with other feelings. We don't need our love to be requited in order to love someone else, just as we don't need someone else to despise or hate us in order to despise or hate them. Often we choose the object of our affection without considering whether that person will feel the same, and often our idea of that person is very different from his idea of himself or his expectations of life or of us."

My mother sets out her arguments in the safety of the surrounding darkness, and every word she says moves her a little further away from the city that, for me, sums up the whole situation. The intentions behind her words become increasingly enigmatic, and I feel myself growing increasingly insubstantial and adrift, however hard I try to hang on to what I want to know, to the reason why we're here together. I find myself letting go of that completely. My mother's very autonomy troubles and frightens me, as does the goal toward which her endless explanations are taking us, explanations I'm sure now she has been working on ever since the argument with my aunt twenty-four hours ago and that were already there in what she said about herself and in the complaints, dredged up from the past, that she continued to talk about after I entered the room. Her words trouble me, because they are a trap and there is no way out of them, they create yet another circle in our very singular relationship.

"People can be absolutely open about themselves and yet we still insist on seeing them differently, investing all our hope in someone who never offered us hope, who wanted something quite different. Is it reasonable, then, when our blindness ends and we see reality for what it is, that we should blame that person, who probably never even intended to be what we wanted him to be? I don't think so."

My mother said this more to herself than for me to hear, and meanwhile, I'm still thinking about Paris and trying to cling to that name in order to dilute the fear beginning to invade me, the fear that, even though she may be lying now, later on, she'll tell the truth, and that truth might set in motion something far worse than the present lie. For a moment, she stays silent, as if she had gotten lost, then she says, "I say this because I can't be sure that wasn't the case with us. It's just pointless speculation. Perhaps he's just as he was when I first met him and perhaps not. I'm the least qualified person to know. I'm inclined to think that the problem is that he's always been two people at once, and that makes life impossible. It's possible for a few years, but later on, life forces you to make a choice, and then it's not possible at all. I don't know, that's just an idea. I also can't be sure that I'm not the one who changed. But we're probably just the same as we were then, which doesn't mean that, right from the start, he didn't love me or that I got ahold of completely the wrong end of the stick. You can't understand, because you've just been a witness, a bystander. Ever since you can remember, you've experienced the past through my eyes. The only thing you know about that past is what I've told you, and you know little about his present. But I know that he loved me. I'm sure of that. He may not have shown it in the way Delfina or I would have liked, but he did love me. Who knows, he may still love me. Abandoning someone or being disloyal to them isn't necessarily a sign that you don't care. Neither is lying to or deceiving them. One often lies to and deceives the person one loves most in order to preserve their love, or to protect them. Whatever he may or may not have done over the years is no indication of his lack of commitment or of his feelings not being genuine. And me saying now that it's all over doesn't mean that I regret the past, that I wouldn't do the same again. The things I tolerated or that satisfied me yesterday might not seem satisfactory or tolerable now, but that doesn't cancel out the past, when they *did* seem satisfactory and tolerable. Besides, I don't think he expects anything else. If he had expected anything, it would have been for me to throw in the towel sooner. I'm sure that he's been living as if on borrowed time. We've known each other for so long. He always knew how far he could go, and I always knew what I could realistically expect. He drove me to despair, drove me crazy sometimes, but that doesn't change anything. For me, he's like a brother, and brothers can be disappointing and exhausting, but you still love them, even though you'd rather keep them at arm's length."

My mother shifts in her armchair, but I can barely see her now. I can just make out the shape of her body against the back of the chair, hear the tinkle of her bracelets and see the beige blur of her jersey as she bends forward over the table to take another cigarette. The flame from her lighter briefly illuminates her serious, concentrated face, her cheeks sucked in by the movement of her lips drawing in the smoke, and then it's gone, to be replaced by the elusive firefly of her cigarette tip retreating once more to the armchair, which again grows wrinkled and mutable, not smooth and still, against the greenish, mauvish blue of the window behind her. It must be about half past seven, no later than that; we haven't even been here for an hour yet, but the brisk winter night has taken over unopposed, and the room lies now in almost total darkness, relieved only by the faint glow of the evening that was and by the dim lights from the building across the street. "One often lies to and deceives the person one loves most in order to preserve their love, or to protect them." While my mother maintains a smoke-filled silence, I think about those words, which, if I thought her capable of such imprudence, it would seem she said deliberately. The two reasons she gives are quite different, and she didn't make that distinction by chance, even though her words weren't specifically aimed at me. The protecting lie is the one you admit to when there's no longer any need to protect, and the lie intended to preserve love is the one you never reveal. I think this reluctantly and wonder how much my mother will keep silent about until the end of her days and how much she is holding back until the time comes for it to be told. And when the smoke-filled silence continues, I think about what she said about love between siblings, which was even less likely to have been aimed at me, but which, nonetheless, stirs and touches me. Can you really feel that someone is your brother even if he isn't? Will I ever feel that, even though I won't know how to identify the feeling because I have no brothers and never will? These two questions burst into my consciousness, bringing with them the echo of things not experienced and possibly never to be experienced, but they fade out and disappear equally quickly, because they are merely a pointless diversion from the disquiet roused in me by my mother's words, her unusual loquacity, the certainty that nothing will change when she stops talking, apart, perhaps, from there being a still stronger bond between us, the noose drawn still tighter, the noose that smarts and tugs even though it's for my own good and even though it is far from her intention to cause me pain. Where exactly is she going? What building is she going to erect on the foundations she is laying down?

"None of this makes any sense, so don't even try to make sense of it. I'm telling you now so that you can know what my life has been like, so that you won't think that I'm acting out of spite. I don't expect anyone to understand my reasons for doing what I did. Seen from the outside, it does seem crazy, the proof being that I'm talking about it now, three whole years after he left. I'm talking to you about it now in order to explain my silence, not so that you'll necessarily understand what motivated that silence. I've never harbored any real hopes in all these years. I don't even know when I actually stopped hoping altogether, but when I did, be assured that it in no way changed my feelings. I have lived very happily with you, and the years have simply passed, that's all. To be perfectly honest, I didn't even give it a thought."

What fills my mind more and more is my mother's grave, determined attitude, her slow, almost menacing way of drawing out the thread. It's the certainty of her presence there before me, quiet and alert, the certainty that no one will come to rescue us, no one will open the front door and interrupt us, *that's* what I'm thinking about, not her actual words but this chosen darkness that wraps about us and fills me with a kind of tremulous unease, while everything around me has ceased for the moment to exist and my mother continues to speak only to me.

"Listen. I'm not denying what happened, I wouldn't dare. I know that what I did must seem strange. I know that the circumstances in which you've grown up have been, to say the least, unusual. I know that much of what happened was due to irresponsibility on my part. What I want you to understand is that, if I *have* been irresponsible, I've been irresponsible with you, but not with myself, because you didn't know the situation, and there's no reason why you would have made the same decisions I did. I've tried to be honest, and I've tried to draw us closer together by allowing you to judge for yourself, but I failed to take into account that you weren't yet a grownup and that I was giving you a distorted view of life by allowing you to think something was normal when it was perhaps just a product of my way of being. It was shameful of me to say to you, as I did just now, that he won't ever come back to live with us, and that, even though you and I hadn't talked about it, you knew. You did know, but the problem is that you should have found out directly from me, not through this web of silences I've been weaving."

Perhaps because she's talking to herself, not to me, and is telling herself things she has never told herself before, my mother's voice sounds sad and somewhat somber and it occurs to me again to think that no one is going to come and rescue us and that what she says now will remain said forever. No one will contradict her or give me a different version, we will have to live forever with what she tells me now. The two of us together forever, as it has been for as long as I can remember, despite that "he" whom she still refuses to name outright. The two of us together forever, along with whatever she may tell me now and whatever the future may bring.

"It's up to me if I accept how things evolved. It's up to me if I choose to behave like a madwoman, to seek satisfactions where there are none to be had, to decide to let time decide for me, but I don't have the right to impose that same passivity on you. There's no reason why you should forgive what I forgive. I've encouraged you to consider as normal what was only normal for me, never once stopping to consider that time was passing and that you would wake up one day. I'm not infallible, and I was wrong. I didn't realize how wrong until Delfina phoned me and told me that you had seen us. The fact that you said nothing about it to me demonstrates that you distrusted me in some way, that you had begun to be dissatisfied with the order imposed by your mother. And I don't blame you."

My mother keeps going over the same ground and continues to apologize for a mistake I don't even care about, because it seems so tiny and insignificant in comparison with the great tide washing over me as I suddenly succumb to the thought that perhaps taking the blame for something is worse and less considerate than the supposed error that the admission of guilt is intended to make good, that perhaps it's more harmful to recant and take responsibility for the silence than to allow that silence to stubbornly persist. That's what I keep telling myself over and over while she continues to talk and while she stubs out her last cigarette and bends over to put the ashtray down on the table. The lie that preserves is the one that remains unconfessed, and a stronger, more potent truth is all that's needed for a suspicion to be erased and for everything to carry on as before. No one will come in through the front door, and the lights from our respective bedrooms will be the only ones on in our apartment tonight. Order will be restored, along with our trust in each other.

"Why did I go to that café and why am I going to sell the apartment? I've been talking for a while now, but I've just been going around and around in circles. I went there because I couldn't not go, because I'm sentimental, and even though I don't think he deserves it, it still touches and hurts me that he should be in trouble. You don't want bad things to happen to someone who has been part of your life, you can't deny him a helping hand if you're in a position to hold one out to him. Besides, selling the apartment is an opportunity to cut all ties. I'm not denying him my help, but I'm making sure it's the last time. I don't trust myself, and so I need all links between us to dissolve, because I just find it absurd and irrational, this readiness of mine to take him back. I don't want him back, and I have no intention of starting all over with him again."

My mother talks as if she were listing a series of imaginary offences, talking more to herself than to me, with a degree of ill-disguised anger and disdain, and this confirms to me that she's not being honest, that there is always an explanation for any decision we make, and it isn't only time that decides. While I'm listening to her and thinking about her, I really don't care if that's the case and am merely trying hard to neutralize myself against the larger truth that I can sense approaching, so that it won't affect me too deeply and thus lose its power when it does arrive; I'm trying hard not to listen to her, in order to avoid meekly slipping my head into the noose of her frankness.

"I'm not condemning him, what drove me away from him wasn't him being in prison or the idea that he was a criminal. I could accept that. What I couldn't accept was his sheer egotism. Egotists don't usually realize that they're egotists, and that somehow reconciles you to them. Since their egotism usually grows up in the shadow of some old trauma, you forgive them easily. You think they feel unprotected and alone or that they behave egotistically because they see you, who love them, as strong and powerful. That's why the love you feel for them rarely dies. It's a tyranny, a trap. The truth is that it's best to keep them at a distance, because otherwise, they'll entangle you in a long chain of discontents, and they'll feel and make you feel, too, that every complaint you make, every grievance, and every attempt to get them to think about what they're doing is just another attack that only aggravates the deep, hidden pain they carry inside them. You can't reason with them, they're blind."

I don't know where my mother is going. Where *is* she going, I ask as her words rise and dissolve. Nothing of what she says makes sense. It doesn't matter that she speaks and corrects herself, or that her thoughts coincide with mine, or that they are fair and acceptable, because she will never be an egotist, and there will never be any deprivations or blunders for which I will need to demand satisfaction. Nothing will change, and her deceit, if it existed, will solve nothing, because it will represent not a break but a parenthesis, and then some explanation will be found or some larger truth will cover it up. No deceits and no concealments, just her and me in this room, just her and me and her words that don't fade but avail themselves of the space left by my thoughts, which come slowly and cowardly because I fear the noose I can feel hovering over my head.

"It's not his fault. After all, the way we behave always has its roots in childhood, and that's especially so in his case. We are slaves all our lives to what happened in our early years, and the circumstances in which we spent our childhood leave a very deep mark. The worst thing that can happen to anyone is to remain enslaved to the past, to become obsessed with the evil done to them by others, because often the worst evil was done by the person who loved them most. Someone who was rich, or was brought up to think he was rich, will resent it when, years later, he goes bankrupt or realizes that he wasn't rich at all, and will think that other people owe him something. The death of a father or mother can mess you up for the rest of your life. Sometimes it doesn't even take a trauma. We are so malleable as children, and our parents' view of life puts down such deep roots and dominates our way of feeling and thinking. That can be very harmful, and parents need to take great care to ensure that their children don't inherit qualities or views that are already a burden to them."

My mother's words persist and seem to speak in veiled terms of her and me, a suspicion I find distressing. I don't want any parallelisms, I don't want her to know what I'm thinking or for her to need only look at me to guess my state of mind, I don't want to discover in her the child she once was and never will be again, nor do I want that child to resemble me. Her words accelerate and grow tangled, and I can only stop them by forcing my thoughts to move more slowly, pausing at random over certain phrases, fixing on bits and pieces that I repeat and preserve with the intention of building a wall to block out the conclusion I can see approaching. There is, however, no escape. My mother isn't going to stop, and every word she says, even though I try not to hear it, will be further proof of her univocal dedication to me, of my infuriating, tyrannical onliness.

"It's absurd. Life deals us quite enough blows as it is without exposing us to still more. When we're growing up, for example, there's a moment when the whole solid world we've been living in so snugly suddenly collapses around our ears, and it seems to us a vile trick. That's when we realize that time is passing and that we have almost no chance of putting things right. We feel deceived and long for an innocence we will never recover. A lot of people never get over it and let life slip by, thinking that they're the only people who've been through that same experience. But we have to get over it, because we don't have to look very far to keep finding reasons to lose heart."

There's no escape, no chance to protest or rebel. There's nothing to be done.

"I've tried to leave you free, tried to do everything as naturally as possible, for you to have all the necessary information so that you could judge for yourself and so that there would be no duplicity, no shadowy areas between us. But there are things that are beyond my control and that I haven't perhaps really kept a grip on. If that's so, then you've got to be strong and just think of yourself. I'm not always going to be here . . ."

There's no escape. None.

"I can put up with a lot. I know what it's like to have the world fall in on you and to feel that life isn't as sweet and innocuous as you had been led to believe. I've had my share of suffering, too, but I've been through it and left it behind me, and above all, I haven't burdened other people with my problems . . ."

There's no escape. None. Only time and death and forgetting and any children I myself might have.

"Selling the apartment, for example. Delfina is right when she says that it's your inheritance, that I should think about you before I sell it, because you haven't had a normal father who's been with you every day, and the apartment would be a way of compensating you. But Delfina doesn't know, and neither do you, that there are reasons why it has to be like that. There are reasons for my silence, reasons I haven't told you about before . . ."

There's no escape. None. My mother's words rise up and cut the air, trying to merge, and her melodious voice wraps around me and speaks of herself alone, and no longer of me or of her and me together. "Listen, everything you heard yesterday is true. We've never spoken about it, but it's true. I didn't tell you, because I felt the time wasn't right. That's why I kept silent, that's why I hesitated." *This is it*, I think. *This is the mouth of the deep hole. My mother is going to climb down into that hole and reveal everything she has never told me, and everything is going to end in order to begin again.* "There are things you don't know," "Delfina is right," "Everything we talked about yesterday is true." *There it is. The mouth of the black hole. It wasn't pure chance. It couldn't be. She spoke so that I would hear her, so that we could talk today. That's where we're heading.* "Listen. I haven't been a poor, unfortunate wretch, and I don't regret anything. I was very young when I met him. You know that, because I've told you. What you don't know, and what you heard yesterday for the first time, is that I left home and ran away with him. And that's true. I fled and said nothing to my father or Delfina. But that has nothing to do with my life since then. That doesn't explain his behavior or mine. I ran away with him because it was clear that I was going to at some point. Maybe I could

304

have done it differently, but I would have left eventually. The way Delfina would have liked me to have done, perhaps, taking all the appropriate steps and securing the blessing of my family, but I would have left. I was in love. I loved him. Running away with him just precipitated matters, that's all." My mother is speaking hesitantly and without pause. I'm listening, I know what she's saying, but I try to focus only on snippets of it. I don't want to listen. I prefer silence to premonitions and honesty; I prefer deceit to kindness and having our bedroom doors open at night, with the light from one room illuminating the other. *Paris*, I think. "We all have sorrows hidden away in our hearts, and we all make mistakes that are misunderstood or discredit us in other people's eyes. But even if they're reprehensible and harmful, they don't discredit us forever. They might not even be mistakes. They happen as almost everything in life happens, inexplicably and unstoppably." Everything is happening and not happening, everything is moving and not moving, and with no cigarettes to mark the rhythm, with the haste that grips us when, after a long and difficult conversation, we can see that the end is in sight, my mother's words tremble before me and make me dizzy. "Even we ourselves don't understand much of what we do and feel. It's likely that our deepest feelings, the ones that make us who we are, that make us behave as we behave, cannot be explained, because they're not born of reasons or real decisions. They are orders that rise up from our subconscious and there's no point trying to justify them. They happen, and the best thing we can do is to accept them as they are, and not think about them, so that they don't entangle us, and not talk about them, unless they affect someone else." I don't want to listen and I'm not going to. "Listen," says my mother. "Pay attention and listen," she says again, as if she were saying pay attention and listen to what I'm going to say but don't say and which is drawing closer all the time, pay attention and listen to the empty space left by that name I'm concealing and not saying. There's no escape and no end. There will be no more conversations after this and no protests on my part. It will be back to the same, identical life, every day and every weekend the same, the light from her open bedroom door illuminating mine. It will all be as it was before, repeated over again. Always the same, always the same debt and the same devotion. "Pay attention and listen." My mother's reasons superimpose themselves one on the other, circling around the conclusion that never arrives because she doesn't dare allow it to, even though it's close and I don't want to listen or pay attention because, if I did as she asks, I would have to agree with her and she would seem admirable and pitiable and worthy of my compassion for her mistake, for her failure not to realize that everything hurts and that everything repeats itself, that neither her words nor her understanding will save her, and nor, of course, will they save me. *Often the people who love you most are the ones who hurt you most. Our needs do not have to be those of the people who live with us and for whom we are responsible. We are malleable. Childhood keeps us in chains,* I think and repeat so as not to have to pay attention or listen, so that what she's saying now does not touch me, and so that I won't remember it. It's all circles and more circles. It's all explanations for things that have no explanation, that happen and can't be avoided, like me sitting here in the dark listening, like having no brothers or sisters, like her bedroom door standing open at night, and her never-failing devotion to me. I think, because it distracts me and allows me to escape from her indecision and her nervousness, which is increasingly evident in the thickening silences, in the cigarettes she doesn't smoke but would like to if it weren't for the fact that the end is approaching and she wants to remain focused and unfettered. I think, and I escape, and I remember, and I refuse to recognize the trace left by the girl who was and will never be again, there in the thick, anachronistic darkness that dilutes and melds us together and that my mother clearly wanted, because she doesn't mention it and doesn't get up to turn on the light. I think, and I remember, and I feel the future approaching, along with the omens telling me that life afterward will continue just the same as it always has. I think, and escape, and remember, but above all, I try not to hear what she's saying, although sometimes I do and I can't always prevent a particular phrase seizing hold of me and not letting go. Like this one now: "It had to happen at some point. It's hard, but I couldn't allow your dissatisfaction and your distrust of me to continue to grow as it has over the last few days. I couldn't allow you to continue to blame him when, if he's guilty of anything, it's of hurting me, not you." Or like this: "It's necessary. I have to do it even though there's a risk you won't understand. No, you will. You will understand, because you know that it would be worse if I didn't tell you." Or this question addressed to herself: "How can I keep silent, how can I continue to feed your incomprehension or your feelings of disaffection when it's in my power to stop that?" Or this, later on: "I would hurt you, and you would live forever with that shadow, the shadow of someone who didn't have the joy of seeing you grow up." My mother circles and circles, each sentence is a step forward, then she stops and ponders that sentence more deeply; these are the circles and repetitions that allow what we have said to settle before we take the next step, the same tactic she used on that trip to Burgos. My mother talks and talks, and for a few minutes, I fool myself into thinking that she will never finish, that she will go on and on and never reach her goal, that tomorrow will come and we'll still be here and nothing will have happened. *She won't, she can't*, I think, to distract myself from the knowledge that she will, in fact, because we need to start all over and this is what she wants. *She won't. She can't*, I repeat, once again deceiving myself as a silence falls, the silence that signals the beginning of the end, and I'm still thinking about Paris and thinking *She won't, she can't*, even though at that moment she will and she can and I only manage to say to myself *No, no, no* before she opens her mouth, which appeared to be closed even though she was speaking, and says it slowly, and calmly. A curve in the road, a particularly tight bend. She opened her mouth, and she said it, and I heard it. She has gone down to the bottom of the hole, and I've heard what she said, and her words have remained stuck in my head, hanging there, like a familiar lamp we know is there, above our heads, because we bought it and took real pleasure in it for a few days, but that we no longer look at, because it's always there and we see it without really seeing it. Her words hang in the air, and my mother falls silent, and I don't speak or think, and she's looking at me, and I'm looking at her, and thinking about what she has just said, but I don't rationalize it or accept it, and it doesn't worry me, because it's as if I still haven't heard or still don't know. *That's it*, I tell myself, but still I don't react or get up from the armchair in which I've been sitting for about two hours without moving, so close to my mother, who, sitting in that chair obscuring the window, *has* moved occasionally, leaning forward to pick up and light her cigarettes. *That's it, she's said it*, I tell myself. And again: *That's it, she's said it*. And again: *That's it, she's said it.* Four times I do this, until my mother leans across the silence and touches my arm and I think that she has, at last, finished, and that we can, at last, get up. These are cold, inauthentic thoughts, I know, strategies I resort to in order not to go too deep into the meaning of what she has revealed, while she, who has been silently watching me and caressing my arm, starts talking again, this time more melodiously and inquisitively, asking for my response to a question I haven't heard. I don't answer, and she continues talking, more hesitantly and uncertainly than before, sometimes trying to sound harsh and authoritarian and pretending to put on a cool, calm front about what she has told me and the next moment, succumbing to curiosity and misgiving about my response that still hasn't come, and understanding perfectly well why I don't speak. She talks and talks and once again circles around what she has told me, involving me, explaining again, her hand still on my arm, although she has left her chair now and is crouching on the rug in order to be closer to me and see what she couldn't see from her chair because the light is not in her favor now. My mother talks and talks until gradually the words grow fewer and she no longer expects any response from me. My mother talks and talks until she no longer has anything to add, and she squeezes my arm and caresses it with her thumb, gradually bringing her speech to a close, because there are no more reasons to give, no new points of view with which to justify what she has revealed to me. She has said everything, and she comes out now only with the occasional sentence, and silence slowly begins to impose itself, until her words cease and she is just watching me and waiting for my reaction, her hand making that painful, monotonous caress. I don't know how much time passes after that, but in my self-absorption, my serene but artificial not-thinking and not-yet-speaking, it seems like a very long time. Until after a while, a while in which nothing happens, just her crouching there on the floor and her thumb stroking my wrist, she gets slowly to her feet, complaining that her legs have gone to sleep, and she kisses me and, standing up now, takes the two steps that will carry her to the door and the light switch. And only then, when my mother has turned on the ceiling lamp, which I suddenly wouldn't be able to describe without looking at it, and the living room lights up and I see the white walls as if they were freshly painted, and I see her in her beige sweater, I see the bun on the top of her head and the bracelets over her tight sleeve, only then can I reproduce in my mind what she said minutes before and which I have been putting off while she talked on and on trying to explain what can't be explained: *He isn't your father*, I say to myself. *We have the same father*. And then everything ends and begins again.

# XXXI

More than fifteen years have passed since that evening, and I'm well over twice the age I was then, but any attempt to explain the feeling of blank astonishment that filled me when I repeated to myself the words that, for several minutes after my mother had spoken them, I hadn't wanted to hear would be poor and inexact. My immediate reaction is of no significance, and no real notion of what I felt could reasonably be extracted from it, because the way we react to those things that touch us most deeply is often not a reflection of our inner feelings but born of an effort to act in accordance with the blow received. If it were up to us, we would say nothing, we would laugh hysterically or give a sigh of relief, and yet we force ourselves to act as we think we should and to shout and slam doors. I was dumbstruck, paralyzed, plunged into a terrible clamor of conflicting feelings, but more than apprehension at the magnitude of what had been revealed or embarrassment at never having once imagined anything remotely similar, what I found most difficult was not knowing what attitude to adopt. My mother was still watching me and would have forgiven anything I did, and it was that waiting and that ready acceptance of hers that drove me to proceed according to her expectations, that and the sudden increase in the feelings of oppression and claustrophobia I'd experienced throughout the conversation.

Time has passed and nothing is as it was, but it's also true that I don't remember feeling then that the world had fallen in on me. I remember feeling confused and afraid, but not the sense of tragedy or drama one might expect. In a way, it's as if the tension that had accumulated while my mother was speaking had prepared me for it. Having drawn me into her circular discourse, she had fixed me with a look of such yearning, and just at the point when I was capable of taking in the gravity of what she had confided in me, I, in turn, looked at her, and I saw that she seemed bowed and somewhat broken despite her efforts to remain apparently unshaken and in control, and then, after studying her hard and feeling exhausted by the suffocating lack of air and space, I got up without saying a word and went to my bedroom, with her following me; I hurriedly pulled on some shoes and, picking up my red parka, which suddenly felt inappropriate and rather childish, I headed for the front door, while my mother, rather unconvincingly and more in order to do what was expected of her than out of any real desire to stop me, issued a series of questions and warnings: "What are you going to do?"; "Are you crazy?"; "Don't be absurd"; "Where on earth are you going at this hour?" I didn't respond, I didn't say a word, and just before I reached the door, I wondered whether I should venture into the room formerly belonging to the person whom I no longer knew whether or not to call "father" and replace my parka with the pearl-gray jacket abandoned there when he left and that, encouraged by my mother, I had begun wearing from time to time on special occasions, but I didn't dare do it and didn't want to delay leaving. Now, from this distance in time, I think I would have come to regret taking the jacket, a gesture that might have been misinterpreted by her, and all I wanted then was to get away from there and to be alone, and certainly not to emphasize her influence on me by bearing away with me the symbol of a union I wanted desperately to shake off.

I wasn't thinking, I couldn't. My head was spinning before I got into the elevator and pressed the down button, and it continued to spin as I saw my mother's drawn, anxious face disappear from view. It was just after half past eight when, from the wood-and-glass cabin transporting me downward, I heard the apartment door close up above, and as my descent grew faster, I felt neither gratitude nor relief that she had allowed me to leave, nor any resentment, either, as might have been the case in different circumstances, because she had given me no reason to behave in a surly manner, to shout and slam doors, or to cry my eyes out. As I struggled to recover from the shock, I had time to reflect, and yet I didn't think about the strange, dark nature of what I'd just been told, I didn't wallow in feelings of either pity or horror. Once I reached the ground floor, I held open the green, wooden door at the entrance of the building for the doorman, who was just putting out the trash, followed him outside, and then set off aimlessly down the sidewalk peopled with shadows hurrying past, their eyes bright with the promise of the night to come. I wasn't thinking, I couldn't. Nothing seemed to matter any more, and I didn't even try to take any precarious consolation in the thought that Paris no longer mattered since my mother had continued to exonerate my father even after her performance was over and I knew everything, and this was palpable proof that I had never really counted—that everything she might have done ever since I could remember, her every sacrifice, her patient waiting, had been not for my sake, but for hers. Right from the very start, I had been excluded from their relationship, there had never been a triangle, just two parallel lines with my mother in the middle, and knowing this did not lighten my load one bit. He and I represented two different things. I would still occupy the place I had always occupied, there was no escape, no betrayal that could outlast hope; I was the one to whom my mother had to answer, I was the one from whom she concealed things in order to protect me when it seemed advisable to say nothing, and I was the one to whom she explained things when common sense required her to. Nothing mattered and everything was useless, because everything had ended and begun all over again. Our singularity had grown more singular, my onliness more obvious and more irreversible than ever.

I wished I could disappear. I wished time would pass more quickly. I wished Delfina lived in Madrid or that I had a father or an older brother I could turn to. I wished I could erase the last few days, I wished I didn't have to go home to face my mother's kindly, inquisitive gaze. I wished I didn't admire her courage in telling me something that others would have kept to themselves. I wished she were angry and vengeful toward a person who didn't need her protection, that she were less calm and collected and scrupulous when she had lied about and, so I thought, concealed from me the final insult he had inflicted on her. I wished I could free myself from the feeling that it didn't matter what she did, and from my awareness of the abyss into which I was being dragged by her honesty and integrity, because my admiration and my dependence would grow in parallel with the distaste and anxiety aroused in me by my own inability to rebel. I wished she were selfish and insensitive, and that I didn't know about her weakness and her past sorrows. I wished many things, but all of them were impossible and would never happen, because my mother would not change and I could never put my reproaches into words. I wasn't thinking, I couldn't. I needed to find something safe to hold on to, something not passed down through the generations, not inherited, and so I set off aimlessly down the street, fleeing from the pressures pursuing me. I wasn't thinking, I couldn't, because I didn't want to surrender one inch more of my body to the new noose she had thrown around me, and what I regretted most was not my failure to realize this while there was still time to escape. What I regretted most was having insisted on finding out rather than doing nothing, having enquired too closely rather than simply forgetting all about it. I would rather she had not spoken to me, I would have preferred not to know, to go back to the situation before my phone call to La Coruña, but it was too late. The situation was the same, nothing had changed, and it was best to simply accept that.

I walked aimlessly, pursued by my mother's flawless image, until I came to a subway station and went down the steps, eager to hide, to conceal the anguish overwhelming me, to silence the uproar beginning inside me and gradually closing in around me, propelling me toward the sounds of battle, silencing my desire to surrender and accept. I had no idea where I was going. I bought my ticket, waited in the musty passageway beneath the lugubrious yellow neon lights for the first train to appear, then went down to the platform and, for at least an hour, traveled back and forth, choosing at random where to get on and off, making unnecessary transfers, and going up and down the same line several times. For at least an hour, I was alone, accompanied only by the clickety-clack of the various carriages I traveled in, by the dull whistle after every stop, by the few passengers who sat silhouetted in their seats like ghosts with neither past nor future, like specters belatedly summoned to a séance in which they were not called upon to participate. I managed to clear my head of all trace of thought and, cut off from everything, let myself be lulled by the swaying of the train, which plunged me into the tormented oblivion in which children must find themselves immersed just moments before they succumb to the hypnotic rocking of the cradle. Like them, I knew that sooner or later, the movement would stop and the thing I was struggling to avoid would engulf me like a particularly heavy sleep. Like them, I simultaneously resisted and longed for it, but my strength was as nothing compared to the far greater potency of the thick fog luring me on, compared to the fear of unreservedly facing up to the darkness.

I don't know when the idea occurred to me, I don't know what secret impulse drove me to it, perhaps some troubled attempt to cling to the past, some misplaced nostalgia for something I didn't know how to value when it was still mine and that I was obsessively trying to hang on to once I saw that I'd lost it, or perhaps, on the contrary, it was a theatrical gesture of farewell to something I didn't particularly mind leaving behind. I only know that I found myself once more on the Calle Bravo Murillo, after hurriedly leaving the train when I saw the name of the station, and that suddenly everything seemed to come together, everything was coherent and crystal clear, everything was consistent and had a reason for being. There was no break, no rupture with what had happened, each piece of my memory fitted perfectly with the next, seamlessly linked. There was no reason why I should be surprised, there was no cause for it, the fault was mine. How had I not realized, how had I never suspected, how had I not dealt better with my suspicions, how had I so misinterpreted my mother's sorrow and sadness, fragility and vulnerability, her dependence on him? It was my fault entirely, I was the one who had been blind, I was the one who had been mistaken and wasted so much time.

It was not far to walk, or so it seems to me now. I emerged from a different station entrance than I had gone into a few days before, but it didn't take me long to orientate myself in that almost traffic-free street, with its troubling resemblance to an empty movie set, like a shopping mall when all the shops have closed and the only evidence of the hustle and bustle that had filled it just hours before is a scattering of a few fast-fading bars. It never occurred to me that the bar might be closed. I didn't hesitate or falter as I had on my previous visit. I was excited and nervous. I felt embarrassed by my earlier naïveté, like a gullible witness conned into fabricating a false alibi, and I was gripped by an uncontrollable longing for revenge. I wanted redress. Even at this late stage, I wanted more than just a walk-on part in this play and would have liked to be given unlimited power to manipulate and alter the plot and my own role in it. I was walking quickly, and every step I took inflamed and bewildered me still more, driving me into the labyrinth of my urgent need for oblivion. I had no plans, I didn't know what I would do when I arrived at the bar, but that fact did nothing to check my unruly desire to build a wall of activity around myself that would temporarily protect me from what had just been revealed to me. The bar that I'd visited only four days earlier, when I was still determined to know what had happened in Paris—and which I'd left feeling unexpectedly comforted, having learned nothing but having felt a sudden, salutary distance from all that it symbolized for me—seemed to me now like the appropriate backdrop against which to manifest my

317

detachment, to demonstrate to whoever cared to listen that I, too, could make decisions and change the course of events, that I wasn't a mere puppet subject to the whims of strings I did not control. What I hoped to find there was the world I was leaving behind, and propelling me in that direction were the faces of my mother and the person who had never behaved like a father, and, it turned out, was not my father.

The bar's neon sign had already been turned off when I spotted it some way away, but I thought I could see a tenuous light coming from the barred window, and so, far from being discouraged, I quickened my pace, while the craziest, most contradictory plans flooded into my mind. I imagined my father would be there; I imagined finding him there along with my mother and forcing him to confess that it was all a lie; I imagined him not being there and denouncing him to the owner, telling him, as he had asked me to do on that distant afternoon when he had turned up at our apartment and given me his card, that I had seen my father in Madrid; I imagined helping his friend, the one with the jacket and the leather boots, to take revenge for the money he was owed; I imagined becoming a member of that same profession and thieving, mugging, and stealing left, right, and center; I imagined calling the police from a phone booth and having all the customers arrested, figuring that exactly the same people would be there as on my first visit.

When I arrived, the folding aluminum security grille was closed, but not padlocked, and seeing that there were still people inside, I opened it a few inches, reached through the gap, and rapped on the glass door; terrified by my own boldness, my thoughts grew suddenly cloudy and my mind went blank. I could make out two other people apart from the old man:

the woman with the red hair who had served me the other night and was now scrubbing the floor outside the restroom, and a tall man with a frank, open smile, who was standing at the bar, chatting. The woman leaned her mop against the wall and made as if to come over to me, but, casually prevented from doing so by her husband, she took up her mop again, still with her eyes fixed on me. I considered running away, but couldn't move. The owner did not take long to reach the glass door, which he unbolted and gently pushed open, and he said, "We're closed. We're just cleaning up for the night."

His voice was friendly but weary, and it was obvious that he didn't want to waste any time on me. I avoided his eyes and looked instead at the woman, who was working her way with mop and bucket toward the back of the establishment. He didn't move, and still I said nothing. I wanted to, but couldn't.

"Is something wrong?" he asked, focusing his gaze exclusively on me, rather than on me and whatever else might be going on in the street. "Are you going to stand there all night? Like I said, we're closed."

This time his voice sounded firmer and more abrupt, but not cutting or unpleasant. Feeling tempted to run away, I still said nothing, and he looked at me more closely, as if noticing something he had failed to notice before, and as if he were trying to use that insight to decipher the reason for my presence there.

"I know you," he said after a few seconds, still looking at me, then he opened the door wider, drew aside the security grille and stepped out to meet me. "You were in here a few days ago. You drank a Coke and then left. You should have been at school. It was in the morning."

"Yes," I said, involuntarily taking a step back, relieved that he remembered, but caught off guard by that reference to school. For a few more moments, I said not a word, then, seeing that he wasn't speaking, either, and finally dredging up some courage, I managed to stammer out, "But . . . but we'd already met before . . ."

"Really? I don't remember. Where exactly?" he asked, visibly interested. I noticed that the woman had stopped cleaning the floor and was leaning on her mop, watching us, and that the other man was also watching from where he sat slumped behind the phone.

"Three years ago," I finally managed to say. "At my apartment. My mother was out . . ."

I saw him screwing up his face in an effort to remember, all the while thoughtfully looking me up and down, and I could see that he came to no conclusion. I told him my full name, but he still didn't react, either pretending or because he really didn't recognize it.

"You were looking for my father," I explained, not knowing what to do now, heartily regretting the situation I had gotten myself into and feeling his gaze becoming ever more oppressive. "You and another man . . ."

"Now I remember," he broke in. "Yes, now I remember," he repeated as if he really were remembering. "Of course, you're that kid. Sorry about that, but you've really gotten bigger since then."

I thought he was going to continue, but instead he stopped abruptly and waited in silence for me to speak. I didn't know what to say and answered lamely, "You gave me your card and invited me to come and see you . . ."

"Did I?" he asked in some surprise. "Well, you've certainly taken your time."

He was trying to be funny and to appear unruffled, but I realized that, now that he had recognized me, he had gone on the defensive, as if having me remind him of that episode from the past made him wary or uneasy. I suddenly found it hard to recognize in him the stranger who had forced his way into our apartment looking for my father. Physically he was the same, the same nicotine-stained fingers, the same scruffy appearance, but just then he seemed much smaller and more inoffensive than I remembered.

"I was only joking. No need to blush. It's just that three years is a long time . . ."

I recalled my first visit a few days before and must have seemed abstracted, because he asked, "Are you all right?"

"Yes, fine," I said at once, as if I'd been caught doing something wrong.

"Listen," he said. "I don't know what you want exactly, but I think you'd better come back some other day. It's really late for you to be out and about. Your mother will be worried. Besides, we're closed."

I nodded and again peered inside, at the woman and the other man, who were still watching us. I wondered if he and the woman had children, and what they would be like. I imagined being his son and immediately thought of my Aunt Delfina and her husband, and my eight-month stay in La Coruña. Then I became aware that the old man was talking, and I had to make an effort to understand what he was saying.

"Come back another day if you like, but you'd better get going for now . . ."

I could see that he was anxious, even eager to get rid of me, and I gave him a reassuring smile. He took advantage of this truce to step back inside the bar, while I set off to the subway station again. I hadn't gone ten yards when I heard him asking in a somewhat shy, uncertain voice, "You say it was your father we came looking for?"

"Yes," I said, stopping briefly and turning my head. He had closed the security grille now and was looking at me, peering around the glass door, his right hand gripping one of the metal triangles of the grille.

"Did he ever turn up?" he asked, more brightly now that his hunch had been proved right and now that I was leaving.

"Yes," I said. "He's waiting for me at home."

That same night, when I arrived back at our apartment and walked down the hallway, I saw that my mother's bedroom door was closed. The light was on, but she turned it off as soon as she heard my footsteps on the parquet floor. The living room no longer smelled of cigarette smoke, and I felt a cold draft coming in through a window left cautiously ajar. I didn't bother to close it. I went straight to bed, knowing that the next morning, my mother would be sure to send me off to school just as if it were a normal day. Just as if we were a normal mother and son.

# XXXII

Since then, twenty-two years of largely normal and perfectly predictable days have passed, but I still remember that crucial evening with the same mixture of darkness and light. In the eyes of other people, I've grown up, but maturity has not brought with it sufficient distance for me to be able to judge what happened then. I'm calmer now, less subject to my emotional ups and downs, but, basically, the same conflicts prevail. I still can't understand where my mother found the strength or how she managed to find the words. I know that, like her confession on the way to Burgos, she believed it was necessary, which is why she spoke out, but her determination, the intrepid integrity it reveals, continues to amaze me and, like almost everything else about her, arouses contradictory emotions. I should be grateful, I should admire her for what she did, and I am and I do, but I still wish it hadn't happened, and I sometimes distrust her motives. Since I cannot doubt her honesty, I try to come up with reasons to suspect her, and I wonder if perhaps she felt she had to do it and if there were other things she didn't tell me. Not that I do this often, because I rarely think about that evening. Incredible though it may seem, it isn't something that obsesses me, and I myself find my own indifference alarming, but that's how it is. I just can't work up much interest; it's as if what I found out then hadn't really affected me.

In that strangely casual attitude to what would normally be such a troubling revelation, it would be ingenuous on my part not to acknowledge the beneficent influence of my mother, who overcame and survived adversity and the obstacles that she herself erected—the final and possibly futile triumph of her rare mixture of strength and weakness, her subtle combination of mystery and stoicism, of sincerity and a stubborn resistance to reveal herself. She never mentioned it again directly, and although I could not, at first, get it out of my head, I eventually forgot all about it, so much so that, when I did occasionally remember it, it took me a few seconds to persuade myself that it was real rather than imagined. I suppose it was better that way, that my mother foresaw what would happen, and that her subsequent silence on the subject was deliberate; indeed, not until the first signs of her illness became apparent did the whole scenario come back to me. As if her gradual deterioration made me the guardian of the memory she was losing, I slowly began to look back at our past life and forced myself to ask questions and to consider what I remembered of that particular fragment of memory. And yet, if the content of her confession to me on that evening twenty-two years ago doesn't really grip my imagination even now, if my gaze wanders off in other directions, and if rather than focusing on any direct implications it has for me, I focus, for example, on the courage she showed in talking to me about it, this means that her saying nothing more about the matter was not the sole determining factor in my strange indifference to what she told me; other circumstances have intervened, of which that indifference is a prolongation and a consequence.

My mother did not change her life after that final performance. She remained true to the criteria that had characterized her before, although she did, perhaps, become more withdrawn, more isolated and alone. She did not remarry, nor, as far as I know, did she ever have any love affairs, and as for friends—who were never very many and tended to desert her as soon as they recognized her inability to give herself— they became still fewer and harder to replace. Only one thing changed: she did not go back on her word as regards my father. She sold the apartment and kept her promise to give him half of the money, and that was that.

Twenty-two years have passed, but I still don't know what he did with his half of the proceeds from the sale. My mother never explained what the debt was, perhaps because she didn't know, and I can't be sure that she didn't just use it as an excuse in her argument with Delfina. The money clearly didn't last him very long, because I understand he spent two more periods in prison. There is, of course, no trace of any lucky breaks he may have had, although I imagine they would have been few and far between. To the best of my belief, my mother never saw him again apart from a single meeting at the bank, of which she told me almost nothing. She never made any attempt to find him, and he kept well away from us. For a long time, I thought cynically that he would turn up again as soon as he needed some safe haven and that it was just a matter of time, but eventually it became clear to me that this simply wouldn't happen. I can't quite explain how, but a curtain, far thicker and more impenetrable than I could ever have imagined, now separated his life from ours. Strangely, this desire for separation came not just from my mother, but from him, too, something that initially made me still more suspicious. Did he no longer need us? Did he sense, from his place of exile, that he would not be welcome? Had my mother persuaded him to keep away and had he, for once in his life, respected her wishes? Or had persuasion been unnecessary, and had he accepted that everything was over between them? There were many unanswered questions, and they all led me, as they do now, to one solution: Paris, the final insult, the final straw—which eludes me and always will.

My father's physical absence did not, however, mean that he was forgotten. My father did not vanish completely from our identical days. After my mother sold the apartment and gave him half the money, there was a brief period while we were getting used to our new apartment when she and I avoided talking about him, but later, although I can't remember which of us was the first to break the silence, he resumed his usual place in our lives. We continued to receive calls from people asking for him, although not as many as in our previous apartment, and we were soon telling each other about these as blithely as we had before. When we had heard nothing of him for some time, we would begin speculating about his whereabouts, and it didn't take long for us to include him in our conversations for no reason at all, either because I would ask my mother about past events in which he had been involved or because she would mention him spontaneously while recalling some other incident. It was a very strange situation. We certainly didn't expect to see him again, the door of our apartment was definitively closed to him—as my mother had demonstrated by making that last confession to me—but in a way, he was still alive and still present. Much of what I know about the early days of their marriage dates from that time.

I've often wondered how this was possible after what had happened, and the reasons I come up with differ depending on whether they apply to her or to me. In my case, I suppose that as well as being a more or less conscious way of preserving a certain illusion of distance between us, of diminishing our cruelly highlighted closeness by drawing into the present the one thing that separated us and that we did not share, it was also a more secret and unacknowledged way of denying the truth about my origins. In my mother's case, the reasons are more uncertain and harder to discern. On the one hand, it seems to me proof positive of her new distance and remoteness from him, that the thought of him had ceased to affect her, and that she was simply trying to reestablish the normality she had so longed for without making too brusque or categorical a break with the past, one that would have been a continual reminder to me of what she herself preferred not to remember; on the other hand, I cannot help but see it also as an irrepressible reflection of her still unextinguished love for him.

Whatever the truth of the matter, there is still a great deal I don't know about them, much remains obscure to me about their strange union and my role in it, there is still much I find hard to absorb. I feel I lack the necessary information by which to judge them, and my own feelings grow confused when I try to find an answer to the remaining unknowns. I don't know if he knew that I was not his son, and supposing that he did, I don't know if he had always known it or if my mother had told him, as she had with me, only at a moment of her own choosing. That last possibility would perhaps explain his long and unexpected silence, but I'm not sure that would be my preferred explanation. I don't know whether to miss him or despise him, I don't know whether to make him the victim or the villain. Again, there are just too many questions that remain unanswered and always will, which means that I can't choose. The only thing I can say is that I feel nothing for him and certainly don't miss his unpredictable presence, even though he is the person I still think of when I say "my father."

I only saw him again once. It was one winter's night when I was twenty-six or twenty-seven, in a bar I used to go to, one of those gloomy, unapologetically squalid dives, the haunt of a motley crew of inveterate night owls, one of those places that only really comes into its own once all the other bars have closed and the city's streets slowly begin to fill up with people strolling unhurriedly into the new day that is just beginning. I'd gone there with a friend, after hours of fruitless peregrinations around other, more alluring establishments, drawn by the prospect of meeting some acquaintance who would invite us to join the last shift of drinkers of the night. We had sat down at a table, in order to avoid a nasty-looking drunk who had cornered us on the way in, and I suddenly spotted him leaning on the bar, surrounded by a group of five or six foreigners rather younger than him. I recognized him at once, despite all the time that had passed since that sighting at a café on that far-off afternoon, and despite the visible deterioration in his appearance. The hair at his temples had turned a rather yellowish gray, and after years of disorderly living, his very straight back, that feature so characteristic of him, had grown bent beneath the weight of head and shoulders; his clothes (jacket, tie, boots, and jeans), although nice and put-together enough, looked unmistakably worn, and his face, the alert, guarded face of someone accustomed to entrusting his survival to the whim of the moment, was a pathetic, faded reflection of what it once was. His companions, though, seemed not to notice this and stood around him in a semicircle, looking at him with the reverential gaze of tourists who think they're having an authentic experience that can be added later to their store of traveller's anecdotes or that will, at least, forever color the way they view the country they're visiting. He was waving his arms around and showed every sign of being drunk, but he nonetheless retained his composure and spoke without pause, while his audience greeted his jokes with somewhat belated smiles. He was holding a glass of red wine in one hand, and when, on the excuse that I wanted to order a drink, I got up and went over to the bar so as to be nearer to where he was standing, I wondered with sudden sadness if those smiles would be his only payment for the special performance he was putting on for them. I didn't approach him, I didn't speak to him, I didn't want to break the spell he had worked so hard to create. I positioned myself just close enough to overhear his conversation, and until long after I had been served, I waited for our eyes to meet, while I listened to him discoursing in French on a wide range of topics, from politics to recent Spanish history, from bullfighting to flamenco, interspersed with a few comments on drugs and Madrid's nightlife. He had been in the right places at the right time, he mentioned the names of important people he claimed to know, he gave facts and figures, and drew appropriate parallels with subjects familiar to his listeners, which showed a fairly thorough if somewhat dated knowledge of French culture and politics in the first half of the twentieth century. The sole opportunity for him to recognize me arose shortly after my friend had left—annoyed at my having neglected him—and once the tourists had left, too. He had accompanied the group to the door, exchanging farewells and promises to meet again the following day, and when he came back inside, he stayed at the farthest end of the bar, leaning against the wall. I was a few yards away from him, but there was no one standing between us, and I was able to study him at length. All trace of his earlier apparent euphoria had gone, and he didn't even bother looking around him at the other customers. He stood there, unmoving, sunk in his own thoughts, taking sips of wine. When he had finished his drink, he put the glass down on the bar, took out a cigarette, lit it, drew himself up a little, turned up the collar of his jacket, and prepared to leave. At that point, our eyes met, and, just for a second, I saw a flicker of doubt cross his face. Then, as if he'd forgotten that he'd already done so, he once again made as if to turn up his collar, and left. He didn't recognize me, or perhaps he did but was too embarrassed to come over to me.

I haven't seen him since. For many years after that night, we continued to receive news of him fairly frequently, then, suddenly, at around the time when the first symptoms of my mother's illness appeared, he vanished completely. No one phoned to ask for him and no one mentioned having seen him by chance in such and such a place. Sometimes, I like to think that perhaps he's finally seen sense and gotten out and is now resigned to living in a village on the coast or in the mountains, accompanied by some charitable woman he has managed to inveigle into staying with him—one last thing to cling to in what has otherwise been a most unfortunate life. At others, I imagine him trying his luck until the very end, or languishing in prison somewhere, or even dead. None of these ideas moves or repels me more than the others. I think I favor the first option, but then, when I think about my mother, I get to feeling rebellious and find the second option rather pleasing. Given the awfulness of her situation, I find it painful to think that he might be living a discreetly contented life, and then I rage against his memory, knowing, at the same time, that

I'm being unfair, and still feeling a twinge of nostalgia for his marriage to my mother and for what might have been.

It's a somewhat similar situation with me and Delfina. Delfina is still alive and phones regularly from La Coruña to ask how my mother is doing, but I don't feel any particular fondness or affection for her. She appears to feel the same about me. When she phones, I notice how difficult she finds it to speak, I notice the put-on sadness, the way she almost holds her breath while she receives the never-very-hopeful news. I also notice her pent-up impatience, her desire to end the conversation as quickly as possible. She insists on knowing all the details, responding to my report in a tearful whisper, only to say goodbye almost immediately afterward. She rarely asks how I'm feeling or if I'm weary after two long years of coping with my mother's illness. For her, I represent memory. I don't blame her. Since that morning in Madrid when she advised me to take no notice of what my mother had said, a lot of things have happened—and not all of it good. She lives alone now, immersed in her own griefs and anxieties, but this isn't because her husband has died, it's because he left her for a woman he'd been seeing in secret for several years. When he left, he took with him their various mutual friends, the dinners and galas at the golf club, and my aunt's busy social life was snuffed out. She never mentions this and never complains, she pretends not to care, and even to feel a certain relief, but I know how ashamed and embarrassed she feels and how bottomless is the pit of her despair; I know that, however much she would like to, she cannot change the past, and however much she longs for revenge, revenge is impossible. Her situation grieves me, living, as she does, in a city that is not her own and having to accept what money her husband gives her, she, who has never worked and never dreamed she would find herself in such a predicament. I regret this and feel sorry for her, but I can also see that the situation has its instructive side, and what reconciles me to her distress is the realization that what has happened to her takes away any authority she might have to judge my mother. I imagine that she herself is aware of this, which is why she remains silent. And that's sad, because without my mother, the bonds uniting Delfina and myself grow weaker and somehow more artificial. Without either of us wanting to, we behave at a distance much as two recent acquaintances would behave in the flesh when the mutual friend who has just introduced them leaves them alone for a moment. We know too much about each other, and that knowledge brings us closer, but without my mother there, we're incapable of giving expression to that closeness. We depend too much on her memory. Her living death has left us with too many differences. I would like to be able to talk to her freely, and I'm sure that Delfina would find comfort in talking to me, but we could only talk about my mother, and that's impossible, because neither of us knows how much the other knows, and I'm sure she would rather not know what I know. Indeed, I sometimes think it's precisely my knowledge of that secret that separates us, but this would imply that Delfina either knew or somehow sensed it, too, and from the way she behaved during the argument she had with my mother, I couldn't say for certain one way or another. She might well know the secret and have simply refused to accept it, or she might just as likely suspect nothing. The way she kept reproaching my mother for having run away from home seems to indicate the latter, but then my mother's insistence on defending herself against her sister's accusations and her own veiled allusions to an explanation Delfina would prefer not to acknowledge both point to the possibility that she did know. I can't be sure either way, I don't know and never will; it's a mystery that, like so many others, I can't resolve or understand, because I can't conceive of what it's like to have a brother or sister and can't, therefore, imagine what labyrinths of communication might open up between two siblings.

It's even more difficult for me to talk about my mother and my relationship with her over those twenty-two identical years. If I allow myself to be carried away by what my heart tells me in moments of despair, I would have to conclude that our whole life—up until the cruel joke of her illness—has merely confirmed my worst fears about the future, fears I once harbored as a child. However difficult it is for me to say, however painful, this is the only sense I can make of the path our lives have taken up to this point. I find it hard not to resent my mother's determination to remain single, oblivious to the burden she was bequeathing to me. I find it hard not to feel bitter toward her for not making things easier for me and for leaving me no one with whom I can share her unexpected misfortune. I find it hard not to feel angry with her for the helplessness and dependence that are the result of her overprotectiveness, and I sometimes wonder if she at any time considered the damage she might be doing to me, all the while thinking it was for the best, or if she could see no further than her own urgent need to keep me safe from the phantom of my origins. I find it hard not to wallow in all that negativity, and yet I have to say that we've lived very harmoniously all these years, and with the exception of her illness, no insuperable problem has come between us. It has all been very simple and transparent, and much better than one could have hoped. I don't recall her uttering a single word of complaint or putting any obstacle in my way. I can't recall her doing or saying anything, however insignificant or unthinking, that contributed to laying the foundations of anxiety in me. We went through all the usual stages of growing up without any great traumas. We went from living together and seeing each other every day to living apart and meeting once a week for lunch, from telling each other everything on a daily basis to exchanging brief summaries of our respective routines. We grew apart physically and emotionally, and my mother had a chance to experience fully the solitude she had so longed for, but none of these things appeared to affect her. She not only happily put up with the successive separations imposed on her by my independence, she accepted even those that were avoidable and were simply a response to my changing moods.

I suppose I'm still divided on this subject, and finding a balance is as difficult as it always was, but the truth is that in moments of despair, in the absence of external justifications, which I know to be real and undeniable, I see no compensation for and no check on my ceaseless efforts to find out the truth. If things were as I describe, that only increases my fear and remorse for having been unfair, but it doesn't, on the other hand, free me from the suspicion that my mother was playing with marked cards from the very start and that, apart from changes she had to make because of unexpected events that were out of her control, we never encountered anything that had not been previously planned and calculated by her. I should be grateful to her for allowing me to stay on the sidelines, I should be glad of the benefits of not having had to make decisions, I should recognize that my not having slithered down into still darker holes is due in large part to her capacity for manipulating and foreseeing the future, but it's the deliberation and sacrifice implied by that conjecture that prevents me from doing so, the idea of her self-abnegation and the very minor role allotted to me. In the end, I put up with everything, I accepted her wishes, I went forward when she allowed me to and have ended up in the place she reserved for me; I've never put pressure on her, never gone beyond the bounds she set, never made things awkward for her or given her cause for concern. Even the fact that I'm still thinking about all this could be considered a triumph for her. It was all planned, part of her strategy, as are my continuing state of doubt, my clinging to the unknown, and my occasional speculative forays into the possibility that there are things she didn't tell me, things that would paint a less perfect, less cerebral portrait of her. Both extremes would have been necessary for her to keep me safe from dangers I would not have emerged unscathed from otherwise. While one extreme protects me from dangers only she could prevent, the other neutralizes the phantoms and adverse reactions springing up inside me. After all, even if it's true that she had no alternative but to lavish all her attention and care on me at the cost of neglecting herself, rather than seeing this as a selfless sacrifice against which I must rebel, I find it more comforting and more pleasant, and more favorable to her, too, to think that she might not have been as cool and cautious as she seemed and was, on occasions, overwhelmed or defeated, that she made mistakes and deceived both herself and me.

Perhaps she did weigh up and foresee everything, even my indecision and my many contrary impulses, and that is the conclusion I tend to reach in moments of extreme despair, when I allow myself to succumb to distrust and resentment and to return to the ingenuous idea of her possible deceit, even though I know that if she did conceal things from me, no betrayal could ever outweigh her devotion. I struggle with this whenever I'm mired in pessimism, but at the same time, I'm still not sure and I immediately feel ashamed of my own exaggerated obsessiveness and drive it from my mind, blaming everything on my own lack of balance. It doesn't matter whether things were done deliberately or not, I tell myself. She might well have weighed up and foreseen everything, even my uncertainty and the contrary impulses doing battle inside me, but even were that so, it would still not justify my disaffection, it wouldn't make her protective shell any thicker or save her from the attacks she was armoring herself against. Underneath her apparent strength, I see how vulnerable and fragile she is— as deserving of compassion as if she had trusted entirely to providence and shown no more foresight than the amount one needs in order to survive from day to day with just a vague awareness of looming misfortune; as confused as if she had found herself forced to improvise and every act or decision relating to me had been the product of an oft-repeated, sterile debate in which any benefits from the winning side of the argument were cancelled out automatically by the losing side; no colder or more egotistical than if she'd let herself be guided solely by instinct and there had been neither despair nor planning, only a need to adapt herself to events as they happened; no less considerate, either, than if she'd limited herself to doing only what she wanted to do, ignorant of the many interpretations and consequences that her actions would have for me; no more devoted and dedicated than she would have been if I weren't her only child and I'd had brothers and sisters with whom to share her attentions.

Time passes, and memories grow hazy, and what never dies loses intensity and inevitably, in hindsight, seems less important than it was. There are no answers to the unresolved unknowns, apart from those I myself can offer, but I shouldn't complain. No word can change the past, and no word is the right word if you say it when what it describes is the past and not the present. In the present, there are no words. Words come later, and then we all use them in the same way, we can all describe things and give our opinions even though what we are describing and giving our opinions about is not ours, even though it never happened to us. We don't need someone to spell out what we can only guess at, because we can never be sure that what he or she is telling us is the whole thing or only part of it, and our doubts will remain unassuaged. I'm tired of feeling that I've been the exact same person for far too long, tired of thinking about my Aunt Delfina, and my mother, and my father who is not my father. I'm tired of the grief and pointless complaining, of longing for what I do not have and might perhaps loathe if I did have it. I'm tired of the anger and remorse, and of the suspicion that it is merely my own egotism that drove me on then and still drives me on now.

Today I went to visit my mother in the hospital, and as usual, I went with my wife. I prefer her to come, too, because I would find it much more upsetting without her. I would feel I was being cruel keeping my mother there rather than at home, and I would be beset by all kinds of anxieties. As happens more and more often, my mother didn't recognize me, but she hadn't deteriorated physically since the last time I saw her, and, within limits, she seemed well. Naturally, I was glad to see this, but when I left, I felt sad to remember her life, how quickly it had passed, and I couldn't help asking my wife, as I so often have before, if she believes that Paris ever really happened.

"What does it matter," she said, "when nothing matters any more."

And she's right.

It's a feeling of dread. It's nostalgia. It's fear. It's the dreams that loom in the darkness. It's time. It's wanting to run to her bedside and say, "Forgive me, it's all right, I know everything, go to sleep."

# TRANSLATOR'S ACKNOWLEDGMENTS

I would like to thank Marcos Giralt Torrente, Annella McDermott, Cecilia Ross and Ben Sherriff for all their help and advice.

# ABOUT THE AUTHOR

MARCOS GIRALT TORRENTE is an award-winning writer from Madrid. He has published several books, including the novels *París* (Herralde Novel Award), *Los seres felices* and *Tiempo de vida* (Spanish National Book Award), the novella *Nada sucede solo* and the collections of short stories *Entiéndame* and *El final del amor* (International Short Fiction Award Ribera del Duero), released by McSweeneys in English as *The End of Love* and longlisted in the 2014 Best Translated Book Award. *Paris* is his first novel in English-language translation.

# ABOUT THE TRANSLATOR

MARGARET JULL COSTA has been a literary translator for nearly thirty years and has translated many novels and short stories by Portuguese, Spanish and Latin American writers, including Javier Marías, Fernando Pessoa, José Saramago, Bernardo Atxaga and Luis Verissimo. She has won various prizes for her work, including, in 2008, the PEN Book-of-the-Month Translation Award and the Oxford Weidenfeld Translation Prize for her version of Eça de Queiroz's masterpiece *The Maias*, and, most recently, she won the 2012 Calouste Gulbenkian Prize for *The Word Tree* by Teolinda Gersão, for which she was also runner-up with *The Land at the End of the World* by António Lobo Antunes.

Lightning Source UK Ltd.
Milton Keynes UK
UKOW05f2244230614

233938UK00001B/105/P